The Ivy Noose

SHAYNA GRISSOM

Contents

CHAPTER ONE

E ach wiry fiber raked against my skin like a fresh scrubbing pad. The thick, hemp fabric was already feeling muggy on the inside. How did people live in this stuff? It was one thing to have a wool cape, but the entire uniform was so unyielding.

Resisting the urge to roll around on the floor like a flea-ridden mutt, I stretched my arms out in vain. The uniform drew tight across my back and shoulders; my arms threatened to burst the seams. I've never been the dainty sort. These shoulders of mine are meant for labor, not pageantry.

"You look like quite the lady," Dad said.

"I feel like I'm wearing a blanket. It's so thick."

My father pulled the kettle out of the fire and poured some hot water into the little pot with a constant tremble. Lord, he was so frail. I half expected his bones to come popping out of that thin skin of his. Come winter, he'd need every scrap of coal I could afford.

"You'll be thankful for that come the cold. They issue new uniforms as the season changes."

An awful morbs hit me then. Will he be here come spring?

Shoving the thought away, I felt my hair. Pinned in a bun so tight I must have appeared perpetually frightened, but the maids at the manor were all expected to dress this way. I saw them many times, coming to the village for various things. Some lived in the village, but others lived in the manor. The Jones manor was the main source of economy for their little village. Becoming a part of it might've been exciting for most, but for me, it was one step closer to ending up like Mum. Like many village girls, she worked there until she got married, had a child, then died. That couldn't be it for me. It just couldn't.

I scratched my wrist under the cuff. I didn't suit the uniform, and we all knew it; it was best that Dad rein in his expectations. "Let's just hope it's worth the trouble."

"I appreciate what you're doing," Dad said. His eyes welled with pride. That alone made the dress worth it. His slate grey hair thinned into a low crown around his ears, and his skin had bagged under his eyes from long nights coughing.

"I wish I could still work—"

"It's time for me to be off," I said, cutting his sentence short. "You have everything you need?"

"Mary will be over shortly."

I bit my lip to keep from saying something regrettable. The widow next door was doing us a huge service by watching my father while I worked. Debt stacked like a woodpile, only it never seemed to dwindle. I couldn't afford to think poorly of the woman any more than I could afford the rent on the flat or the looming store credit.

"Dinah," he called just as I got to the door. I didn't turn, only paused and waited for him to say whatever he needed to say. "Please try to maintain a sweet disposition. This job requires a certain level of respect for our betters."

Betters my arse.

Being born to a wealthy family didn't make them better; it just made them rich. I slammed the wooden door so hard it banged against the rough-hewn frame and swung back open again. It was a half-mile walk to the manor. It could have been a five-minute walk to the baker if he had just hired me.

But there I was, fancy as you please, marching to the poshest house in the county. It wasn't all bad. Scratchy as the uniform was, it kept me warm just as promised.

Frost glittered in the honey-colored sunrise, and the dirt path beneath my feet well-worn from carriages that hurdled past the village on the way to Chester. The trees were shedding leaves in a variety of russet colors. It was too beautiful a day to pout about having a good-paying job that was heaped with opportunities.

The baker wouldn't give me a job, but I was told I'd be starting in the kitchens. That wasn't so far from the fragrant yeast rising the dough. A room potent with the smells of rosemary, sage, and thyme. Butter browning in the pot. All the things one should smell in the kitchens.

Working in the Jones manner had other perks, too. A minor lord was still a lord, and a glowing letter of recommendation could do wonders for a girl like me. Moreso than if it were to come from the village baker or his lazy son.

And why did he always reek of onions? Even as a boy, he was like that. It must have been a condition of some sort.

Something cut through the air with a great woosh. Spinning past me at a hurtling speed. I turned just in time to see Rodger, yet another village idiot, racing up the road on a half-rusted bicycle.

"Hey, look at you!" he shouted from the safety of his bike seat. "Someone finally squeezed you into a dress."

Before I could think of something clever to say, he raced over the solitary puddle on the road. Mud slapped against my uniform, and icy specks hit my face. So shocked by the immaturity and brazenness, I stood and gasped at the state of my dress.

"Have you no decency?" I cried out.

On my first day at work, no less! Rodger gave a forced laugh before riding toward Chester. In truth, I suspect he did not see the puddle but was too proud to admit the wrongdoing, but I was furious.

Served me right to hope I'd make a good impression. I trudged along the road until a grove of trees gave way to a tall, iron fence with spiked tops. The gate was made of similar bars, and on the front was a plate with the name Jones cut away from the metal. Hedges lined the pathway before rounding a giant fountain. The property was pruned and picked to perfection weekly, and there wasn't a single leaf on the ground despite the numerous trees.

It was hard to imagine the likes of me roaming around a place like that, especially covered in mud. Maybe they'd have some rags to wipe down my uniform. What a state I must have looked, trespassing through such a pristine garden.

The manor itself was a three-story red and white building. It had a brick wall that went along the backside for privacy. It was the tallest building I had ever laid eyes on, and the turrets reminded me of some great castle. Only it weren't a castle. It was more like the size of a boarding house. All shutters and brick with climbing ivy wrapped around the chimney.

I pinched and pulled at my uniform—straightening it to the best of my ability before sucking in a deep breath between cold lips and going inside.

Mr. Davies said to enter through the servant's door. It was an unmistakable entrance with a whitewashed door and frame. I lifted my hand to knock but hesitated. Was I supposed to knock? I never held a real job before, let alone a servant's position.

My father's words echoed in my head as I struggled to determine the proper etiquette for the situation. It was never a strength for me, but I needed this job, and one never had a second chance at a first impression.

The door opened before I could make up my mind, and a tall, gaunt man with a wiry moustache stood in its place. "What are you doing?" he asked.

"Mr. Davies," I stuttered.

He frowned, looking me over before ushering me into the kitchens. "Come in. Don't just stand there."

The kitchen alone was bigger than my flat. There was a full-size cast-iron oven detailed in copper finishing against a main wall, insulated between two work counters, where women in the same uniform had their backs turned. There was enough workspace to accommodate half a dozen workers. Cooking and baking tools of every design were just waiting for utility. It smelled of finely milled flour and herbs drying along iron hangers, just like it ought to have.

Closing my eyes, I clasped my hands together and inhaled. Yes, this was a blessing. This was the change I needed in my life. It was a rough start, but when I looked back on it, this would be a day I'd remember fondly. I just knew it.

Mr. Davies flopped a dishrag in my face. "Clean yourself up before anyone sees you."

Heat flared from my cheeks as I was reminded of the state of my uniform. I took the rag and wiped away what I could.

"A boy rode straight into a mud puddle beside me," I explained.

"You remind me of your mother," he said. "She and I were not close, but I was sad when she passed. She was a good woman."

How many times had I heard that? It's not that I doubted it. She was a wonderful mum, but what made her good to me wasn't the same as what made her good in the eyes of men. She must have kept tidy. Smiled when spoken to. Wore her burdens the way women wore those silly hoops under their skirts. Hidden but capacious enough to keep her from fitting in those spaces where she didn't belong.

Now here I was, picking up where she left off. Only, I did none of those things.

I scratched off the last specks of dirt on my cheek with the rough cloth, ignoring the sting of it. My cheeks must've been red from the cold and embarrassment as it was.

The urge to throw the towel at him was restrained only by my desire to prove to my father that I could conduct myself well enough for the posh. Returning home only a few hours later would no doubt send Mary buzzing through the village. I couldn't go back a failure. Dad needed a hot fire throughout the winter and less worry on his thin shoulders.

"This is where you will work," Mr. Davies said, pointing a calloused finger at the sink full of dishes. "I assume you know how to properly wash a dish?"

I ground my teeth together and gave a single nod before stepping up to the sink. I rolled up my sleeves and began washing like my life depended on it. Determined to wash the dishes so efficiently that Mr. Davies would be forced to find other work for me to do. The sleeves cut into my arms and the lye stung my nose, but I didn't care. I would prove myself and move up the ranks. I would show them all, one heirloom teacup at a time.

"Mr. Davies!" a woman cried as she bustled through the swinging door. It was Harriet. Her cheeks were flushed, and her heavy chest heaved. "Mr. Jones requires your assistance."

Mr. Davies paled and said, "Is it Mrs. Jones?"

Harriet nodded, and Mr. Davies left the room without another word. Harriet placed a hand against the wall with her other hand on her hip as she recovered. The maids stopped kneading their bread loaves.

The elderly woman with flour dusted across her apron asked, "What happened this time?"

"She's having another one of her episodes," Harriet said.

I didn't want to be an eavesdropper, but I was curious. No one liked a gossip, especially me, but everyone who worked here was so hush-hush about it in the village. I didn't know anything about the people I worked for. My fingers were pruned like dried dates, so I moved to drying and stacking while the ladies talked on.

The younger of the three, the one with mousy brown hair, said, "She's been having a lot more of those lately. Are they calling the doctor?"

Harriet nodded. "She won't get out of bed today. Be a love and bring her up some food?"

The younger maid took out a silver tray and began setting it up with tea, biscuits, and fruits. "Not tea, Marie," Harriet said. "The missus doesn't like tea."

"What sort of woman doesn't like tea?" I asked. My eyes went wide, and I buttoned my lips before another stupid word could come out.

It was rude and intrusive. I ought to know better. Still, I had been like a ghost in the room. Was it so wrong to want to be included in the conversation? All three women regarded me, and I was suddenly ashamed of making a joke in what was a tense situation. Stellar job, Dinah. The whole house would hate me before too long.

"The American kind," the old maid replied.

How exotic! My mind reeled with the possibilities. What a glamorous woman to be employed under. The dislike of tea was instantly forgotten. "Beg your pardon. I'm afraid I don't know much about the family. Is she sick?"

Marie stared at me, absently pouring tea into a floral teacup before placing it on the tray. That wasn't going to go over well.

It was Harriet who took pity on me. "I suppose Mr. Davies didn't tell you a thing."

I shook my head like the foolish child that I was. Fully distracted from the dishes, I leaned against the sink, ignoring the wool working through my underclothes even when it itched to all hell.

"Mr. Jones married last spring," Harriet explained. "He's old money, she's new money, you know how that goes."

No, I didn't, but it didn't take a posh education to understand rich people only associated with other rich people. "I see."

"Yeah, what a bum deal that was," the old woman said.

"Anne!" Harriet scolded. "She's got a condition."

Anne rolled her eyes and went back to beating the unfortunate dough into the counter.

"Any one of us could get it," Harriet said. "It's a female condition that changes at any time. That's why her doctor agreed to move across the pond."

"It's a load of rubbish if you ask me," Anne grumbled.

I returned to my work, my mind full of questions about this American woman and her *condition*, as everyone referred to it. What was she doing that had everyone in such a state? Imagine sending a whole house spinning at a drop of a mood.

"I don't know where any of this goes," I said, hoping to change the subject.

Anne showed me. The teacups were the last to be put away as they had to go to the cupboard in the formal dining room. I followed behind the old maid, who would occasionally swing her arm out and give a brief explanation. "That's the parlor where Mr. Jones is usually found," or "That's the wine cellar."

A long table centered the formal dining room. It was draped with a lace runner, and several candelabra lined the table. The room itself was drab, and the curtains were ragged, breaking the illusion that this house was something exquisite. Even the fanciest of fancy in this village was nothing more than a pauper lord. Grand home indeed. The chandelier was a curvy gold thing that held six candlesticks in the center of the room. Along the wall was a foggy glass cabinet with an assortment of teacups.

"There you are," Anna said before turning right back around for the kitchen.

The house wasn't large enough to lose my way, but avoiding Mr. Davies was something I was keen on. I hurried back to the kitchen as fast as I could. Voices echoed along the entryway. It was Mr. Davies with two other men.

"How are you?" A man asked.

"Business is good, at least we have that..." another said.

"How is my dear patient?" The man asked.

Returning to the kitchens, I released a stayed breath and finished up the remaining dishes. I put away various things in the kitchen. Mostly as an excuse to familiarize myself with where things belong. Anne's bread loaf was a hard, mealy thing that struggled to rise even beside the oven. It occurred to me that if her bread was awful, I might get a chance to trade positions with her. Best mind my own business.

I was tidying up the center table when Mr. Davies checked on us. "Ah, you're done. Come along."

A splintery broom was pushed into my pruned fingers. "Sweep all along here."

The hallway extended into the entryway and clear toward the other wing of the house. Try as I may, I couldn't find a single pinch of dust along the creaky wooden floor. It may have once been brilliant, but now, it was a house full of relics. Even the water closets were outdated by current standards. Still, it was nicer than cold feet making their way to an outhouse, but I couldn't help but feel disappointed by the state of the manor.

It was a brick-and-mortar ghost. Without life or affections. My flat had more warmth even in the dull ache of morning after the fire died. It was a forlorn relic from someone else's time. Who were the Joneses, and why did they take no pride in their home?

Mr. Davies was off once again to boss around another unfortunate maid. The way he walked was jarring, like he was marching off to war. As if something was incredibly pressing all the time. Imagine feeling that important. My cleaning of a clean floor served a purpose, but it was not for the benefit of the floor.

I often wondered how nearly a third of the town was employed in this one manor. There was only so much polishing that could salvage this antique furniture. Candles half-dwindled everywhere, and there were wax stains on the floor of the entryway where the chandelier remained tarnished and unlit.

As far as I could tell, there were no kids running around. The couple were newlyweds, so that made sense. The parents, Mr. and Mrs. Jones senior, were long gone, so there were no elderly to care for. Just a small staff for a couple of grown adults. If Mrs. Jones had money, why let the place remain this way?

Outside the parlor doors, I found it. A single rogue dust bunny that escaped the clutches of the last sweeping. It was important that I had something to sweep into the bin; otherwise, I ran the risk of appearing incompetent or, as I feared, not needed.

It was a tangle of blonde hair, probably pulled from a brush recently. I herded the little hairball all the way to the steps when a smartly dressed young man opened the pocket door as he and his guest emerged from a bedroom.

Mr. Jones was not much older than I. He wore a black suit that matched his slippers. Blond man with a clean shave. Well-bred by the looks of it. He wiped his forehead with a handkerchief despite the chill in the house and unbuttoned his jacket to place his hands on his belt.

"She's not getting better," Mr. Jones said. "She hasn't left her room since we came home."

The man I presumed to be the doctor was a slight man with greasy black hair parted down the center. His mustache had more wax on it than the floor I swept. That reminded me. I resumed sweeping in blissful oblivion like the good little maid I was.

"Perhaps it is time we consider other avenues," the doctor said with a soft, fatherly voice. "We all knew this was a possibility."

Mr. Jones turned his gaze over the stair railing. There was a sadness in his face that didn't belong on a man so young. I remembered when his mother died. The news sent the entire town into mourning. Fredrick Jones couldn't have been more than fourteen then. It was always hard to lose a parent so young. I was six when my mother went toes up, and I still looked for her in all the usual places. Cozy by the fire with her knitting needles. Humming a little tune while she cooked up some toast...

"I know," Mr. Jones said. "My father was sympathetic to her condition as well."

The face of a stern, old man eclipsed the scene. It was Mr. Davies, and he was once again unhappy. "Are you quite done?"

My eyes fell to the floor, and the fruit of my efforts had been lost. "It's gone," I said.

"What is, Ms. Mayweather?"

"The hairball."

Mr. Davies closed his eyes for a long moment as if he were tired. "Dinah, I am a very busy man, with a limited staff, managing a large household on my own. I need to know that you are here to work and not to eavesdrop. We pay far more than the gossip columnist in Chester."

He was worried that I was a snitch! I was poor, but I had principles and human decency. I shook my head stupidly. The thought hadn't even occurred to me. Mr. Davies was right, though. They paid well here. The wages were more than any gossip columnist paid. Enough to cover all the bills and grow a savings account for the inevitable. After that, I could move to Chester and forget all about this rotten little village.

"Mr. Davies, I'd never—"

"Good," he said with a nod. His shoulders eased at that. My earnestness must have come through because the constantly ruffled butler relaxed. "Back to the kitchens then."

"Do you think she can attend the dinner with me tonight?" I overheard Mr. Jones ask the doctor as their heels clopped down the steps.

Mr. Davies remained in the entryway to see the men off, but before I made it toward the kitchen, I heard the doctor say, "Oh yes, what I gave her will put the pep back in her step tonight!"

Giving one more glance toward the hallway, my mouth pursed at the notion. What kind of woman needed so many vitamins to take a step outside her door?

Greeted with a new pile of dishes. Anne was already putting her loaf in the oven. The poor thing hadn't even risen yet. It wasn't my job...yet. I rolled up my sleeves and heaved fresh water into the sink from a bucket and got back to work. Grateful to be rid of the situation in the entryway. Something about the way they talked about Mrs. Jones. Like she was some farm animal to be managed... I didn't like it. Was that how all posh men treated their wives? Like Broodmares?

The men at the pub weren't gentle about it, but at least their disdain was obvious. They drank and sang songs while their wives labored for hours to give them a son, then complained the next day when supper was late. God forbid their wives have girls. What use were girls other than trouble? Couldn't plow a field or take over the family business.

"She told Rosa she is going to jump off a bridge," Harriet said as she mutilated the chicken in the cast-iron skillet. Hadn't the poor bird suffered enough? To be at the hands of this woman had to be a crime. Boiled before stuffed and fried. They must have had a cook give notice recently and had no choice but to pick up where she left off.

Anne had her face in the oven, but after she tossed in a few more logs, she closed the door and said, "What was Mr. Jones senior thinking by marrying his son to her? They have plenty of money."

"With the state this place is in, I'm not so sure," Harriet said. "Mrs. Jones must be rolling in her grave."

I couldn't help but scoff while wiping down a fine China plate that cost more than my entire flat. "That's the thing about posh people," I said. "It's never enough."

It was an odd moment. I half-expected the two women to ignore me, but just like that, I was inducted into their little group. Harriet stopped stuffing herbs into the back end of the chicken.

Anne nodded with agreement before saying, "No, I suppose not. But Mrs. Jones holes up in her room all day; she doesn't do anything for the household. That's not how the lady of a manor is supposed to act. It's like no one taught her better."

"I can't say I know anything better myself," I said, aware of my own inferiorities.

"You're the Mayweather girl, right?" Harriet asked. I was taken aback by the transition in the conversation. I looked over my shoulder at Marie, who flinched under my gaze. "I didn't mean anything by it," she added.

"I am," I said.

"Your mother worked here before she got pregnant with you," Anne said.

I didn't need the reminder as much as Anne needed a wooden bowl whacked against that horse face of hers. "I know."

Anne's blue eyes glanced at me for a moment before she resumed chopping potatoes as if gauging the moment. Whatever she said next could either make us enemies or good friends. If my tone didn't tell her, my face did, but I was much younger than she, and I could make her life a living hell.

"You best be careful," the old woman said. "That old Mary has eyes for your pops. You might get stuck with two old geezers to care for."

I'd sooner burn down the flat. My scowl set Anne in a fit of giggles as if she read my mind, and I couldn't help but laugh too.

"And if you're not careful, you're going to serve the Joneses some burnt chicken."

Her eyes went wide before she spun around to tend to the stove. The chicken she pulled out was brown, but perhaps they wouldn't notice. "Don't worry," I said. "Being overcooked might cover the abuse it suffered at Harriet's hands."

Harriet put a hand on her hip and feigned offence. "Well, if you're such an expert, why don't you give it a go tomorrow?"

My moment had arrived.

CHAPTER TWO

W hen I went home that evening, I didn't walk alone. Harriet walked with me in the dark. She carried a single lantern, and the light glowed warmly on the ground. It was nice having someone to talk to for a change. Marie stayed at the manor, but I didn't know who else did.

"Anne and Marie aren't coming?" I asked. I omitted Rosa because I hadn't met her just yet. She had spent the day holed up with Mrs. Jones.

"Oh no, the others live in the manor. Someone has to get the house started in the morning and be there if the Joneses need them."

That made sense. Houses that size must have been freezing without their great big fireplaces. No doubt Mr. and Mrs. Jones required bed-warmers and whatever else it was that posh people were immobilized without.

"What about Mr. Davies?" I asked.

"He stays behind as well. It's just the four of them most nights. Sometimes I stay if the Mrs. is feeling too poorly, but they have some fancy dinner tonight, so I imagine they will all be relaxing a bit."

Did the lady of the house really cause so much trouble? "I thought she didn't leave her room."

"She don't unless the doctor gives her all that stuff from his bag," Harriet said. "She has these fits sometimes, and we're afraid she's going to seriously hurt herself. Sometimes she will scratch at her face to keep from having to go."

"I see." It wasn't that I couldn't relate. On the contrary, I was quite envious that I hadn't thought of it first.

If I had scratched at my face, screaming, maybe Mary would think twice before barging into the house. It was genius, really, but I couldn't say such a thing. "That's horrid."

"The doctor says that hysteria is more of a mental thing. It was thought that the uterus caused different problems depending on where it migrated to in the body, but this doctor is real smart. He said the uterus don't move at all, and that something is wrong with Mrs. Jones's psyche."

Scratching at faces, migrating uteri, baking in the kitchen, this job was becoming more interesting by the minute. I didn't mean to be morbid, but honestly, how bad could this woman be? "Well, at least the rich girl has a fancy doctor to cater to her psyche. Maybe that fancy doctor will have a look at my father, too."

Harriet's side eye was not lost in the darkness. The dirt road had grown slick with the cool night air. The intermingling of moisture in the air and dirt had spread across the land, and tinges of the farmer's manure added to the earthy pallet.

"You're a bitter one," Harriet said. "I suppose if I were in your shoes, I'd feel the same."

"Spare me the pity," I said harshly. "Me mum is dead, and my poor Da is sick. Last time I checked, there were orphans living in the street with smog in their lungs."

"That doesn't mean you can't be sad about who you've lost."

"Sadness costs too much," I said. "I can't afford it."

"I think you're just scared," Harriet said. "There's no shame in being afraid of death and what it does to you."

I swallowed the lump in my throat and went on as though I didn't hear her. Harriet went too far, but I didn't want to appear upset. Acting up only proved them right. It was better to shrug it off like nothing bothered me.

The village emerged from the trees, displaying a dimly lit little square dotted with six lanterns. At night, the bakery hosted folks to come and drink since we didn't have a proper pub. My mouth watered, wishing I could sit down and have myself a pint, but it was frowned upon for ladies.

No, we had to suffer our drunk husbands and squalling children without libations. The menfolk would kick me out further than I could spit, and I could spit a good several feet.

"Well, I'm off," Harriet said. "You'll find your way, yeah?"

"Yeah," I said, releasing Harriet from the moment. "My father will need rescuing from the widow Mary."

The maid gave a gruff chuckle. "See you in the morning then."

I went to the front door of my home, and I fully meant to enter just then, but another idea came to mind. A dry smile wrapped across my face, and I hesitated. Once Harriet was out of sight, I left my yard and waded through the dark. I knew the village like the back of my hand. Weaving in and out of the neighborhood, I came across a slightly less shabby flat than my own and grinned.

Parked against the fence was a bicycle. It was shiny and new just last year, but Robert left it outside in the rain so often that it was already flaking with rust. I took the bicycle and walked it into the darkness of a tree line where no one could see me. The chain clinked as it rolled, and I constantly searched around, making sure no one could see me up to no good.

There, I picked up a good-sized boulder, making sure to knock off the slugs and mud. It was a nice rock, and it would do its job well.

With both hands, I bashed the front wheel of the bicycle. I smashed it over and over until the tire frame was bent inward. Once that was done, I yanked the seat away from the rest of the frame and threw it into the woods for good measure.

That was for the jabs about me and my dress. The mud. The lewd comments outside the bakery, and for any other time he or anyone else gave me a hard time.

His parents saved up the money to get it, and he treated it like he treated everything else, like rubbish. I would have loved to have a short ride to the manor; I had no doubt Robert would have ridden the bike to splatter more mud on me the next day if I didn't do something. My dress was soaked in cold sweat as I stifled a laugh. I had never acted out like this before, but something about working at the manor emboldened me.

It squeaked and thumped along the road as I gently replaced it in the spot Rodger had left it. Sated with revenge, I returned to my flat, where I found my father asleep in the same chair I had left him in. The fire blazed hot, thanks to Mary, who was seated beside my father, knitting as if she owned the place.

Mary's wide forehead shone in the firelight behind her red hair. She leaned forward when I walked in and said, "Well, how did it go?"

"It was fine," I said. "I washed dishes."

"And what about the girl Fredrick married? What is she like?" Mary asked.

I had no desire to spread gossip, especially not to my neighbor. Mary would spread the tragic story of Mrs. Jones to the entire town before daybreak. Mr. Davies was so relieved when I promised to keep quiet about the lady of the manor, I didn't want to disappoint him.

"I haven't met her," I said. "I was too busy in the kitchen.

Frustration clouded Mary's face. She bundled her knitting needles into the yarn and stood up to leave. "I should go. He needs his rest."

More needed to be said. Mary was unsatisfied with the conversation, and she was the type of woman who needed catering to. Unbaling my fists, I relented. She did us a good turn many a time, and I would be decent enough to notice.

"I thank you for watching my father," I said. "I know you being here has comforted him greatly."

This put a smile on Mary's doughy face. "Really dear, it's no trouble."

That night, I hung up my uniform and fell into my bed.

Mum may have worked at the manor before me, but that didn't mean we were destined to the same fate. Lots of people worked at the manor. Some moved away from the village. Others quit and moved on with their own businesses. There would be nothing to stop me from pushing on once... I hated myself for even thinking it.

As my mind drifted off to sleep, an image of an empty flat came into view. A catalogue on my mother's old vanity, other odd images came to mind. Long, smooth legs with pointed toes and soft arms that draped over the knee. Of the trails of soft pink georgette fabric draped over a thin frame, and effortlessly curly blonde hair falling all around me.

Expensive rosewater hung in the air. I had never known a dream to have scent before, but it was as real as the pillow I rested my face on. No one I knew owned rosewater unless it was homemade. It was as though the dream were a premonition that someone beautiful was about to enter my life. Just so long as I didn't botch things up.

#

The morning was quieter than usual. I didn't notice it at first, but as I washed the dishes, the silence in the kitchen grew ominous enough for me to pause. The tiny hairs around my nape started to rise in warning of something. Like I was being watched.

I turned around half-expecting a specter of my mother, or a crazed Mrs. Jones wailing and tearing her hair out. It occurred to me that I didn't know what the lady of the manor even looked like.

There was no one in the room. That was the reasoning behind the silence. Neither Anne nor Harriet was in the kitchen. Not even Marie, though she didn't work in the kitchens often. Since my expressed interest in preparing food, the three of us rotated the duties. Today I did the morning dishes, which left Harriet and Anne to see to breakfast. When they were not at their stations, I just assumed breakfast was served early.

The kettle was hot, and the eggs were out. Sausage and tomatoes lay abandoned on the counter. Bread had been sliced, and there was a half-opened jar of berry preserves on the counter. The milk was picked up, but it wasn't poured into the carafe.

Needing an excuse to leave the kitchen, I finished preparing breakfast. Mr. Jones always ate by himself in the parlor or the dining room, so I took the tray to the door and knocked. There was no answer.

"Mr. Jones?" I asked before opening the door. I found the room empty. The fire wasn't lit, and the chill in the room bit at my knuckles as I clutched the silver tray.

There was a commotion from upstairs. A shout followed by a shattering sound. I held my breath and waited. It sounded like a fight, but with who? I searched the entryway and halls for someone, but the rest of the manor was weirdly empty. "Mr. Davies?" I called.

My voice echoed up to the crystal chandelier and went unanswered. If something was wrong with Mrs. Jones and I didn't help, they might blame me. At the same time, walking in on an ill woman without orders was a good way to lose my job. Another clipped shout came from upstairs. Anxiety hardened in my gut.

Turning around, I jumped back. There was a person directly behind me. I nearly dropped the tray, but Mr. Davies caught it. "Dinah, what are you doing?" he asked.

He had a way of appearing at the worst time! I gasped and stumbled a step back, my heart pounding like a snared rabbit. Frightened me half to death.

"I didn't know where you were, where anyone was," I gasped. The damned corset restrained each breath. "I think they're fighting up there."

Mr. Davies frowned. We both went silent so that Davies could confirm the commotion. There was little by this point. I hoped he didn't think me a liar.

"I was seeing Mr. Jones off. I was surprised to find no one in the kitchen," he said.

That explained why the parlor fireplace wasn't lit. I myself had yet to meet the lord of the manor. He was always off on business trips. I wasn't even sure what he did. "My guess is that Anne and Harriet went upstairs to serve Mrs. Jones."

But that was Rosa or Marie's job. Mr. Davies did not go into the room unless Mr. Jones was there. It wasn't appropriate for a man to be left alone with a woman in her bedroom. Only the doctor was permitted to be alone with Mrs. Jones.

The door opened, and both Anne and Harriet emerged from the upstairs bedroom. Their otherwise pale faces were enflamed, and they were huffing and puffing franticly. I closed my drooping mouth and watched the two older maids bumble down the stairs. Their hats were missing, buns undone as if they had gotten into a brawl and lost. Long, red lines were drawn along Anne's right arm, and Harriet's uniform was torn at the collar.

"What is going on?" Mr. Davies asked. "I found Dinah wandering the hallways with a tray—"

"It's the missus," Harriet gasped. "She's having one of her episodes."

"Where is Rosa? Marie?" Mr. Davis asked.

"Gone," Anne said. "Both of 'em. Picked up and left. Rosa said she couldn't watch that woman mutilate herself anymore, and Marie followed. They were too young to be lady's maids. I fear we just made things worse, Mr. Davies."

I wasn't at all surprised by that. Anne was a crusty old woman, and while Harriet had a good heart, she was a lot of bluster. Mr. Davies was beginning to panic. He started to pace back and forth, stroking his moustache. "I should call for the doctor," he said. "But by the time he gets here, it may be too late."

"We're not going back up there," Anne declared. Harriet locked arms with her fellow maid and nodded.

"Just until the doctor arrives—"

"That woman is insane!" Anne cried. "She nearly yanked my hair out."

"That vase flew out of nowhere! Didn't even see it in her hand," Harriet said.

"Look at my arm," Anne gestured to the scratches. "She's ripped at her face and pulled chunks of her hair out. It's like she's having some sort of seizure. She's convulsing and flailing about. It's unnatural, I tell you. That woman is possessed!"

I had to bite my tongue to keep from laughing. Oh no, a possessed posh woman. Someone get the smelling salts! It reminded me of the old goat penned up on a nearby farm. The kids were so frightened of it.

They would stand outside the fence and shriek at its every movement, then wonder why it charged them. This woman was no different, and I didn't care for the superstitious nonsense everyone else in the village ranted about.

Mr. Davies paled at the mention of the vase. "Oh lord, not the Cloisonné Hu-Form!"

A tragedy to be sure.

The woman upstairs was suffering immensely without the aid of her doctor, but no, not the vase. Meanwhile, I was standing like an idiot with a tray, as if I had somewhere to go with it. This wasn't my problem. I had bread that needed making. I turned to return to the kitchen when Mr. Davies called, "Dinah..."

I closed my eyes and clutched the tray as though it were my last grip on sanity. No, no, no. Everything was going so well. The last thing I needed was to get mixed up in all this. I didn't know the first thing about upper-class women. It sounded like a good way to get fired, or worse, get something expensive thrown at me. I heard about maids who broke things; they had to pay for them even if the fault wasn't entirely theirs. I'd be one vase away from indentured servitude.

Not daring to turn around, I said, "Yes, Mr. Davies?"

He let out an exasperated sigh. "I require your assistance."

"I really ought to see to the kitchens," I said. "Anne and Harriet will maim the bread."

The threat of bad bread wasn't going to be enough in the face of an upset woman breaking priceless vases. I turned around and faced the group and understood there was no saying no. Harriet wrenched the tray from my hands, and soon I was being guided by Mr. Davies up the stairs.

The red damask carpet runners muted my clumsy steps, and I looked over my shoulder to see that Anne had hurried to the kitchen and Harriet was saying a prayer with her hand tracing a cross over her person. Traitors. Saving their own hides. I swallowed the dry lump in my throat. I wasn't scared. I was just tense from holding that tray for so long.

"Now," Mr. Davies said. "When you're up there, it's important that you don't say or do anything to overstimulate the lady. Just try and keep her distracted until the doctor comes, and that should be around dinnertime. Mr. Jones should be home by then as well."

Mr. Davies was fidgeting. He was probably more nervous than I was. "What if she breaks things?" I asked. "Will I be held responsible?"

"No," Mr. Davies shook his head so fervently his moustache waggled. "You won't be held responsible for anything she does. The Joneses were duly informed about her condition before she married into the family."

Why me? I understood that Mr. Davies could not be with the woman unaccompanied as he was no family, but there had to be someone else. A laundress? A priest, maybe? Why did Mr. Jones marry her in the first place?

Before I could ask, we were at the door. Mr. Davies gave me a sullen nod and said, "Best of luck."

I hesitated at the door. What could I possibly do for this woman? I knew nothing about Hysteria or the woman behind the door. I had to do something, though. This woman was in pain; the least I could do was sit with her. I looked down at Mr. Davies, who was gesturing with his hands, urging me into the room. I took a deep breath and readied myself for whatever happened next.

I knocked on the door, and no one answered. "Mrs. Jones?" I called.

Mr. Davies was motioning for me to just go in, so I did. The thick, blue curtains were partially drawn as if someone had tried to open them but stopped. The ringed canopy was made with a matching fabric, and the carpet was a lighter shade of blue. There was a fireplace and a full furniture set accompanied by a loveseat and a table.

It was the typical Victorian bedroom if you subtracted the shards of broken vase I had to step over as I entered the room. There was an adjacent room off to the side. I assumed it to be another bedroom.

"Missus Jones?" I called.

There were muffled sobs coming from the bed and a sifting of pink fabric. I got closer and saw a shock of wheat-colored hair wound in great curls that fell across her bare shoulders and onto the bed. Her back was fully exposed to me. Silky soft skin that had never seen a whip or a day of hard work. The morning light caressed the curve of her back and along her toned hip. She turned in her bed, facing up, exposing a face, chest, and arms covered in long, red lines dotted in blood.

My breath went ragged. I felt horrible for ever thinking her condition was a shod for avoiding work. Those weren't little scratches; they were deep, painful rips in her flesh.

"I'm sorry," I said, forcing my gaze downward. "I just wanted to make sure you're all right."

The woman's cry was trapped in her throat as she twisted and writhed in her bed. I backed against the door and stifled a gasp. She was like a woman possessed. Her arms bent back in a most unnatural way. I couldn't just leave her like this. If that mean old goat got his horns stuck in the fence, I'd help. It was no different with her. She was not possessed. She was sick.

Slowly, I approached the bed. "You're all right," I told her.

Mrs. Jones's eyes were rolled so far in the back of her head that the whites of her eyes glowed in the soft candlelight. I thought about the frenzied articles in the news about institutionalized women. Such things weren't just black and white on a bit of paper... These were real women, just like her, suffering.

"Hey," I said. Uncertain of what to say as I sat beside her convulsing body on the bed. "You have every right to be upset."

Was I reaching her? It was impossible to tell. I gently pushed her down at the stomach, and she was as rigid as a dead body. I jerked my hand away. Shame washed over me then. I was afraid of her, just like everyone else. If I were her, I'd hate that.

Rosewater.

A potent, floral rosewater wafted from the woman in the bed. Her golden hair...just like my dream. I shook the thoughts from my head. Plain old Dinah didn't have premonitions.

"Listen here," I said. "I'll have none of you hurting yourself. You can be sad, you can cry and shout, you can break every priceless item you want, but the next time you cut yourself, I'm going to give you a slap. Lady or no. They can fire me, but you'll think twice before hurting yourself again!"

Where it came from, I couldn't say. I didn't want to be fired, especially not for slapping the lady of the house, but I was angry at her for hurting herself. She could do anything but that. Mrs. Jones deflated in her bed. It had worked, or maybe her convulsion had simply run its course.

Her eyes snapped open then. Wild blue eyes raged at me as her hands took the form of claws. She swiped at me, but her nails raked uselessly against the thick wool of my uniform. She was exhausted. Those nails needed trimming for sure. Why had no one done it sooner?

"You can hurt me all you like," I told her. "I can take it."

She fell back against the pillow, blonde curls cascading over the fancy embroidery. Tears rolled down her temples. I struggled not to tear up myself. What afflicted this woman so? I took her hand and held it for a long while. I said nothing more until she stopped crying.

"Where are your nail scissors?" I asked.

Mrs. Jones made eye contact for the first time. She was a striking beauty. Her soft, full lips and shapely nose. Her features timeless and strong yet feminine in every way. She didn't answer, but I had a hunch they were somewhere on that vanity with the hand-painted roses.

I rummaged through the vanity before finding scissors with a gold sparrow on the handle. Mrs. Jones eyed me like a feral cat eyed the village boys.

"What are you doing?" she asked. Her voice was a low, husky tone enunciated in a foreign accent. I had never heard an American speak before. It sounded nothing like the impressions folks gave after a few pints.

"I'm just going to trim down those claws of yours," I said.

I took her soft hand in mine and went to clip when she whipped her hand away and struck me across the arm. "How dare you!"

"How dare you!" I said, my temper flaring. "Hurting yourself like this."

"Get out!"

There I was, trying to help her, and she thought she could bully me off. No sir. This woman was spoiled and needed to be told off. She might have frightened the other maids, but her behavior was all too familiar.

"No." I wasn't going to leave until I trimmed those nails. "My mother acted like this when her fever became too great," I said. "You don't scare me."

"And why not?"

I took her hand a second time and cut the jagged, broken nails, stained pink with blood. "Because you're not dying."

She stopped arguing then. I hadn't meant to say it, but something about this had my temper going. Perhaps it was because my mum spent so much time in bed. It brought me back to a time when I was little and helpless. I wasn't a child anymore, and neither was Mrs. Jones.

When I finished one hand, she gave me the other without a fuss. When I finished, I traced my thumb along the edges of each finger, searching for snags. Soon, her fingernails were smooth with her fingertips. There would be no more of that on my watch.

"Are you all right?" I asked when I was done.

She sniffed and let out a small laugh. "When people ask if you're all right, they don't want the real answer. Especially not in this country. I could ask a shoeless beggar if they were all right and they would say, 'yes'".

"You're not wrong," I said.

Perhaps that was the wrong thing to say, but what did I know about comforting distraught posh people? She wasn't screaming or convulsing at me, so there was that.

"English people are known for our stiff upper lip. We take everything in stride but die a little inside with every hit we take."

She turned to me then, and I understood why Mr. Jones married her. She was the kind of woman men wrote poems about. Even with the long, red claw marks across her neck, chest, and arms. Blood was drying and caking in spots along her scalp. On the floor was the occasional lock of blonde hair coiling like a golden snake in the morning light.

This woman wasn't going to see my hands tremble, but it must have shown on my face because her wet eyes smiled with a coy recognition. She pulled her nightgown over her shoulders and sat up. The neck of the garment fell wide across her shoulders, exposing a marred décolleté.

"When I called out for someone, I didn't expect you. Hand me my cigarettes, will you?" she motioned to the silver case on the tallboy.

Just what had she meant by that? Perhaps she was the one who asked Mr. Davies to hire a new maid. "Most wouldn't expect me to serve a lady, ma'am."

"Indeed not." She emphasized the ending sounds of her words so poignantly. It was a sign of a formal education, unlike my own slang, whichI tried to control at work. This woman attended elite schools and knew far more than I ever would.

I tripped over my maid uniform but managed to save myself from falling with the arm of the loveseat. Her eyes followed me to the tallboy where I retrieved her cigarettes and matches. She was still facing the closed window when I approached with the case in hand.

"You're not as they are," she said, taking the case from my hand.

Even an American could tell I didn't belong any more than a fish riding a horse. Her recovery was quick, and her sudden confidence put me at ill-ease. I hoped she wouldn't tell anyone the things I had said to her. I fumbled with the match, but when it sparked into a quick flame, she leaned into it, her breasts nearly exposed with her reach.

"No, ma'am."

"Penelope," she said. "Please call me Penelope."

Her eyes were so sad. She struck me as someone who was lost and profoundly lonely. Harriet warned me to not get too familiar with the Joneses, but how could I not in a moment such as this?

They're not like us...

I couldn't afford to get familiar or involved. Harriet was right. They weren't like us. She asked me to call her Penelope, but what would Mr. Davies think of that? If I married some rich bloke and joined the upper-class society, no doubt Penelope would make it a point to tell everyone at her fancy parties that I was once her maid. She would mock me and laugh. Under her employment, she could decide who and what I was.

The moment I no longer served her purpose, I'd be sent packing with little regard for my well-being.

"Please try to cheer up, Mrs. Jones. You've got a wonderful life."

She sneered at me and threw her lit cigarette on the carpet. A tuft of black smoke accompanied a sputter of sparks as she stared at me, daring me to put it out. The natural inclination in this moment was to hurry and stop it, even if it was a source of amusement for her.

"You're all the same after all."

Her own flames lit my own. She had baited me, and I couldn't help but nip the hook. Yelling at her was not an option, though I desperately wanted to. The skunky smell of the burnt carpet filled the room. Before she could object, I yanked open the windows. She squinted against the daylight. A tit for tat.

"All right," I said. The Anne and Harriet approach didn't work. I had to try my own way. I sat down beside her on the bed. The informality of the action startled her. "What is it like then?"

"Ever since I came here," she said, "people keep barging into my room, waking me up, urging me to eat. I can't eat first thing in the morning. Everyone is rushing about, and they keep telling me about what they are doing. Why?"

I opened my mouth to speak, but she went on.

"Fredrick keeps dragging me to all these parties. They hate me. They laugh behind my back—I just know it. I'm not one of them. They think me absurd and stupid. Maybe I am."

There she was, confidant one moment, then blown out and defeated the next. Her nightgown had slipped off one rounded shoulder as her curls tried to braid themselves into the garment. I could relate in some ways. Sure, I wasn't highborn, and I didn't know if her peers hated her the way she said, but I knew what it was like to be an outsider.

"The people at the village laugh at me too," I said. My hands were clasped tightly together in my lap. "I'm not the most ladylike, and I never really got on with any of them."

"I do like a rugged girl," Mrs. Jones declared as her eyes scanned me up and down.

The brazenness of it. All I could do was blink. She laughed and took out a second cigarette, lighting it herself this time. The way she said it made me flush and reminded me of the stocking advertisement. The smoke coiled above her head like a halo.

"Boys are rotten bastards anyhow," she said.

"Aren't they, though?"

We both snickered at that.

"Freddie isn't a bad sort," she said. "He's kind, but he doesn't know a thing about women. I just miss my home. I had friends... I knew my place in life."

"I envy you for that. I'd give anything to get away from this place and get a fresh start."

She nodded as she took a long draw from the stem of her cigarette. "I thought that's what I wanted too. The lady of a grand manor, mingling with Dukes and charming English aristocrats—away from my parents."

"I don't know much about the posh life," I said with a relenting sigh. "But I know nothing is what it's made out to be. Even then, sometimes the stuff you assume is bad turns out to be okay."

She stopped squinting enough to look at me then. The pace of my heart quickened, and I swallowed.

"Are you so certain the boys don't like you?" she asked, extending a long arm, offering me a puff off her cigarette. I knew Mr. Davies wouldn't approve, but given the situation, perhaps he would forgive me.

"It doesn't matter," I said. I didn't know why I was saying this, but I felt like I could tell her anything. "'Cause I don't like them none."

"Well, I can't fault you for that. Do you like being a maid?"

Nothing could shock this woman. I had heard that ladies in the bigger cities were acting more modern these days, smoking and drinking and the like, but Mrs. Jones was something else. I wished I could be like that. Like consequences couldn't touch me. It must have been the American upbringing. They were far more modern over there.

I took the cigarette and took a draw off the filter. Harsh tobacco filled my lungs. They contracted, threatening to make me cough, but I forced it down. The warmth of her lips on the filter made me light-headed.

"Beats staying at home with my sick father and Mary. Or being evicted."

"New York is so different," she said. "People are blunt, not like they are here. They mean what they say. I always know where I stand with them."

I passed the cigarette back to her, grateful to be rid of the thing. Still, I enjoyed the rebelliousness of it. It was an open door to activities that were barred to me. As a high-status woman, she could get away with it, but the likes of me could never go about smoking. "We don't say things outright," I said. "We like our protocols."

"Do you ever," she scoffed, pulling her nightgown over her shoulder. "What a mess I must look like to you."

"Not at all," I said, and I stared her in the eyes when I said it. I wanted her to know I was serious, but the exchange left me as breathless as her cigarette.

I turned away first. My station demanded it of me. "I don't think you're a mess. You just need to assert yourself is all."

As distraught as she was, I'd never seen a woman so beautiful. She put the catalogue girls to shame. It didn't feel right, looking straight at her.

"Assert myself?" She laughed, nodding at the vase fragments on the floor.

"You're just trying to scare them off to defend yourself, but they don't hate you. None of us do, we just don't know what you want."

This made her scratch and tug at her scalp again.

"What I want? Not once has anyone asked me. I know I need to be a good wife. I hate that I can't control my moods. My doctor comes and loads me up with his medicines. It's the only way I can get out the door without losing my mind."

Something about that doctor made my gut feel all rotten inside. "The maids will continue as always until you tell them otherwise," I explained. "All you need to do is give them a new protocol and they will follow it."

"Just like that?" she asked with a snap of her fingers.

"You are the lady of the house. Everything will turn on your six-pence."

She smirked and said, "I'll never understand you people and your money."

"You're rich enough that you'll never need to."

It was bold, and I regretted it for a moment, but she burst into laughter. "I like you," she said. "You say it how it is."

It was never described as a positive trait before, but when she said it, a cool confidence came over me. "Anything you want done, just say it, and it will happen. You'll see."

"I don't want to be given a single cup of tea again."

I recalled the mornings when Marie or Rosa made tea even when Harriet said she didn't like it. Was it an intentional goad at Ms. Jones?

Maybe they got off on upsetting her. Then again, it might have just been habit. Maids compelled to put something on the tray to drink.

"What do you drink?"

"Strong, black coffee, none of that crème."

I nodded. We didn't have it in the kitchen, but Mr. Davies would make it happen. "What would you like to eat?"

"A poached egg."

That was it? Explained her slim frame. "Not even a piece of toast to go with it?" I asked. "I make an excellent bread."

She gave a nod of indulgence. "Well, for you, I suppose."

Joy overflowed in my chest. I smiled and jumped up. "I'll see to it straight away."

She batted those long black lashes at me, and I feared I'd never be able to say no to anything she asked. I left the room and leaned against the door. The pine smell of wood polish roused me from what felt like a waking dream.

My head had cleared of Mrs. Jones's intoxication. Lingering tobacco and rosewater evaporated, and my thoughts leveled. Closing my eyes, I tried to banish the odd hopes that clawed at my heart. Penelope...

It was only when I opened my eyes that the remedy for disillusioned infatuations was staring me straight in the face. Gone was any idea that Mrs. Jones and I could be friends or anything else. Mr. Davies was staring down at me, cheeks red and mustache twitching. It was a jarring departure from fantasy into the reality of my station.

"What happened?" he asked.

He was so animated and desperate. I felt bad for leaving him here in his panic when I was quite enjoying myself. "She doesn't want tea."

"She what?" Mr. Davies's eyebrows rose several inches.

"Mrs. Jones," I reiterated. "She doesn't like tea. Says she never wants another cup served to her. She also wants a poached egg with a slice of toast for breakfast."

Mr. Davies struggled with the information. His brow creased as the questions filled his head. No doubt he was wondering how I acquired this information. To be the mouthpiece of the lady—of *thee lady*—filled me with a smug excitement.

"She also does not wish to eat so early. Ten o'clock should be fine."

"But Mr. Jones eats at eight."

"Then we will have to serve two breakfasts," I said. "It's important that Mrs. Jones's wishes are seen to. She isn't confident that we are willing to listen."

The tried and true butler he was, Mr. Davies straightened. "Well, that won't stand. If Mrs. Jones wishes a late breakfast without tea, it will be done."

"And if you could procure some coffee," I added. "Just black coffee, she would enjoy that very much."

At this, his face lit with excitement that had me staggering back. "I know just the man!"

As I marched down the hall, determined to put some weight on Mrs. Jones. I didn't blame her for not enjoying the bread Harriet made, but still, to forego eating altogether was unacceptable. If I didn't eat on the regular, I'd be tearing my hair out and throwing vases, too. No doubt New York had fancy dining halls and French restaurants at every corner, but they didn't have all that in the village. I'd have to make do with my skills and hope it was enough.

Unbidden images of her full lips moving, taking long drags off her cigarette. I shook it off. There was to be none of that. Besides, Mrs. Jones was just a little too flirtatious to be sincere. Maybe she realized how captivated I was by her and decided to take advantage of it. What would the likes of her want with the likes of me?

False or not, I couldn't dismiss the encounter. Even if she was just having a go at me, it was nice.

In the kitchen, I smiled to myself as I carved her a slice of bread from my finest loaf. I was never very good at poaching eggs, but after three failed attempts, I managed one. The egg slid from the wooden spoon onto the buttered toast while humming an old nursery rhyme.

"Someone's in a good mood," Anne noted from the sink.

Harriet regarded me with some concern but kept her comments to herself. We didn't have the coffee she requested, but I opted for some fresh milk.

"She doesn't want tea," I said to the two maids. They only stared at me, gape-jawed with vacant eyes.

"All of that over some tea?" Anne asked.

"I suspect there's more to it than that. I think Rosa and Marie vexed her something awful."

Anne raised her eyebrows and made a sound of agreement. "Those two were always up to no good. Wouldn't surprise me."

Mr. Davies was waiting in the entryway for me to return. When I came with the tray, he took it from me and said, "Mr. Jones has returned early and is with the lady now."

With Mr. Jones back from his jaunt, Mr. Davies was once again permitted to enter the bedroom. Well, that was that, then. They would hire new lady's maids that would hopefully be more agreeable to Mrs. Jones. I could go back to baking in peace.

As I worked the dough, thoughts of Chester came to mind. What kind of apartment would I have? Maybe something above the bakery where I would work. The flour Mr. Davies procured was fine and well-milled. Proper bread flour. It was free of bugs, but I sifted it all the same.

Harriet and Anne leaned over the counter to stare at the pile of dough as if it were some alien creature. I placed a damp towel over the top of it and moved on to the cake. "Never had a head for baking," Harriet said.

"I couldn't tell you a good loaf from a bad one," Anne said. "How do you know when it's done?"

I poured a soupy, yellow batter into the tins. In the oven, it would go just until it stopped singing and the room was filled with the freshly baked cake scent. "It's supposed to double in size," I replied.

It wasn't some baker's secret. This was common knowledge that had somehow been forgotten in this kitchen. Wives everywhere knew this unless they relied on the baker, but most couldn't afford to.

"I don't see the point in baking our own when we can just buy it," Anne complained.

"Hers tastes a lot better," Harriet said. "Besides, the boy doesn't always get here in time.

"You don't knead the bread enough," I explained. "You should be able to stretch it until you can see through it."

"Before or after it doubles in size?" Harriet asked, prodding the lump under the towel.

"It's an awful lot of work when we can just buy from the baker," Anne said.

"But you won't want his once you've had mine," I said.

The two women scowled at my confidence. It wasn't polite or wise to make such bold claims, but I had made this bread countless times, and I knew it to be true. It was the first recipe my mother ever taught me. Just a basic loaf suitable for any dinner table. I had been making this bread since before I could spell out the alphabet.

A chalky dust cloud bloomed when I clapped my hands. The silky-smooth granules found their way into even the smallest of cracks in the counter. When the bread was pulled from the oven, Harriet and Anne hovered over the loaves and closed their eyes to inhale.

"The smell alone is worth it," Harriet commented.

"It smells like a proper bakery in here," Anne said.

Once it cooled a bit, I cut up a slice with a long, serrated knife and gave them each a slice. One would have thought Anne was seeing God in that moment. Her eyes were turned upward as she chewed. Harriet had devoured her slice and had the knife in hand, going for another.

There was no reason that sod in the village should make money off this family while I was here. By not hiring me, he lost his biggest customer. This job was turning out to be a wonderful thing indeed.

That evening, the stars glowed brighter than I had ever seen before. I gazed at them in admiration. It was too bad I didn't have one of those cigarettes. The evening was warmer than usual, and my uniform circulated the humidity around my body. If there was ever a good night to act rebelliously, it was tonight.

"So, you met the lady," Harriet started. She remained silent for so long that I forgot she was walking beside me.

"I did," I said, leveling my tone.

Harriet's side-eye was a nuisance to my otherwise wonderful day. She awaited the opportunity to remind me that the lady of the manor and I were not of equal standing. It was impossible to be close to her. Harriet wanted to tell me things I already knew. Shoes weighted by reality lowered me away from the stars and back to the village where my father was waiting.

"I think she just doesn't know what to do with herself," I said. "She feels like an outsider in her home as well as with Mr. Jones's friends."

"She told you this?"

I nodded. "She said she hates parties because she doesn't think the other poshes take her seriously. That's why her behavior is so frightful. She knows it doesn't solve anything, but she can't control it."

"And Mr. Jones does love a good party. Whatever the doctor gives her makes her act drunk," Harriet said. "It's no wonder they think her strange and amusing."

Like a brawler's punch to the gut.

So, there was merit to Mrs. Jones's fears. It was a vicious cycle. Her nerves would get the better of her, and the doctor would give her medicine that made her act strangely. She would attend parties under the doctor's influence. Mr. Jones's friends would laugh at the drunken wife, which confirmed her fears of inadequacy in British society.

"I don't know if I like that doctor," I said.

"He's a specialist in the field, and he's studied at the best American institutions, but I do wonder if his treatments are not making things worse for our lady."

I frowned with the full understanding that I would be forced to watch it play out. "It's Mr. Jones's concern, not ours," I said.

Harriet gave a solid nod in agreement.

There was only so much women had a say in. All we could control was our reputation, and even then, it was as easy to ruin one as it was to blow out a candle. I had to be careful with how I conducted myself around Mrs. Jones. Not just for myself, but for her as well. I needed to be a proper influence. How was I to teach a lady to be proper when I was anything but?

Back at home, my father appeared more improved than ever. He smiled warmly when I came through the door. "There she is!"

"Here I am," I said with a smile as I hung up my cape. "Where's Mary?"

"She is in the loo."

Hopefully, she'd fall in. "Well, I have some things I need to tidy in my room—"

The door swung open behind me, and Mary's shrill voice sounded. "Dinah!"

I rolled my eyes. "Mary."

"I heard Rosa and Marie quit today," she said. "Rosa, the poor girl, was beside herself. She said that she'd had it with Mrs. Jones and her episodes and that she couldn't take anymore."

This was enough to get even my father's attention. He leaned in and said, "What sort of episodes?"

How dare she go spreading that about the town! I'd tell Mr. Davies tomorrow. Rosa was never getting a job at the manor again. Marie just followed Rosa into the poorhouse. Now the old busybody was sniffing for clues. I had to calm myself. If I said something in anger, Mary would know there was merit to the rumors.

Unclenching my hands, I took in a deep breath and said, "The lady of the manor is American," I explained. "She has a different way of talking, and I think Rosa took offence. She proved to be an unsatisfactory maid. Mrs. Jones is a proper lady. Well educated, just... American."

This set Mary on her heels. Father leaned back into his chair, satisfied with the answer. "Marie is William's girl, isn't she?"

"Aye," Mary said. "She's a bit simple."

"They're young," I reasoned. "I think Rosa was antagonizing the missus, and Marie just didn't know any better."

The rumor that the maids lacked the emotional capacity to understand the well-educated and exotic American would reach Chester before the week was over if Mary had anything to say about it. Disaster would be averted.

"I'm going to bed," I announced before kissing my father on the head. "Goodnight."

"Goodnight, my dear."

That night when I lay in my bed, I thought about Penelope. I tried not to, but I always found my way back to her bedroom. The sheerness of her nightgown and the soft glow of her curls in the candlelight. Her voice, sharpened by her American accent, came unbidden to my mind. When I drifted off to sleep that night, her laugh echoed in the once uninhabited silence.

CHAPTER THREE

It was my turn to do the prep work in the kitchens. I was outside sitting in a chair, plucking the feathers out of a chicken in the chill of an English morning. It was soothing, really. My fingers were caught between the heat of the constant movement and the biting cold. Harriet said it was going to be a harsh winter, but the harshest winters were the shortest ones.

While outside, I was privy to the baker's boy knocking on the door with his basket of goods. Anne answered the door. Too far away to hear what was said, I inserted my own dialogue.

"Here I am," the baker's boy said. "God's gift to mediocrity."

"We'll have none of that stale bread from you," Anne said.

"But why?"

"'Cause we got our own bread, and it's better than yours," Anne croaked. "And you smell of onions."

The baker's boy stood there as she waved him off and shut the door in his face. He stared at the door as if he thought they would change their minds. I returned my attention to the chicken. It was rude and smug to snicker at the idiot who assumed no one else could manage a loaf of bread. Did he assume most of the village just lived off air?

Mr. Davies came around the corner of the house. "Dinah," he said. "Mr. Jones would like a word."

Fear seized me in the way I had been seizing those feathers. I examined his face for any clue as to why, but he was as unreadable as an old Latin bible. "What about?" I asked as he ushered me to the parlor.

The butler didn't answer; he simply opened the door. I hesitated for a moment, but he nudged me through the door. "Ms. Mayweather, sir."

Mr. Jones looked up from his newspaper and said, "Come in."

The parlor was a man's space to be sure. Black enameled wood framed the red velvet cushions that circled around a low table. The carpets were red with green floral squares, and the curtains matched the sofas. The height of the fireplace mantle was the proper height for a man, standing nearly five feet in height.

I entered the room and tried to figure out something to do with my hands. "Hello," I said, not daring a horrid curtsey. No matter how Mary tried, I never could manage the formal greeting.

"Please," he said, folding the newspaper neatly. "Sit down."

The parlor turned a bit as I made my way to the love seat opposite Mr. Jones. I couldn't afford to lose this job. There were no other prospects for me. I couldn't even prostitute myself to the village boys—though I'd sooner die than do that. If I was let go, I'd have to leave the village and go to Chester without a sixpence to my name. I would have to send as much as I could back to my father as a good daughter did. Maybe he could live with Mary. She'd agree to it if I sent money.

Maybe the workhouse was where I belonged.

Mr. Jones's blue eyes were pale as a cloudless sky. His jawline was longer than his youthful plumpness could keep up with, giving him a drawn appearance. The blonde stubble—signs of a burgeoning beard—glittered in the daylight.

He considered me thoughtfully for a moment before speaking. "What did you say to her?"

I didn't say anything apart from threatening to slap her. I didn't do anything if I omitted smoking cigarettes with the lady or forcing her to cut her nails. I shook my head in denial. "Nothing."

Maybe if I fell to my knees and begged for my job, he would forgive me.

"I got word my wife was in the midst of another fit," he explained. "When I came home, she was calm. Happy, even. She didn't tell me anything, but Mr. Davies explained what had happened."

Oh. My mind went blank as it dawned on me that he was attempting to praise me. I reassessed the situation. A hysterical wife, rioting staff, followed by a peaceful evening. "Well," I said. "You see, Rosa has always been a bit cruel, and Marie just did whatever Rosa did. I think they may have agitated your wife."

The news came to Mr. Jones as a revelation. His eyes went wide, and he crossed one leg over the other. "Really?"

"Yes," I said. "In fact, Rosa went about the village trying to spread rumors about what happened. I told my father and the widow Mary that it wasn't the lady's fault. Rosa refused to listen to anything the lady said, and she was just so frustrated by it."

"The tea," Mr. Jones said in recognition. "She told me that she was constantly being given tea despite never drinking it. She told Rosa she didn't drink tea, but it's a hard habit to break."

We giggled together like old friends. "Yes, it flows through our veins."

He laughed at that, exposing a set of white teeth. "I just can't get over the change in her after you spoke with her. Mr. Davies said you weren't in there for more than an hour."

Was our time together truly so brief? "If I may be frank, Mr. Jones."

"Please."

My tongue lashed about in my mouth as I struggled to find the right words. "I think Mrs. Jones just needs someone to talk to. A proper lady's maid with more experience. Maybe even an American, like herself."

Mr. Jones made an agreeing noise. "I think you're right. Rosa was intended to be a companion, but they didn't hit it off. I think she needs someone brighter. Someone like you."

"Me?" I said breathlessly. I couldn't possibly spend so much time with that beautiful creature. I spent five minutes with her, and I was smoking. Who knew what sort of trouble I'd find myself in? Rich women could afford to make such mistakes, but for me, it was a steep downhill fall into ruin.

"She needs an English companion. Mr. Davies doesn't think it's a good idea for some reason. I think it has to do with village gossip, but as we can see, gossip goes both ways. Merit over gossip, I always say."

I didn't think for a moment that he always said that. It came off as desperation more than anything. Mr. Jones was determined to keep a lid on his unhappy marriage, and he'd employ anyone who could help him save face. He'd hire the one who kept her quiet, and for some daft reason, he thought that person was me.

"You'd be given a raise, of course," he added.

I swallowed hard. "Raise?"

"A lady's maid gets paid more than a kitchen maid," he explained. "An additional pence each check."

Nine pence a week. That was over a half pound more than my already generous wage. I couldn't afford to say no. With that kind of wage for a few years, I could open my own bakery in Chester. When my father died, I could move into the manor, and the money would just pile up.

"I'd be happy to serve the lady," I said. I tried to curtsey, but my legs were too wobbly. I should have known better than to try, but I wasn't in my right mind. All I could see were the coins piling up in my savings jar.

"Good. It's settled then," Mr. Jones said as he stood up, signifying our conversation was over.

I followed the master of the house out the parlor door, where Mr. Davies waited.

"Mr. Davies," he said. "Ms. Rosa is not welcome in our home again. Dinah will be the lady's maid. Also, bring me a salt soak. My feet are swelling again."

"Very good," Mr. Davies said with a bow.

The rest of their conversation was distant for me then. My eyes were on the door above the stairway. I didn't know the first thing about being a lady's maid. I would be with her most of the day. What would I do? There was only so much hair to brush. Whatever I did, I just needed to do my job. Keep her happy, and I'd make out for the better.

The parlor door shut, and I found myself alone with a rather stern-faced butler. "Well," he said. "I suppose congratulations are in order."

Mr. Davies had made his opinion known to Mr. Jones and now to me. I didn't entirely disagree with his opinion. I had no idea what I was doing. It was only a matter of time before they all knew I was unfit for such a role.

"I should get to it, then."

Before I got my foot on the first step, Mr. Davies took me by the elbow, forcing me to turn. "I must urge you to maintain the utmost professionalism. I know what you are, you know."

"And what is that, exactly?" I shouldn't have said that. He could have me sacked for it.

"You're a Tom. I know one when I see one." The butler's eyes fell to the floor as if he were suddenly ashamed. "Please excuse me, Dinah. I have no reason to make such accusations. Just...be careful. Not for Mrs. Jones's sake, but for your own."

I swallowed hard and nodded. "Of course."

Reclaiming my elbow with a swift jerk of my arm, I clung to the railing as I ascended the stairs. I had been shaken around enough by the morning's events. I didn't need him adding to the already crippling self-doubt.

How dare he call me out like that! I could be imprisoned for such things. The sheer gall of men was infuriating. If I had said something like that to anyone, I'd be shipped off without notice. Men had far too much privilege for their own good.

Then again, it was that male privilege that brought me to the door of Mrs. Jones.

I'd do my best to be a good lady's maid for her. Not because of the pay, the warnings, or even because I fancied her. I was already aware that I'd be spending the rest of my life alone without Mr. Davies reminding me. But because I could do the job the same as anyone.

If I could make Mrs. Jones better, maybe it wasn't too late for my father, either.

CHAPTER FOUR

I knocked on the door. "Mrs. Jones," I called before I entered the room.

She was standing beside her armoire, fighting with her corset. Right away, I could see the staggering difference in our undergarments. As a working woman, my stays were there for reinforcement and nothing more. Mrs. Jones's corset was a steel cage that pinched at the midsection. It was no wonder she was prone to fainting at parties. How on God's green earth did she manage in such a thing?

She didn't so much as glance over her shoulder, as if she didn't care who saw. "Help me with this, would you?" she asked.

I approached from behind, grabbing the laces. "Ready?"

She gripped the vanity. Her reflection in the mirror was one of sheer grit and determination. "As ready as I'll ever be."

I pulled the laces, drawing the corset tighter against her flesh. She didn't require a corset in the comfort of her own bedroom, but I wouldn't question her reasoning for wanting to wear one. The corset was nearly fully closed, flush against her skin when I tied it off.

"All right," she said, swaggering away. "I need a break for a moment."

I stood there, unsure of what to do next. Should I make the bed? See that her basin pitcher was full? The uncertainty left me paralyzed as she lit up another one of her cigarettes. I was full of nervous energy. Eager to please and fulfil a role I didn't quite understand. There was an unspoken formality, renewed from my promotion.

"Mrs. Jones," I said.

She regarded me then, her cigarette hanging between her fingers. She gave a thoughtful nod between draws from the stem. The room bloomed with smoke. "I know," she said. "This is new for you."

I untangled my hands from one another and nodded, feeling vulnerable and uncertain.

"Look," she said. "Back in New York, I didn't have a whole army of maids helping me. The apartment was too small for all this nonsense. Just follow me around and look busy; no one will notice the difference. I understand they gave you a substantial raise."

She understood... My eyes welled up and I bit my lip. Mrs. Jones knew I was no lady's maid, and she didn't expect one. I nodded, not trusting myself to do anything else without crying. A lady who didn't know the first thing about maids and a maid who didn't know anything about being one. What a funny pair we made.

"Good, you deserve it for putting up with the likes of me. I'm not accustomed to being fussed over. My father didn't approve of it. Just tidy up as you see fit."

"Yes, ma'am."

"It's Penelope," she said. "Call me Mrs. Jones in public if you must, but it's Penelope when no one is around."

That was it then? I just cleaned up here and there and stayed with her so she wouldn't be lonely. I could do that. How did Rosa botch this up? I searched the room to find that Penelope had picked up after herself. Her clothes were all neatly hung, and her belongings were in the vanity drawers.

She even made her own bed. Fluffed the pillows and everything. I didn't even make my own bed unless I thought Mary was going to barge in and do it for me.

"Though I do want you to continue making food when you can," she said. "You have a real knack for baking. Until I had your food, I just assumed all British food was terrible."

"I'll try to work it into my duties," I said. How I would manage that, I didn't know. I supposed I'd have to find time. Perhaps she napped. It would've been grand if I could rest whenever my day became too much.

She sat down in front of her vanity. "Style my hair," she said. "Try to hide the scabs."

Penelope scarcely left her room, as far as I knew. Why she needed to do her hair or wear a corset was beyond me. I would have thought it would aggravate her condition, but I supposed there wasn't much else to do. Dress, eat, undress, and go to bed. It wasn't much of a life, but it was hers to make.

She pulled up a pile of hair and frowned at it. "Help me with this, will you?"

Using her brush, I tamed her wild curls and pinned her hair into a Gibson—well as much of a Gibson as I could manage. I was never one for fashion. Her hair was so malleable in my hands, her curls twisted and folded into a neat pile that hid the scabs on her scalp. She turned from side to side, examining my work, and smiled.

"Good," she said. "Shall we?"

Now it was my turn to be nervous. I untangled my fingers that I was twisting about and straightened. I wasn't just the kitchen maid anymore. I was a lady's maid, and I needed to act the part. "Where are we going?"

"Freddie and my doctor both say I must leave the bedroom. I'd rather jump out the window and end it all than walk amongst so many strangers."

"What happens if you don't?" I asked.

Her eyes flittered down to her table before she fixed her paralyzing gaze on me. "Go madder than I already am, I suppose."

Her hands trembled as she braced my arm. She was afraid but determined to make it down the steps all the same. "You must think me a fool," she said.

Penelope's hands shook so hard, it sent tremors up my arm. Here she was, thinking she'd pass out from fear but doing it anyway. If anyone was the fool, it was me, fleeing the room every time my father coughed or tried to hold a conversation with me. I was the true coward, not her.

"I think you're very brave," I said. "When something scares me, I make a run for it."

"That's not an option when everything frightens you."

Perhaps not, but I couldn't help but admire her. Sure, she was posh and madder than a wet hen, but her boldness and honesty were something I wished I had more of.

Maids stared as we came down the stairs and scurried away, not wanting to interrupt whatever was happening with the lady of the house. I gripped her arm, aware of gossip that would follow. "You don't have to do this, you know," I said. "You don't need to prove anything to anyone."

"No," she said through gritted teeth. "I'm going to walk, and if I faint, so be it. If I vomit all over the floor, well, you'll have a mess to clean up."

I snorted with laughter. If that was supposed to frighten me, she had another thing coming. "Puke is nothing," I said. "Try living with a man who coughs up chunky blood."

Penelope's face screwed up. "Poor thing, it must hurt something awful. Is there nothing to be done?"

I shook my head. A funny thing happened then. Penelope straightened somewhat. It was as if the details of my father's illness stayed her tremors. So, I kept talking. "It started last spring. It was just a cough at first, but now he is nearly chair-ridden."

"Has he seen a doctor?" she asked.

"Last year," I explained. "Not that it did any good."

"Still," she said. "Something to ease his pain would be better than nothing. If I ask Mr. Davies to send a doctor, do you think he would? We would pay for it, of course."

Overwhelmed by the prospect, I didn't know what to say. It was so earnest and considerate. She barely knew me but was willing to spend good money on a doctor for nothing other than to ease his passing. Guilty wasn't even the proper word to describe how I felt.

I managed a nod before choking out, "Thank you. That means a lot."

"Don't thank me yet," Penelope said, glancing down at her with a smirk. "If I vomit, you will have your work cut out for you."

We made it down the steps and out the door. The wind pushed at our faces, and Penelope let out a slight groan before she leaned on me. "Nothing bad will happen," I said. "You're with me."

I don't know why I said it. Any number of things could happen, and I would be powerless to stop it. I might be able to fight off a prowler, but she wouldn't get far in that corset. If a flock of angry birds could mistake her hair for a nest, I would be too short to wave them off the top of her head. Like a giraffe, she was.

I couldn't quite think of anything else happening on the manor grounds.

Still, it felt like the right thing to say. Her boldness was waning, and I wanted to bolster that confidence even if it meant lying.

"I'm okay," she told me, though I suspected she was telling herself as well.

The garden was caged in with a short hedge that gave way to a white rose trellis gate. The path continued down the center, a rough but plucked path that straddled a lush green lawn. Tall trees and bushes sat toward the entrance, and white pillars marked sections for the more exotic plants, as well as a single swing that hung from the last two pillars in the back. The entire garden was enclosed behind a brick wall, a security measure for the previous ladies of the manor who valued their privacy above all else.

Come spring, the wildflowers birth a savage haven for bees. So much was dull and covered for winter, but even then, I could envision the potential.

We walked, Penelope and I, arm in arm. Steam erupted from our mouths as clouds in the chill autumn air, as the manor fell away from us. Penelope's stride became more stable the further we got from the house before she finally gave in to freedom.

"It's so nice to be out in the open air," she declared. "I didn't realize how confining that house was."

"You've left before," I said.

"Yeah, but I was under the influence of the doctor's medicine. That stuff can make anyone feel invincible."

Again, the unsettling sensation in my stomach. Just what was that doctor giving her? I had no reason to distrust the esteemed doctor, but I couldn't bring myself to accept him.

It probably had to do with my own upbringing. Doctors were called when things were bad. Might as well have called an undertaker for all the good they did. Nothing but bad news ever came from doctors. I didn't dare bring this up to Penelope, whose appearance brightened at the mention of him.

"I wish I could feel the way his medicine makes me feel all the time," she declared before sitting on the swing that hung between the pillars. Dormant ivy wrapped around the columns in thick ropes. They, too, would grow and expand in the spring.

I pushed against the small of her back. She projected her legs outward, the skirts of her dress flaring as she leaned back and giggled. Soon, Penelope was swinging in the air, squealing with delight. She was laughing with pure joy, and it was a gorgeous sight to behold.

We remained there for several hours. Seldom speaking, just relishing the outside air as much as we could before winter took hold. Her fingers were icy to the touch when I asked, "Shouldn't we go inside?"

She glared at the house with contempt. "I suppose we must."

"You don't have to stay in your room," I told her. "There is a lady's parlor and a small greenhouse."

Penelope considered this before saying, "Let's take lunch in the greenhouse."

I had hoped she would say that. I didn't have an excuse to go in there otherwise. I passed by many times and never rummaged up the courage to peek.

It was a small enclosure, not much larger than Penelope's bedroom. Green-tinted panes of glass created a house full of orchids, English roses, climbing vines, and lemon trees. In the center of the greenhouse was an iron table with two matching chairs. Penelope sat down at the table and unpinned her hat from her blonde hair.

"Do you want some coffee?" I asked.

"Yeah, and maybe some of that bread you made."

I hesitated at that. I hadn't made any bread. If I had known she wanted more, I would have made an extra, but those were dinner rolls. "Bread?"

"That thing they served for tea yesterday."

Right. She was referring to the sponge cake.

Penelope didn't know what it was called or the difference between an English cake and bread. I wasn't about to openly correct her. She had only been here for six months after all. I was just grateful she was eating. I had seen far too many trays returned untouched when I worked in the kitchens.

I left her in the greenhouse and came into the house through the formal dining room adjacent to it. I could have entered through the parlor, but I didn't want to risk interrupting Mr. Jones if he was in there. In the kitchen, Anne and Harriet were washing dishes and cooking up what smelled like sausage.

"Mm," I said. "It smells wonderful in here."

Harriet gave me a nod while she prodded some sausages in a skillet with a large fork. "How's life with the missus?"

I glanced at Anne, who shook her head at the mention.

"It's okay," I said. "We took a walk. She had a go on the swing."

Neither maid appeared nearly as excited about it as I was. Penelope had left her bedroom unaided by drugs for the first time since she arrived. Yet, everyone in the kitchen was behaving as though it were just an ordinary day. I supposed it was just another day for them. Were they upset that I had been promoted?

"Better you than us," Anne said while wiping a table down with ferocious swipes. "That one is—"

"We're just glad it's working out," Harriet said over the top of Anne, lest she say something regretful. "She's really taken a shine to you. Mr. Davies said that you're all she talks about."

Butterflies took flight in my stomach. "She's very kind," I said. "She didn't have maids in America, you know."

Harriet's red cheeks puffed at that. "No servants at all?"

"I heard her father was rather eccentric. Self-made man and all," Anne added.

I sliced up a piece of the sponge, making sure the strawberry filling remained intact. Waiting on the counter was a bag of roasted beans. I opened it and took in the scent. It was a strong, smoky scent that overwhelmed my senses.

"Do you have any idea how to make this?" I asked Harriet.

She shrugged. "Mr. Davies got it. Maybe he knows."

"Witchcraft, if you ask me," Anne grumbled.

I giggled at that. Anne was such an old codger. Still, I had promised Penelope coffee. I didn't want to return empty-handed. Besides, if the coffee tasted like it smelled, it would be a nice compliment to the cake.

The butler was nowhere in sight, and I didn't have the patience to look for him. I poured a handful of beans into a teapot and poured boiling water straight from the kettle. I let it steep like I would a strong Earl Grey before pouring it into a cup. It was dark and tasted bitter, but I hoped it was right.

I returned to Penelope, who was staring wistfully out the window. She took a sip of the coffee and cringed. "You're absolutely darling, but you make terrible coffee."

Butter held together better than I could in that moment. No one had ever called me darling before. There was something so sweet about it. It was probably just something Americans said. I needed to get used to that. She didn't mean anything by it.

"I didn't think you'd notice," I countered. "Not knowing the difference between cake and bread."

Penelope smirked and glanced at the cake. "It tastes more like a bread than a birthday cake."

"There are more than one kind of cake," I said, seating myself across from her.

"Whatever it is," she said taking a bite with her fork the wrong way, "it's delicious. Just the right amount of sweetness."

She smiled when she took a bite, savoring the flavor I had taken such care to provide before extending the fork to me. I shouldn't have, but she would have been offended if I declined. I took the fork and carved out a bite for myself.

It didn't get any better than this. Sharing a piece of cake with fresh strawberries, the scent of her coffee, relaxing amid the exotic blooms. We remained there until Mr. Davies found us and announced that Mr. Jones wished to eat dinner with his wife in their bedroom as they always did. Penelope did as she was told, as we all do, leaving me to take the plates to the kitchen. On her way out, Mr. Davies gave me an accusing scowl, as if just being near her would somehow tarnish Mr. Jones's wife.

I returned to the kitchen and got some started. Humming a little tune while I washed the dishes, I caught Anne encroaching on my dough, hovering over it like the grim reaper she was.

"Not yet," I told her. "It needs to rise."

Both maids were at attention now. Harriet, with her hands on her hips, asked, "How do you know it's done the second time?"

"It should bounce back when you poke it. Honestly, how have you never made a loaf of bread before?"

"We always just bought it." Anne scratched her head before giving the lump of dough a dismissive wave and returning to her chores. Of course, not only did they get paid enough to just buy their bread, but they also never made it at work. Poor people weren't the only ones who made their own breads. I was going to make bakers out of them yet.

CHAPTER FIVE

I t became a ritual of sorts.

I would come into the room around ten, she would eat, and I would help her dress before we walked and lunched in the greenhouse. This wasn't to say that it was always easy. Some days, Penelope trembled so violently in my arms that I feared she would crack her chattering teeth. Other times, I would be chasing after her with a hat and umbrella, she was so eager to be free of her bedroom.

But regardless of her state, Penelope put one foot in front of the other and made it outside. There was something so exciting about her little gains. The way she smiled at me. Like no one else in the world understood.

Not that I always understood. She said queer things from time to time. One morning, she rolled over and asked, "Did you get my message?"

Her face fell when I frowned. "Mr. Davies didn't tell me anything."

She rolled her eyes. "The doctor said I need to focus my energies to get messages across, but I can only seem to do it when I'm in one of my fits."

Harriet mentioned something about the doctor and his work with the psyche. It must have been some sort of exercise he developed to get her through one of her seizes. Like how people set their children to task to keep them out of trouble.

"Well, there's always a next time."

That morning, Mr. Jones declared that he wanted to hunt the pheasants. There had been complaints by some caretakers that they were being overrun by the long-tailed birds. Mr. Davies was opposed to the idea, but Penelope thought it exciting.

"Sir, it's not good to excite yourself so early in the morning," Mr. Davies called and chased after the young lord as he burst from the front door wearing a hunting jacket and donning a rifle.

"Davies, don't scare off my game!" Mr. Jones said.

Penelope and I watched the outburst from the swing and giggled as the butler frantically chased Mr. Jones across the lawn. "Does he like hunting?" I asked.

"He does now," Penelope said. She caught my confusion. "Freddie gets bored easily. Last month it was chess, and the month before it was Billiards. He goes through every crossword and every magazine or newspaper he can find. He's always busy and always working."

Mr. Jones did work a lot. He was always coming and going. "What is it Mr. Jones does, exactly?"

"He's a land agent," Penelope explained, pushing back on the swing. "He manages the properties of richer men. That is why he's so intent on social gatherings. He requires popularity and word of mouth along with his good name."

Was this also a burden on Penelope? It had to be. She must have felt a great deal of anxiety at these social events, where one wrong move could affect their livelihood. Her illness was more than just women's nerves. It was complicated and entwined with all aspects of her life.

A loud popping noise echoed in the distance, and birds took to the sky in droves. I was startled by it, but Penelope just laughed. It was strange how the smallest things could frighten the lady senseless, but things that scared the wits out of me didn't bother her at all.

"Not today, Freddie!"

"Hunting doesn't frighten you?" I asked.

She shook her head. "My father took me hunting as a girl."

That was rather unusual. Hunting was not something proper ladies did. Not that Penelope was what I would describe as a proper lady. That's what made her so exciting. She said her father was an unconventional man, and I was starting to understand. Imagining Penelope, dressed in her corsets and full hooped skirts, on a hunting trip was laughable. "He took you hunting?"

"I'm a good shot, believe it or not," she said. "I think my father wanted a son but had to settle for me."

"That's not so strange," I reasoned. "The grocer had three daughters, and they know their way around a cash register and can carry nearly as much as me."

"I bet they can hunt too." Penelope grinned and winked. I suspected she was right. The world was changing. With industry booming, women and children worked in all sorts of ways. It was no longer the times of my mother, when working as a maid was all a proper woman could do before marrying.

"Do you like your parents?" I asked.

Penelope's face soured. "Is it wrong to say no?" she asked. "They provided me with so much, yet they dominated every aspect of my life. I attended fine schools, and when my nerves became too great, they found the best doctor money could buy. When I became sick, my mother became overbearing and my father distant. Part of the reason why I married Freddie was to be far from them, but even an ocean isn't far enough."

The hedges shook wildly, and Mr. Jones emerged with an injured bird flapping wildly in his hand. He held it up by its feet. "We're having pheasant for dinner!" he announced.

"Oh, Freddie, that poor bird," Penelope scowled.

He regarded the bird before slinging the gun over his shoulder. "It's just a bird, my love."

Grabbing the feet with his free hand, he twisted the bird's neck. Bones snapped, and the fowl went limp. Mr. Jones smiled at his wife and said, "There we are."

Such things did not bother me. I plucked many a chicken and saw them get killed, but Penelope blanched, and I realized it meant something different to her in that moment. The bird was powerless in the grasp of Mr. Jones. Just as Penelope was in the hands of her parents, her husband, and her doctor.

She forced a smile and said, "Wonderful."

"I didn't mean to upset you," he said, frowning at her. "I apologize. I should be more sensitive to your disposition, but it's for the best, you know."

The best for whom? It certainly wasn't in the bird's best interest. Nor was it in Penelope's to watch the bird flapping around in pain. I kept my mouth shut like a good maid did.

"Of course, dear."

"That's how I'm going to die," she said, staring at the vines growing along the house. "An ivy noose will wrap around my throat and slowly strangle the life out of me."

Damn, Mr. Jones! That bird being killed like that in front of her was awful. She might have gone hunting, but I was betting she never killed anything up close and personal like that. Her father probably had dogs or a man to take care of the kill.

The urge to say the right thing bubbled up in a frenzy. I wanted to fix it. To make her better without the doctor or the drugs that she was so fond of. Not because it was my job, but because she was trying so hard. I watched her every day, and there wasn't anyone in the world quite like her. I wanted her to succeed.

I took Penelope's hand, but her stare remained fixated on her imminent death. It was like a trance. Her hands were colder than headstones. "You're like ice! Shall we go to the greenhouse?"

"I'd like that," she said, refusing to let go of my hand.

#

It turns out you must first mill the coffee beans before brewing them. Along with the beans, Mr. Davies brought a machine to make the coffee, but Anne didn't know what it was and put it in one of the cupboards. Mr. Davies found it and was brimming with excitement to show me.

He pulled out a glass device, the top portion of which reminded me a bit of a fish tank with a cord that dropped down into a bulbous glass container with a handle that positioned the whole thing over a burner. It was a work of mastery, really, but I was intimidated by it.

"What do you take me for?" I asked him.

"Oh, it's actually quite simple," he said. "Come, I'll show you."

I supposed it wasn't all that scary, just new. I stepped beside him while he demonstrated how to use the vacuum coffee pot. "You take the top off like so, and you pour hot water into the bottom."

Mr. Davies ground out some coffee before returning to the machine. "Now," he said. "We put the top in properly. Up goes the heat."

He turned up the burner, and the boiling water rose to the top. He poured in the coffee and said, "Stir it well. We want it nice and foamy now."

The burner was turned down once nearly all the water had left the bottom chamber. He had me stir more gently a second time before turning the burner off completely. Dark, murky water swirled in the tank for several minutes before the coffee left the tank and slowly filled the round bottom. The only thing that remained at the top were coffee grounds.

My eyes went wide. No wonder Penelope loved this drink so much. It was just as exotic and temperamental as she was. We took the top off and lifted the bottom bowl to pour it into a teacup.

"And that is it," Mr. Davies said.

I took a sip. It was bitter and overwhelmed my sinuses, but I had to agree it tasted much better now that it had been made properly. It was much like Mary making tea; the old windbag had lost her sense of smell in her old age and always let it steep for too long.

"Be sure to clean out the filter when you're done, and that's it," he said.

Penelope loved it. She clasped the cup with both hands, closed her eyes, and inhaled deeply while the garden around her appeared to breathe with her. "It's just like how they make it back at home."

"I'm glad you like it."

"You don't drink coffee here at all?" she asked.

"Mr. Davies said it was more popular when he was a boy, but it was too expensive for the common Englishman, so tea became the standard."

"I see, well, I'm grateful. You've gone out of your way just for me."

"It wasn't just me," I blurted out. Her blue eyes widened. "Mr. Davies was the one who got the coffee and the coffee maker. He even showed me how to use it."

"That old man? I thought he hated me."

I sighed, weary of her paranoia. "How many times do I have to tell you? No one hates you."

"The kitchen hag does," Penelope said, holding the cup the way a man would.

I snickered at that. "She's just hateful—it's not directed at anyone in particular. Anne really isn't that bad when you get to know her."

"I'll take your word for it."

The rain started to come down in huge wet splats against the greenhouse ceiling. The noise was deafening, but it was peaceful in a way that only rain could be. Water came down in cascades all around us; it was like standing inside a waterfall. The room began to swelter, but Penelope didn't seem to mind. She was observing the ivy vines as their tendrils searched the leaded glass for freedom.

"Fredrick has another one of his parties tonight," Penelope grumbled. "I hate those things. I'd sooner jump off a bridge than get into a carriage."

I didn't want her to go either, but I had no say in the matter. While Rosa found Penelope's humor discomforting, I had no qualms matching it. People didn't understand that it was easier to make light of pain rather than feel it.

"Well, don't go doing that or I'll be out of a job."

Usually, she would laugh at something like that, but this time her stare remained fixed on a wilting pink orchid. Her hands were trembling, and she put them under the table to hide it. She was trying to keep it together for my sake. I was at a loss for what to do. Should I distract her, tell her she would be fine? It was an awful thing to be so powerless, and in the confines of her class, Penelope was perhaps even more powerless than I was.

In typical English fashion, the rain had suddenly stopped and revealed Mr. Davies moving toward the entrance. "Pardon the interruption, Ma'am, but the doctor is here to see you."

"About time!"

I stood as she did, and without another word, she left. She didn't so much as say goodbye, she was so eager to see the doctor. It was fine. She didn't owe me any formal goodbyes. I was just her maid, after all.

I went through her room and tidied up the clean room when Penelope burst into the room again and gave me a kiss on the cheek.

"I'll miss you while I'm gone," she said, fleeing the room again.

A laugh escaped my lips as my skin got hot all over. She was a funny one. I didn't know what to make of it. She kissed me. I rubbed the spot where her lips met my skin and sighed like a lovesick boy at a pub. It was just a kiss on the cheek. Girls kissed one another all the time. To make more out of it was setting myself up for trouble.

Penelope was kind, that was all.

#

I had just slid another sponge cake into the oven when Mr. Davies entered the kitchen. "Mrs. Jones would like some coffee."

It was late in the day for coffee, but she was going out tonight with Mr. Jones. Perhaps she was tired and needed a little lift. I set to work brewing the coffee with the vacuum pot before hurrying up the curving staircase that led to her bedroom. I knocked, and there was a soft moan.

That probably meant enter. "I brought your coffee, Mrs. Jones."

"Penelope," she slurred in the dark room. "I told you."

I scoffed at first, but before I could give her a hard time, all the humor left my body. She was draped over the loveseat in a formal gown. Her pink satin dress was low-cut and garnished with pearl beading. Her hair had come undone since this morning when I pinned it. The corset prohibited her from slouching, so she was sort of splayed on the sofa, threatening to slide down at any minute.

I closed the door behind me and set down the coffee before propping her back up. "What happened?" I asked.

"Never been better!" Her head lolled to face me, and she smiled.

It was like she was drunk. No wonder people at those parties found her so amusing. They must have thought her a lush. Is this really the state her doctor left her in every time he came to visit? "Maybe some coffee?" I asked.

She nodded and swung an arm up as if she intended to grab the cup. "Here, let me," I said before holding the cup to her lips.

This couldn't be right. Whatever this doctor was giving her was too strong. She wasn't in any condition for anything but her bed. Penelope drank the coffee. Her eyes regained some focus, and she slurred less, but she was still so lethargic.

I paced the room as she lay on the loveseat. What was I going to do? She was drugged into near comatose. This couldn't be normal. What if the doctor gave her too much?

"Stay here," I said. It was a silly notion that she could go anywhere on her own in this state. Leaving the room, I ran down the swirl of stairs shouting for Mr. Davies until he came rushing out of the parlor.

"What is it? What's wrong?" he asked.

"The missus," I started, straining to control the tremor in my voice. "She's…"

I stopped. Mr. Davies's expression was not one of alarm but of knowing. He couldn't be serious. This was the state they took her out in public?

"How could this be allowed?" I whispered to keep from shouting.

"The doctor knows what he is doing," Mr. Davies explained in a soothing voice. "He is well-trained and versed in Mrs. Jones's case. He's cared for her since she was a child."

"He did this to her as a child?"

"Well, no," Mr. Davies stumbled. "I don't know, honestly, but from what I understand, Mrs. Jones suffers from a hereditary disposition. Her mother had it. When she and Mr. Jones married, it was clear that she would need ongoing care, and it was a risk the Joneses were willing to take."

For the money. Penelope was beautiful and loaded—what more did they need? Just keep her drugged until kingdom come, and there would be no problems. I wanted to shout at Mr. Davies.

"If you were her father, would you allow this?" I asked.

There was a flash of rage in the butler's eyes, but he smoothed his hair and straightened. "You care for her," he said stiffly. "That is good. More than anything, I think that is what she needs, but remember your place. The men in her life know best."

If I ever wanted to hit anyone, it was Mr. Davies in that moment. It took everything I had to let that go. I looked to the parlor door, and the butler nodded.

"He loves her very much. I can assure you of that. The doctor thinks of her as his own daughter. She's come leaps and bounds since she came here, and even more since you've been with her. Just give her time."

I swallowed and blinked back the tears. Mr. Jones did seem like a nice man, and he wouldn't let anything bad happen to his wife, would he? Going against a proper doctor probably wasn't the right way to go either. What did I know of medicine and psyches? Nothing. I was a barely literate village girl, one kind second cousin away from a workhouse.

I was just shocked to see her that way. "She was worse before?" I asked.

"Mrs. Jones needed to be sedated the entire boat ride from New York," Mr. Davies explained. "Mr. Jones was so alarmed he thought perhaps the marriage was a mistake, but the doctor promised she would get better, and she has."

I didn't know what else to say. Mr. Davies put a hand on my shoulder and said, "Go home, Dinah, your work is done here for tonight."

That was the way out of it. Penelope was much sicker than she let on. While her treatments were terrible, they provided a sense of relief for her. She even said so herself. I was being unfair to her doctor, who had been working with her for years. I told myself these things, and things similar, but the knot in my chest hardened and refused to ease.

The village lights hovered in the distance. I was nearly to my humble flat where my father and Mary awaited me. They'd want to hear about my day, and when I left the room, they noticed. Maybe I'd sit down and have a real chat with him. I'd tell him about how Mrs. Jones was sending a doctor for him. He'd be really chuffed about that.

There was movement around the flat as I approached. I squinted to get a better idea of what was going on, but I could hear Mary's wails cutting through the dark. Something had happened. I quickened my pace, and my feet couldn't carry me fast enough, so I broke into a run. There were several people surrounding the flat, all weary and saddened, and my stomach lurched so hard, it knocked the breath from me.

My father was dead.

CHAPTER SIX

I t was Mary who came out to greet me. I shoved past her and a small
crowd of villagers to find my father in his chair. It was as though
he were asleep. Serenity had taken over his face, and he was wrapped
in his favorite blanket. He looked so small. Like a sleeping child more
than a dead man. I half expected him to open his eyes and start talking.

It didn't feel real. None of it.

"Oh, Dinah," he would say. "I must have dozed off."

"Did you get some rest today?"

"Oh, as much as I can get with this blasted cough."

Only there was no cough. It was the only difference between him
being dead or not. He sat in that chair, did nothing but cough when
he was alive. Now, he was dead, and he sat in that chair all the same.
Something withered inside as I pulled his blanket up and around his
shoulders.

"Goodnight, father," I said.

A loud pounding banged against the front door. I opened it to
come face to face with the crowd, Mary, and the Baker with a hammer.
In Mary's hands was a laurel wreath. She smiled apologetically.

"I already covered all the mirrors," she said.

"What are you doing?"

"Funeral proceedings, my dear."

My dear was only something I tolerated from my father. "I want none of that in here."

"Dinah!" Mary said, her face stricken and tired. "We need to respect your father's death."

He's dead, I wanted to shout. What does it matter now that he's gone? They couldn't give me a moment alone before doing all their bizarre rituals?

"Dinah just needs some time," the baker said. "Why don't you go to bed? We'll take it from here."

"Must we turn my house into a public circus?" I asked. I didn't want this. If I just went to bed, he'd still be there. He was still there, wasn't he?

"Just the traditional things, my dear," Mary said. "We watch over his body for several days, keep the mirrors covered. Flowers, candles, and maybe a photo."

That sounded like money. I crossed my arms and said, "I can't afford that."

Mary frowned. "You have money, dear, several jars full. I've seen it myself."

Now half the town was here and judging me for not wanting to pay for a funeral. It could have paid for some medicine if he had just stayed on a little longer. I could have done something. The pain in my stomach came on so quickly, and I didn't want them to see that I was seconds away from breaking into sobs. They didn't understand. Having a funeral meant that it was all over, and I wasn't ready for any of it.

"Fine, whatever. Just let me sleep."

I slept so lightly that every little bump from the next room would jolt me awake and remind me that my father's dead body was in the other room. Like some crazed spectacle people could not get enough of. They did all this with my mother, too, and I really wish they hadn't. I was just six when she died, and it was so hard to make peace with my mother's dead body just sitting there in the living room—especially when it started stinking.

It was like they wanted to make sure I wouldn't forget, even for an instant, that I was totally alone in the world. I cried into my pillow until my eyes and ribs ached. I was lost in grief, but relief was a sharper pang than loss. God help me, I was glad he was dead. What kind of horrid person wishes for someone's death?

At some point, I had fallen asleep and woke with a start. I had slept in. Panic set in as I threw the sheets off. Tumbling out of bed, I pulled on my corset and maid's uniform. I barely had my hat on, and my shoes were half-buttoned when I broke from my bedroom to find Mary and Mr. Davies waiting.

"Mr. Davies," I said, clasping my hat over my hastily made bun.

He stood and gave a slight bow. "We got the news from Harriet. I wanted to give my condolences."

My mind was still fogged from sleep. I was still under the impression that I was late for work. "I'll run all the way to the manor," I said.

Mr. Davies waved me off. "No, you must take the day off. Several days if necessary. Mrs. Jones insists."

"She knows?"

"Of course," he said. "She sends her condolences as well. She and Mr. Jones have a bouquet of flowers on the way as well."

That meant I had to stay here, with the corpse and Mary, and anyone else who wanted to wander into my home and pay their respects.

There was no way out of it now. Still, knowing that Penelope cared filled me with a heady joy I shouldn't have felt at this moment.

"Why are you smiling, my dear?" Mary asked.

"I am happy to be among such wonderful people at a time like this."

It was the truth. I needed them to care because I was too afraid to. My father was reduced to a piece of furniture, and I flip-flopped between shoving him back in his chair or chucking the corpse out the door. I never liked Mary, but at least she knew the decent thing to do. Maybe she cared more about my own father than I did. What would my mother think if she could see the treachery of my heart?

"Right," Mr. Davies said. "I'm off, we will see you at the manor when you're ready."

Mary waited until he left before speaking. "They really do treat you lot right. Makes me wish I worked for them as well."

"They are kind people indeed," I said, but my thoughts were only of Penelope.

"Mr. Davies has a daughter about your age. You're related, right?"

"He's my mother's cousin." An uneasy feeling came over me then. I had no idea Mr. Davies had a daughter. He gave no indication he had children when I railed at him over Penelope just yesterday.

His daughter was probably in some boarding school or in Chester, perhaps. Maybe she and her mother lived far from here. I turned to Mary and said, "We have no other family than the people in this village. No one who will come. I want him buried before too long."

I turned to face my father, then. Decay was setting in as his face began to swell. They had put him in a rough pine casket, and flowers were beginning to pile all around him. Had I slept in all morning?

Mary hesitated and turned to my father for assistance, only he was no longer here to make me mind her. It was just me now, and we both knew I had more say over the funeral rites than she did. They were not married, and she was not kin.

The flowers were costly, as was the casket, and the burial. They applied a layer of bricks over his casket to keep graverobbers from stealing the body. It was all so numbingly familiar. There I was, right back where I left off thirteen years ago, clutching a handful of dirt, unwilling to let it go.

The priest said words I didn't hear. Mary let out a wail for dramatics. I stood there, staring down into that hole, my heart full of loss, of guilt, and relief. He wouldn't hurt anymore, but I wished that I had a chance to tell him that I was sorry for being so resentful. It's not like he asked to get sick. He tried to have that conversation with me half a hundred times, but I just couldn't do it. It would never happen now.

Half the village came to the funeral. Even Mr. Davies was in attendance. I hadn't realized my father was so popular. It was good that everyone came out, even if it was only in the end. Even in the cold, while it threatened to rain, the crowd remained steadfast in the mourning garb they hadn't worn since the last funeral. I didn't even have a mourning dress, and I was too stocky to borrow one, so I just wore my maid's uniform.

As the funeral ended, people left in pairs down the hill and back to work. Only Mr. Davies and I remained. "My condolences again," he said.

"Well, I suppose now I can live in the manor."

We both stared at my father's grave, right next to my mother's. One day, it would be me right beside them. I wondered if anyone from the village would bother to show for my funeral. I wouldn't blame them if they didn't.

"Yes," he said. "However, I would advise you not to get too attached to Mrs. Jones."

I faced him then; he was ghastly pale, and his shoulders slouched as though he were the mourner of this funeral. "What do you mean?" I asked.

"It was determined—before the marriage—that if Mrs. Jones was unable to handle life as a married woman, she would be taken to a place where her needs could be met."

Several long moments went by before I fully grasped what Mr. Davies was saying. It knocked the wind from me, and my balled fists shook with rage. They were going to institutionalize her. "Was that Mr. Jones's idea or the doctors?" I spat.

Mr. Davies sighed. "Her family, his family, and the doctor. They never expected her to get better, and I need you to know that before you get too invested, because it may not end happily."

I bit the inside of my cheek to make sure I could still feel pain and winced. "Does she know?"

Mr. Davies shook his head before lowering it. "A daughter is her father's responsibility until she becomes a wife, then she becomes her husband's business. We can't stop it. It's best just to not think about it."

I could only scowl at him as I marched down the hillside. A horrid family sold her off to another horrid family before locking Penelope in an institution. Mr. Jones received the funding that got them up and running once again. Her parents got rid of their insane daughter. The doctor was also a conspirator in this somehow, but he might have been the only decent one among the bunch.

I paced my flat, furious about what was transpiring. There was nothing I could do. I was just a maid, with a pittance of savings, and she was a high-born lady—a married one at that. Like it or not, she was technically Mr. Jones's property. As I calmed, I regretted the way I treated Mr. Davies. He was just trying to warn me of the situation.

He didn't appear exactly thrilled by the prospect either; he was just as powerless to stop it.

Maybe it was a good time to leave. Cut my losses and just run for it. I couldn't bear the thought of watching them cart Penelope away. I could still work in the kitchens, of course, but could I stay after knowing what they did? Even worse, everyone had this information, all but her. Now I was hiding this from her, too.

I plopped onto the loveseat where my father once sat and stared into the fire for hours. He was gone, not just in spirit, but truly gone. It was surreal, and I was raw on the inside from holding it in for so long. I kept waiting for his cough, but it never came. The house was foreign to me now, as if I were an invader sitting on a stranger's loveseat.

My freedom had come at last, but I found myself conflicted. I had wanted him to pass on, but now I just wanted things to be as they were. I wished he were there so I could talk to him about Penelope's predicament. What would he say if he were here? I regretted not confiding in him more. He was sick, not stupid, but I didn't want him to worry about me any more than I wanted to worry about him.

I could drop off the uniform and collect my wages on the way to Chester. Or I could go back to work and stay with Penelope until they took her away from me forever. Remaining involved, knowing how it was going to end, or start over? Care for her and watch her succumb to a horrible fate, or run away and forget it ever happened?

Lying on my bed, I stared at the ceiling for most of the night. Registering the change in temperature as my indication of how far the night progressed. The warmth fled my tiny room as the evening wore on. The chill apparent on my skin worked its way into my bones by the early morning and was followed by the dawn, which brought on a dampness. Everything ached, and my stomach soured.

What was I to do? I could be free of that declining house owned by a lesser son. If I left for Chester now, I could use a letter of recommendation to get another job and save myself the agony of what was to come. I could do what I had planned before I met Penelope. It would have been the safer and wiser choice, and yet...

I couldn't leave her. I would regret it in the same way I regretted the way things ended with my father. I left too much unspoken with my father, and now there was nothing I could do to change that. If I left Penelope now, she'd never know how much I enjoyed our time together. Or how much I appreciated the way she loved my baking and how nice it was to have a friend.

No, she'd think she had done something wrong, just like my father probably assumed I hated him for getting sick. I couldn't let her go out like that. I wasn't sure I could let her go at all.

CHAPTER SEVEN

I went back to work the next day. I couldn't stand it one more moment in that empty flat reeking of death. He wasn't there anymore, so what was the point of remaining?

Both Harriet and Anne paused as I walked through the door. The butler was drinking a cup of tea and reading a book. So absorbed with his book, Mr. Davies was not moved from his seat. His eyes locked on the book.

"Mr. Davies said not to expect you for several days with the funeral and all," Harriet said.

"It's done," I said as I set up the coffee machine. "What are you reading, Mr. Davies?"

"Just an article," he said, rubbing the bridge of his nose. He shifted slightly in the chair before wiping his eyes as he closed the book. Was he crying? I scanned the room, and no one seemed to notice but me.

"I best get back to work," the butler said, tucking the book into the breast pocket of his coat. He averted eye contact as he left.

"What was he reading?" I asked Harriet in a whisper.

"Nellie Bly, I think it was."

The name sounded familiar, but I couldn't quite place it. Whatever it was, it upset the butler greatly. I piled the tray with the usual things Mrs. Jones liked and took them upstairs to her bedroom. It was still early, so I didn't believe her to be awake; I just wanted to be away from everyone else.

As I expected, the room was draped in darkness. No grand canopy, no spiraling four-poster bed. These could be any kind of carpet and not the lavish Oriental-made variety. There was a sliver of daylight illuminating the table, where I sat the tray down before sitting on one of the loveseats. There I stayed in the darkness and waited for the stirrings of Penelope.

Unfortunately, it wasn't all that long. The scent of the coffee filled the air, and the crinkling and shifting of fabric signified that even the scent of the drink was enough to rouse the missus. She let out a moan before calling, "Dinah, is that you?"

"Yes, it's me," I said. "I came up early, so take your time."

"Bring me that coffee, would you?"

My eyes had adjusted to the dark. Her blonde hair was a beacon of light as dust particles floated in the stream of daylight. I did as she asked and brought her the cup of coffee. She took several long sips before saying, "Mr. Davies said you'd be out today."

"Well," I said. "He's buried. There's no use sitting at home about it."

"I'm sorry for your loss. You must be devastated."

I couldn't take any more condolences. She meant well, and I appreciated her flowers and the fact that she cared at all, but I just couldn't lie to her. The weight of my father was heavier in death than in life. Every time I walked by his empty chair, I half expected to turn around to find him sitting there, watching me with his dead eyes.

"Hello, my dear," his corpse would say. "I'm so proud of you."

"Thank you, father."

The bones in his neck would pop as he turned in my direction. "Even if you wanted me dead. Even if you couldn't wait to put me in the ground. Do you want to know what your mother looks like down here?"

I shook the grotesque imagery out of my head. He was at peace now with my mother. I sat down beside Penelope and sighed. "That's the problem," I said. "You see, I'm not devastated. I'm not sad in the slightest. I'm glad he's gone."

Penelope's face was unreadable in the dark. I flinched, imagining she thought me a terrible person. There was a shuffling by her night-stand before a match was dragged across a box. A small flame burst into life, illuminating a face that wasn't full of scorn.

"Was he mean?" she asked, drawing off her cigarette.

"No," I said. "He was a good man. He worked the farms and always told me how proud he was of me. He never struck me, and he never tried to match me up with the village boys the way Mary did."

"He was sick for a long time, though."

"Yeah. When he worked, things were different, but when he stopped working, everything became so hard. When it became clear he wasn't going to get better, it was like the man he was just slipped away, leaving just a shell. I hate that he suffered for so long. He was a burden on me, and I resented him for it. I think he resented it too."

It all just came spilling out at once, and I couldn't stop it. Penelope sat and listened all the while. Puffing on her ridiculous cigarette as the smoke surrounded her.

"It's not how he wanted things to be, but he couldn't just stop being sick. All that was left to do was die. I've already grieved his death, and now people are trying to make me relive it all over again. You must think me an awful person."

"No," Penelope extended the cigarette, to which I took. "It's like Auntie Gertrude."

Ashy flavor coiled in my nostrils and over my teeth, but I enjoyed it. If I couldn't drink a beer in the pub, at least I could do this under my lady's behest. "Same situation?" I asked, passing the cigarette back.

"My great aunt Gertrude was a magnificent woman," Penelope explained. "She had rings on every finger, and her waist was impossibly small. She was so popular and funny. If it weren't for her, I'd still be stuck at home. She was the one who knew Fredrick's father."

She leaned back against her pillow. The thin fabric of her night-gown was like a second skin. The rise and curve of her breasts gave way to the valley where her stomach caved. Her hips were slim, and her long legs were tucked under the blanket. Of all the times to be gawking at a woman, now was not the time.

"One day, she insisted she lost something, but couldn't recall what it was. She was frantic and so distraught they called the doctor."

"Not long after, Gertrude couldn't so much as remember her own name. She didn't even know her own children. Her family was relieved when she passed on. The same doctor who attended to her is now my doctor. Our family was so indebted to him. He stayed with Gertrude nearly every waking moment. He cried when she passed away."

So, the man did have a heart. That was more than anyone else in Penelope's life. The doctor was the only thing standing between Penelope and the institution. When I overheard him pressing Mr. Jones about something, I assumed it was malevolent in some way, but he might have been advocating for a new and better treatment for Penelope.

I supposed I feared doctors more than anything. Well, except death itself. My father used up all the money we had on one when things got bad for Mum, and he couldn't save her. As an adult, I realized there was nothing he could do at that point, but as a child, it seemed like she got sicker after they came. He said she had a tumor in her belly.

Surgery was a possibility if we could afford it, but there was no guarantee that the cancer wouldn't come back. We couldn't afford it, but even if we could, Mum refused because she didn't want to stay in a hospital. Were they really that bad that she'd rather die than stay in one?

I thought about what Mr. Davies told me, about how they wanted to put Penelope in an institution. I didn't know much about those places. I saw pictures in the newspaper once. Women all tied to iron-barred beds while men in white coats stood over them. I wouldn't want to stay in one, so I could only imagine how Penelope would feel about it.

There was no discussion about keeping it a secret because I already understood the consequences. If she had any idea what they were plotting, she would come undone. All the progress we made would come falling down like a bunch of dominoes. Lying to protect her, lying to save her. It felt so wrong, keeping things from her, but what else could I do? She deserved better, but a maid two steps from a workhouse couldn't provide it.

"What does the doctor give you anyway?" I asked.

"Oh, only he knows that," she said. "He is a modern doctor and believes hysteria is in the mind and psyche. He keeps all his medicines in his bag and mixes a special injection for me depending on how I'm feeling that day."

People kept on mentioning it, and I didn't understand. "What is the psyche?"

Penelope had a queer grin just then, as though she were about to divulge a secret. I leaned in, eager to know each and every one of hers.

"The psyche is our mind's connection with our soul," she explained. "Our spirit, if you will. Most people aren't even aware of theirs, but some can reach this untapped potential and use it in special ways."

I didn't know what to make of that. Were we talking about spiritualism or the occult? "Are you talking about psychics?"

Her lips parted, giving way to a perfect smile. "Well, for some. For others, like myself, it can be troublesome. The doctor has studied it in depth. He has endangered himself in many ways, trying to find solutions, but nothing helps other than the drugs."

It wasn't Penelope's mind or uterus that was causing her ailments; it was her very soul. How could I ever hope to reach that? A soul couldn't be mended like a sock. Nor could it be hidden like the patches of missing hair or the scratches down her arms. This was something beyond me, and I didn't quite know if I could believe such a thing.

"I... The doctor really thinks this? You think it, too?"

"I've seen things, Dinah. Things I can't explain. I've seen my death. I've seen so many things. Things I couldn't possibly know. Sometimes he gives me medicines to try and bring out my abilities, but Mr. Jones protested."

Just what was she seeing? I wanted to ask about her death, but that was far too forward of a thing to ask. It felt intimate somehow, knowing her death. Then again, it might shed some light on her fears.

"How do you die?"

Penelope threw her head back and smiled as though she were giving a cherished beauty secret. A little petroleum ointment around her eyes or a dash of powder before dessert. "I'm slowly suffocated by a noose, only no one can see it but me."

I shuddered at the thought. Mr. Jones might have been right. Whatever Penelope was witnessing was nothing short of morbid. She noted the frown on my face and said, "It's fine! He is a renowned doctor."

I nodded but remained unconvinced. It sounded more like some kind of science experiment than medicine. It reminded me of a peddler who came to the village from time to time. He always had bits of lace and new stockings, but he also sold bottles of tonics that he claimed came from faraway places that could cure toothaches and the like. I got some once for my father for his cough; it smelled like watered-down licorice, and it didn't do shit for his cough.

This was different, I supposed. This medicine certainly did *something* to Penelope. He was a world-renowned doctor who studied medicine at the best schools, not a village peddler.

"So now that your father is gone, are you moving to the manor?" she asked.

"I had thought about it."

"It would be nice to have you around all the time," she said, patting my hand. "You should speak with Mr. Davies about it."

"I will."

For better or worse, I would remain with Penelope. I would do my best to convince Mr. Jones that institutionalizing her wasn't necessary. If the doctor was helping her, I would do everything in my power to help him. To gain the doctor's confidence might help me gain a foothold on this whole psyche thing.

As for Mr. Jones… Penelope could run a household. She just needed more confidence in herself. No one ever tried to ease her into this life; she was thrown into it. Maybe I could teach her how to tread the water.

CHAPTER EIGHT

The transition from the humble flat to the manor was swift and seamless. What little that once belonged to my parents was sold, and the flat was empty of my belongings within a few hours. I didn't have much to begin with. Most of the furniture came with the flat, apart from my mother's vanity and a few dishes. I kept their pair of teacups, my brush, and a hand mirror.

"I think you should have this," I said to Mary as I returned the blanket she once knitted for him.

She frowned as if she expected more. Mary benefited from our arrangement, but now she would need to find some other widower to fuss over. Nonetheless, she took the blanket, but she didn't wave goodbye as I walked back to the manor. The first snow of the year was falling, and I smiled as the white, fluffy flakes fell on my nose.

I wouldn't be walking to and from work in this weather, I'd be snug and warm in a manor kept heated throughout the day and well into the night. No more rationing lumps of coal or damp firewood throughout the icy months. Winter was a beautiful thing when freezing to death wasn't a concern.

My room was small, but clean. I took up Rosa's old room downstairs, across from the kitchens. There was an iron-framed bed with thick blankets, a plain wardrobe, a full-length mirror, and a nightstand. There was also a free-standing wash basin with a wash tub. It was everything I needed. It was perfect.

It was late morning when I entered the kitchen to get Mrs. Jones's breakfast ready. Anne glanced over her shoulder before resuming work. The butler came striding in, all pink in the cheeks and excited about something.

"We got some meats from Italy this morning," Mr. Davies said. "Do you think the missus will want some?"

I hadn't the slightest idea if she would. Penelope was a fickle eater. Meat was something she picked at. If it was boiled or still on the bone, she wouldn't touch it. I made it a point to slice anything before bringing it to her, and that seemed to help, but even then, she avoided the fatty bits.

"I'll ask her."

Still resentful from our last discussion, I managed a stiff nod before leaving. It wasn't his fault, and I knew that, but it stung all the same. The bright snow light from outside danced along the crystal chandelier in the entryway. It sent a spectrum of lights all around the crown molding and red floral wallpaper. Outdated and shabby as it was, the winter lights made it seem cheerier somehow.

I could only imagine how beautiful it would be come spring. All the flowers blooming after a harsh winter. The image of Penelope on a blanket on the lawn, eating strawberries and champagne. She would laugh and give me a wink that made me blush. I shrugged off the fanciful daydream.

People made rash decisions while grieving. More than once, I'd see a man passed out on the pub doorstep, sleeping it off in his own piss.

The last thing she needed was for me to admit how infatuated I was with her. If anything was in need of confessing, it was the conspiracy her husband and parents were in on.

Penelope was up and about when I came in. She was still in her nightgown, waiting for me to come and help with her corset. "Morning," I said.

"How did the move go?" she asked. "Was Mary happy to see you go?"

I set the tray down and grinned. "She wasn't too happy when I didn't give her another sixpence."

"You really think that's all she cared about?" she asked, sitting in front of her vanity. "Older people don't like change. First, your father, and now you are gone. You lived there a long time."

I grabbed handfuls of her golden hair and pulled it up into a style. "Perhaps you're right," I admitted. "I always resented her. She inserted herself into our lives right after my mother died. There was no conversation about it; she just took it upon herself to be a thorn in my arse for the last thirteen years."

"Old women are always meddlesome. My mother had my marriage arranged when I was ten."

A knife twisted in my heart. They had been plotting to institutionalize her since she was a child?

"Nothing formalized, of course. She just got very cozy with the Joneses."

I didn't have words to say. Her hair slipped through my frozen fingers.

"Are you all right?" she asked, turning around to regard me.

"I'm fine," I stammered as I finished pinning her hair. "Oh, we got some cured meats from Italy. Would you like to try some?"

She tilted her head and observed me for a long moment before a grin worked its way across her face. "I love those thin-sliced meats with cheese and olives. That's all I ate when we spent a summer in the Mediterranean."

"Well, call me green," I said. She stood up, and I began lacing her corset. Imagine going to Italy or Greece. I had only seen pictures on stamps at the post office. White stucco buildings with deep blue water and an orange watercolor sunset.

"Maybe one day we will go," she teased. "Whenever I get through this problem of mine."

Would they ever get that chance? Penelope would hate my pity. There had to be a way to make the parties easier for her. Why couldn't they host them? Surely, she would feel more comfortable here than in a stranger's home.

"Why won't Mr. Jones hold parties here?" I asked.

Penelope drew back the curtains and felt the fabric with disapproval. "In this house's current state? I'd die of embarrassment. Fredrick wouldn't allow it."

The house was rather drab, even if it was the nicest house I had ever seen. Mr. Jones was employed by dukes and lords to oversee their properties and manage their farms. What would they think if he lived in a home that hadn't been renovated since his grandmother's or even his great-grandmother's time?

"I suppose you're right. The home could use some redecorating."

"Redecorating?" Penelope scoffed. "It needs a hot match to one of these eighty-year-old drapes!"

She had given me a brilliant idea. Penelope needed to show Mr. Jones and the doctor that she was improving. What better way than to remodel the manor? Then, they could host parties here; it would be a win for both her and Mr. Jones. "You could make suggestions on such things," I hinted.

Penelope's eyes shifted, and she said, "I don't think anyone needs my opinion."

"You are the lady of the house," I said, giving the corset a good pull. "Trust me, they would feel much better if you gave some input."

She was conflicted. Her head lowered as she wrung her hands. "I don't know, the house needs so much work. I don't know if I can do it."

"You'd have me to help," I offered, though I knew little about decorating or home remodeling. "Mr. Davies would be thrilled."

At this, Penelope relented. "You think so?"

Mr. Davies would swoon at the thought of orchestrating a renovation. "Of course."

It was too cold for our daily walk, but we took tea and coffee in the greenhouse. We continued our discussion on all the things Penelope would change if given permission. She walked about the house and even jotted notes. "We need new wallpaper. The furniture is solid but needs refurbishing and upholstery. Oh, Dinah, I don't know if I can manage all this."

I didn't understand half of what she was saying. How could one person know so many terms? She even went on about the plumbing at great length. I wasn't certain I could manage my hold on the conversation.

"You can do anything if you set your mind to it," I said. It was cliché and not entirely true in most circumstances, but it had already taken the idea and run with it to the ends of the earth.

It was colder than usual inside, and the roof was blanketed in snow. Penelope looked up and laughed. "So, this is what it feels like to be buried in snow."

We were experiencing this for the first time together. Our first winter in the Jones manor. For lunch, we ate the cured meats with cheese and bread. Penelope wanted wine with the meal in place of her coffee. I found Mr. Davies carrying luggage to the entryway on my way to the kitchen.

"Mr. Jones is going on a trip?" I asked.

"Just for a few days," he said, lugging a heavy carpet bag to the arched double-doors of the manor.

"Mrs. Jones has expressed interest in remodeling the house," I told him in a whisper.

Mr. Davies's eyes widened. "Splendid! I'll send for fabric samples and..."

The butler carried on about all the things they would need and the people he would call on. Laughing to myself, I could only nod as I picked up some of the words that Penelope used. Try as I might, it was all just a bunch of posh hogwash to me.

"I'll let her know how enthused you are about the idea."

Harriet was singing when I entered the kitchen. Her voice was a deep, feminine timbre. She was singing in a language I didn't understand. I tried my best to sneak in unnoticed, but she stopped singing as I entered. "Please keep singing," I said. "It's so lovely, I wish I knew the words."

She smiled softly. "It's an old Celtic song I learned from my mother. I honestly can't tell you what it means. I know it's a sad song, though."

Why was she sad? Perhaps she didn't have a reason. Sometimes people just wanted to be sad. Winter had that effect. Anne wasn't in the room. I thought to ask why, but I didn't want to interrupt Harriet's song a second time. I took some of the pre-sliced meats and sliced up some cheese. I found a table wine in the cabinet. It was a red wine; I hoped it would be to her taste, as I still didn't know where the other wines were.

There was a thin, black figure standing in the greenhouse with Penelope. The shadow shifted around the table. As I got closer, I realized it was Mr. Davis, and my alarm waned. The green glass had a way of distorting the contents inside.

"I'm back," I announced.

Penelope was gripping her hands under the table and chewing on her lip. Her eyes were pleading with me to help, but it was an excellent opportunity to assert herself. She needed to tell Mr. Davies her ideas. "I think she took notes," I said.

"Are these it here?" he asked, bowing toward the notes. Penelope nodded but kept silent. "May I?"

She nodded. Mr. Davies skimmed through her notes, nodding in approval. "I can get the people for the job, send out fabric samples, and I can speak with Mr. Jones on the subject if you like."

"You would do all that?" she asked.

"Of course!" he said. "Your notes are so detailed. With an eye like yours, this place may be fit for a ducal visit one day."

Penelope flushed at the compliment. Her watery blue eyes pleaded with me to take over, but I couldn't. She needed to make these decisions without constant coddling. If my mother hovered over everything I did, I would have never burnt a loaf or tried to bake dough so overworked that it snapped back into a hard little ball. If I had never failed, I would have never truly succeeded. Penelope needed to learn that, too.

"Is there anything else you require of me?" he asked.

Penelope shook her head, and the butler left with a bow. Penelope drank the wine with a shaky hand. "God, he makes me nervous."

"Mr. Davies?" I turned to regard the butler as he left. There was nothing remotely threatening about him.

"He's always there. Always watching and waiting."

That made me giggle. "Penelope, that's his job."

Her eyes went wide. "To stand there in the corner of the room?"

It did paint an odd picture. I imagined myself and my father attempting to eat our watery stew in our hovel while Mr. Davies stood ominously in the corner. The shadows from the fire danced across his sunken eyes and gleamed on his well-oiled hair. Mary would ask for tea, and he would leap into action. It would have startled my father, but he was too stiff from rigor mortis to bolt from his seat. He was dead.

I shook off the morbs and focused on Penelope. "To see to Mr. Jones's every need."

"My father never had ongoing servants in the apartment. All we had was a weekly cleaning and laundry service. He said it wasn't worth the hassle. I think he valued his privacy, and I can see why."

"Your family is loaded but lives in a flat?"

She picked up a slice of prosciutto and folded it into her mouth. "That's the way of things in New York. We lived in a penthouse apartment in downtown. It was huge by New York standards. I told you my father was unconventional. We never saw the housecleaners or the laundresses. If he saw them at all, he'd fire them on the spot."

It was bizarre. "Why did he hate them so?"

"My father accumulated his own fortune. He built his factories with his own hands. We seldom joined in social events unless Auntie Gertrude made us. We didn't exactly fit in with the upper echelons. New money and old money only meet at the altar, they say. My father wanted to feel like the man of his house, and my mother just wanted his money."

The grievances Penelope had were mostly directed at her mother. She admired and respected her father, even if he distanced himself from her when she became sick.

"That explains why you're so clever," I told her. "You must have inherited it from your father."

She smiled at the finger sandwich she had made and savored the first bite with her eyes closed. "You really think Mr. Davies likes the idea?"

"Oh, I know he does. I haven't seen the man excited about anything until the talk of coffee and redecorating. Mr. Jones would be relieved to have the house restored as well."

"Freddie does complain about the house," she said. "It's a lot to take on, but I think it would be worth it."

"More wine? I asked.

Penelope held up the bottle and tipped it upside down. I drank a cup with her, but she had drunk all the rest. "Maybe not."

She wrinkled her nose and hiccupped. "Oh, come on, just a little more."

"Setting ourselves up for a world of pain," I warned.

"Just do it!" She said before a hiccup snuck up on her. The ashtray was full, and she was lighting up another.

I'd ask Mr. Davies if there was a bottle half or nearly empty.

"Mr. Davies," I called as I came into the kitchen. I stepped into the room expecting Anne and Harriet in the kitchen with Mr. Davies fussing over something, but I found Harriet and Mr. Davies sitting on some three-legged stools. Harriet was crying.

"What's going on?" I asked.

Harriet scrubbed the tears from her plump cheeks. "Oh, it's just life, doing what it does."

"Anne is retiring," Mr. Davies explained.

I didn't imagine Harriet would cry over Anne retiring. The realization dawned on me then. Just when I didn't think I could feel any more loss. There was only one reason why the tough old bird would retire. "She's sick, isn't she?"

"I'm afraid so," he whispered.

"Like my father or my mother?" I asked.

"More like your mother, I suppose," Harriet said. "There's a tumor in her belly. It's doubled in size in the last month."

I inhaled a sharp breath and nodded. Exactly the same as my mother. It may not have been in the same organ, but I knew the outcome all the same. "Anne will go quickly then," I said. "Trust me, it's better that way."

There were equal parts horror and sadness in their faces. As if they hadn't lived long enough to know these truths. The silence in the room had grown awkward. "We need more wine," I said. "Maybe a bottle nearly gone?"

"Oh, yes, of course," Mr. Davies recovered. "Has she put any more thought into what we discussed? I can procure her some decorating magazines from Chester."

I grinned and nodded. "I think she'd love that."

"That would be lovely," Harriet said. "Just imagine that high-fashion, New York style here!"

"It's strange, though," Mr. Davies said. "I think she's rather intimidated by me."

So, he was aware. "She never had a household staff," I explained.

They both gasped in unison. "No maids?" Harriet asked.

I shook my head. "Nope, they had a laundry service and a cleaning service. Her father had a queer sort of rule about them. They had to remain unseen. Up until now, she thought you were just standing over them, making sure they were using the proper dinner forks."

Mr. Davies straightened on his stool. "I was made aware of this eccentricity in her upbringing, but I fear it's more than that. She has an aversion to men in general, I fear."

"Is that why she was afraid to go outside by herself?" I asked.

"I suppose it is. She was terrified of the men working in the yard, and she would sob uncontrollably if left unattended at one of Mr. Jones's events." Mr. Davies's voice lowered with what he said next. "Mr. and Mrs. Jones also have great difficulties in the bedroom because of it."

A lead weight sank in my gut. She didn't mention any of this to me at all. Why downplay something that had such a profound effect on her? I suppose we were similar in that regard.

"Did something happen to her?"

Mr. Davies was blushing. No doubt he was ashamed to be gossiping with the maids, but this was important. "Her first episode was after a male professor had struck her," he said. "I don't have all the details, but when the doctor learned of it, he told the Hathaways that Penelope shouldn't be subjected to a man's temper."

I clutched the fabric of my dress and bowed my head. So that's what started it all. It was a harrowing reminder that my friendship could only go so far in Penelope's recovery. I was no doctor. What would have become of her if the doctor didn't intervene? I didn't know the first thing about how to make her better. All I could do was continue to support her to the best of my ability.

"Thank you, Mr. Davies, for telling me," I said. "I'm so sorry about Anne. I don't mean to come off so rough, but the pain—"

"I understand completely," Mr. Davies said with a frown. "We all know you've seen enough of it."

I returned to Penelope with the wine only to find her asleep with her head resting on the table. She had drunk far too much, just as I suspected. I set the bottle down and gently roused her by rubbing her back. Penelope moaned my name, and I laughed. "Yes, I'm here, silly woman."

I scooped her up and carried her up to bed. Mr. Davies caught me halfway up the steps. "Do you need assistance?" he asked, bounding up the steps.

"I worked hard labor during the summer months," I explained. "She's light as a feather."

"Good lord!" Mr. Davies said. "I pray I never anger you!"

I grinned. "Pray you don't."

CHAPTER NINE

M r. Jones still wasn't back from his business trip yet. Word was that the snow was falling heavily in Manchester and that he might be delayed. When there was no coach that night, I set up a small dinner plate for Penelope and brought it up. I no longer knocked unless someone was watching, but when the door swung open, she flinched and rushed into a shadowy part of the room.

"It's just me," I called.

"I'll be right out," she said from her corner of the room. Her voice trembled, and I grew concerned that she was on the verge of the fabled episodes the others warned me of.

I rounded the changing screen to find her with a water pitcher and a washrag. She was fully naked, and god was she beautiful. The fluster shaded across my face, and I backed away. "Sorry," I said. "I was worried you were in trouble."

"Anne used to run a bath for me twice a week, but she stopped doing it," Penelope said.

My heart sank. She didn't know that Anne was sick, and she was too afraid to ask someone else to prepare her a bath. I should have known, but I just didn't think of it. Something like a bath was really my job anyway. "I'm sorry, Penelope," I said. "I should have thought of it."

"It's no trouble, really," she said from behind the screen. "In New York, the indoor plumbing was state-of-the-art. I could do it myself, but this system is different. I just don't know it yet."

The bathroom in their bedroom had warm running water—the only room that had it—but a maid would need to start a fire in the boiler downstairs to heat up the water first. She probably tried to start her own bath only to find the water too frigid. "I'll start up a fire to heat your water. It takes about a half hour to heat the water if I remember right."

She didn't say anything. There was a faint sniffing, though, and I knew she was crying. How terrible would it be to feel like you have no control over something as simple as a wash? I thought I knew helplessness because I was poor, but all women felt it, no matter their station.

"You know," I said. "These baths need an update as well. I imagine Mr. Jones would love a nice hot shower in the morning, like he has in Manchester. It would be nice if you had a toilet in the same room as the bath, with actual plumbing."

Penelope chuckled. "When he complained about the 'damned boiler,' I never put two and two together. You have to light a fire each time I want a bath?"

"Mr. Davies came back from Chester with home decor magazines. He is practically foaming at the mouth over them."

She laughed, but I could hear the wetness in her throat from crying.

"He and Harriet both are thrilled to have "New York style" in the manor."

"You're just buttering me up," she said.

"Ask them yourselves, but I bet you anything Mr. Jones would love to update that junk heap. I know we'd love not having to light boilers for your posh arses at the crack of dawn. I'll get that fire going."

I'd let her chew on that on her own while I built the fire in the boiler closet downstairs underneath the room. In a home of regal staircases and crystal chandeliers, past all the detailed wainscotting and crown molding, resided a closet downstairs, directly underneath the bathroom. It was an ugly little unfinished room.

No carpet touched these floors, and there was room enough for two people facing the square boiler built into the cinder wall. Above it was a tank that presumably held water that could be forced upward into the tub. In this room, the bones of the house were exposed, and copper tubes forced their way through carved-away holes and into the bathroom. Even the most regal and beautiful of things still harbored a dirty little closet or two.

There was wood stacked beside the door, along with a bucket of kindling. A long shovel rested against the wall beside the boiler. I opened the rectangular doors and built a nice big fire before shutting in the heat. I fed the beast enough wood to make the whole boiler hot to the touch before returning to Penelope.

She was staring intently into her vanity mirror, scowling at her creamy, smooth skin. She examined her neck and smoothed the lines around it. Perhaps she hadn't heard me come in, but I was rather loud. I thought to say something, but what she did next took the words from my mouth.

With a raked hand, she clawed down her neck, leaving angry red welts from chin to chest. I forgot all about her bath water and rushed to her. She moved to do the same, but this time, to her face. A clawed hand dug into her scalp as she meant to drag it across her cheek, but I grabbed her hand before she could.

"What are you doing?" I uttered.

"I'm useless," she said. "A useless, terrible wife, a disappointment to everyone. He won't want me if I'm ugly. They never want you when you're ugly."

She fought my control, but I had her wrists from behind and pushed them downward to her sides. "You are so much more than a pretty face," I told her. "So much more."

Her watery blue eyes met mine through the mirror. We were close enough that her sable-soft hair pressed against my face and neck. My tears were entwined with her curls, and I vowed I'd never let go if that's what it took. Penelope sobbed and heaved before collapsing on the vanity.

"I can't stop myself from feeling this way," she cried. "I know I shouldn't give in to it, but I do, and then I'm racked with all this guilt. I'm tired of being a burden to everyone. I can't do the things he wants me to."

The way she said that it seemed as though she wasn't talking about Mr. Jones. "Penelope," I said, kneeling beside her, pulling her gaze from the mirror. "You're the best thing to have ever happened to me."

She flinched, but I wouldn't let up. "When my father died, you let me tell you how I truly felt. You didn't judge me. You share your meals with me and your cigarettes. When I lived in the village, no one ever made me feel like I belonged. With you..." The words caught in my mouth. There was a fear that my feelings for her were too much and that she wouldn't receive them. "I feel like I belong."

Penelope was silent, and she wouldn't look at me. Had I gone too far? That line between employee and friend had been crossed, and I was about to pay the price. My stomach sank low, and I reminded myself of the ever-growing savings in my bedroom.

"Do you really feel that way?" she asked, her lips trembling. "I was afraid I came on too strong. It's hard to tell with you."

More bung-eyed by what she said than any wine in the cellar, I kissed her forehead. Imagine, the likes of her fancying someone like me. And she thought I wasn't interested! I wondered if all Americans needed things to be so overt.

"It's just hard," I said. "For me to tell people how I feel. We Brits don't talk a lot about feelings, and feelings like ours could get us into a lot of trouble."

Penelope slipped free of my grasp. "I'm nothing but trouble, darling. They wish they could keep me in a cell."

Did she know about the institution? The plot formed in her late childhood to send her away was supposedly withheld from her, but Penelope was a clever woman. She must have put it together. "Why?" I asked.

She smoothed her hair with a nervous motion. "I was in bed when the vase shattered, yet I threw it all the same. Even strapped down to a bed, they can't hold me."

What on earth was she speaking of? I shook my head, hoping she'd elaborate, but she turned away. Unwilling to speak on it further. A horrid rattling sounded from the pipes in the bathroom. I clutched Penelope's hand, and she snickered. "That means the water is ready."

At any moment, the hot water could come exploding from those pipes, spraying them with boiling hot water. "That is terrifying."

She stood and said, "I'm going to bathe. I'm fine now."

Her voice was so calm it frightened me. What would she do all alone in there? My mind searched all memories of the room. Was there anything sharp in there? I didn't recall seeing anything. Such things must have been long removed for her safety, and I shuddered at the thought. I had no doubt she would hurt herself given half the chance.

I remained in the room, though I said nothing in fear that she would make me leave if she grew aware of my presence. Every few minutes or so, I would freeze, petrified by the silence, only to be relieved by a splash from the tub. Her nightgown fanned across the bed, and I waited until she emerged from the room, wrapped in a towel.

"Feel better?" I asked.

She rolled her eyes dramatically. "So much better," she said. "I'm so sorry to frighten you. I just get that way sometimes."

"Just promise me that when you feel that way, don't hide it, tell me about it."

She smiled. "I'll try."

An unrelenting chill enclosed the manor that night. Penelope's fingers were stiff with cold, and goosebumps scratched painfully against my uniform. "Goodness, it's cold tonight!" I said, stacking more wood into the fireplace. Even the wood brought in from the cold took longer to burn before submitting to the flame. Red-hot coals radiated as much heat as they could, but Penelope and I were reduced to sitting on the floor, huddling near the fire.

"This is ridiculous!" Penelope said through chattering teeth. "New York winters are cold, but we had radiators."

I had seen radiators advertised in newspapers, but I had never seen one in person. It seemed strange to me that such things could even work. "They actually work?" I asked.

"Oh yes," Penelope said. "We still had fireplaces, of course, but we didn't rely on them like this house does."

On cold nights like this, I was grateful that I no longer lived in the flat. It was drafty with gaps in the door frame and windows. Unlike the manor, we had a limited supply of wood and coal, and it had to last us through the winter. My poor father would have frozen half to death if he were alive.

"The dead don't feel cold." I heard his voice so distinctly it was as if he was in the room with us. "We don't feel warmth either."

My eyes searched the room, but there was no one there, but I heard him clear as day.

"Are you okay?" Penelope asked.

She had hinted that she was in touch with things that the normal person wasn't. At first, I thought my father's presence was all in my head, but maybe it wasn't. If Penelope could sense him, it would prove I wasn't losing my grip on reality.

"Do you...sense anything else in the room?"

Her brow furrowed, and she stroked my cheek. "I should have liked to meet him."

My heart was thumping, and I didn't know if it was her touch or her words. "You can feel his presence?"

"No," she said. "It doesn't take a psychic to know you miss him."

I was relieved in a way. My imagination always got the better of me. Maybe I just missed him so bad that I recreated him in my mind. I wish I didn't, though. It was disturbing. "He would have gotten a kick out of your accent."

Penelope grinned. "Sometimes people ask me to say random words just to know how I pronounce them. I can't be the first American to come to England."

"No," I said. The term Dollar Princesses was coined some time ago. "Just the first one to come to this village, I think."

"Fancy that."

Flames licked at the fresh timber and released a fresh, woody scent as it crackled. It was my imagination, I told myself. Just like when I imagined him sitting dead in his chair. Nothing more. My shivers were from the cold, but the hairs on the back of my neck would not soothe.

CHAPTER TEN

The snow had melted along the roadways but still clung to the trees and blanketed the rooftops. The trotting of horse hooves shook the crystals on the entryway chandelier, which signified Mr. Jones's return to the manor. We were instructed to all wait outside for him. Even the laundresses and groundskeepers were expected to wait for the lord of the manor.

Mr. Davies lined us up by rank and fussed over our uniforms. Not once had Mr. Jones mentioned care for elbow patches or apron stains, but the butler wanted a formal welcoming all the same.

Mr. Davies assessed everyone. When he got to me, he nodded with a frown. "I dare say, you've grown into this uniform. Your posture and demeanor have greatly improved since you first arrived to us."

I beamed at the butler. It was an unexpected compliment that made me smile. "Thank you, sir."

He stiffened as though he didn't want to be happy about praising me and turned to see Mrs. Jones emerging from the front door. "Do you need some assistance, Mrs. Jones?" he asked.

"No, I just wanted to greet my husband," she said, fidgeting with a weighty emerald earring.

"Very good, ma'am," he said. "As the lady of the house, it is tradition that you stand here, in front of the help."

Penelope moved to the place in the driveway that Mr. Davies indicated, making a brief glance at me as though she wanted to make sure she was doing it right. I silently clapped and gave an encouraging smile amid the sea of wide-eyed help. I was so proud of her I could scream. Never before had she ventured out of the house to greet Mr. Jones. She always stayed inside where it was safe from the unknown dangers that plagued her mind.

The carriage was a glossy red affair, fully enclosed for the passenger. It was pulled by two brown and white horses with white fluffy hooves. I knew nothing of horses, but a few people had them in the village, mostly for working. For my ninth birthday, my father arranged for me to go on a horse ride, but the horse was being pulled along by Mr. Granger. A kindly old man if there ever was one with wild white hair and a bright pink scalp under his top hat.

The carriage wheeled to a stop, and the coachmen stepped down and opened the door. Mr. Jones's long legs came out, overshooting the step before placing one foot on the ground, then another. The wind tousled his light hair. Despite his greenish appearance from the carriage ride, he was every bit the handsome gentleman. His eyes went straight to Penelope, and he grinned. "Oh, don't tell me you missed me," he said.

"I'm surprised too," she joked.

With a black gloved hand, he took her hand and led her into the house. It was a good thing that they got along, but I bristled at it. The way she threw back her head and laughed at something he said.

Unclenching my jaw, I reminded myself that he kept her out of an institution.

Mr. Jones and Penelope went straight upstairs and closed the door behind them. I had been cast aside for the evening. "Leave them undisturbed, Dinah," Mr. Davies said, dragging a large bag through the doorway.

"Of course," I said.

That afternoon, I took out some of my aggression on a sourdough. I kneaded away the images that came to my mind. His hands disrobing her, caressing her skin. Did she enjoy it when he touched her, or was it simply a duty she performed? The sheets shifted and twisted in my mind like the dough being shaped in my hands. I slammed the lump onto the table. Harriet eyed me from the sink.

Anne's spirit was ever present in the kitchen. Harriet sang her sad song. And whenever we joked about something, there was a moment where we both waited for Anne's quips, but they never came. They would never come again. Harriet was sadder these days, but her mourning was compounded by some other sadness. I wanted to ask, but it wasn't a proper thing, asking about pain.

"She's come a long way these past few months." Harriet ventured.

It was meant to be a compliment. Something to raise my spirits. As if I were lost without Penelope to fuss over. "Makes my job easier," I said, moving from one counter to another. Loaf number three was starting. I decided a good, enriched dough would do. Something with lots of butter.

"Keep that up, and we'll have to start selling those," Harriet teased.

I was about to say something I shouldn't, but Mr. Davis came bursting into the room. His cheeks were pink, and he was absolutely tickled. "She dismissed me!"

"Did she pinch your arse too?" Harriet asked.

"Of course not!" he blustered. "She and Mr. Jones were having a discussion in the parlor when she asked me to leave. She wanted to speak of undergarments and did not wish to do so in front of me."

"She's full of surprises, isn't she?" I quipped. "Today it's leaving the house and dismissing servants from the room, what will it be tomorrow? Full-scale redecoration?"

"It's so wonderful to see her come out of her shell," Harriet said. "Is she still doing the scratching thing?"

"I caught her once and stopped her, but other than that, no," I said.

"How did you stop her?" Mr. Davies asked.

"I held her blooming hands down!"

Mr. Davies's mouth dropped. "Best not tell that to anyone else," he said in a hushed voice.

"I know it's not proper, but I was afraid she was going to hurt herself," I explained. "It wasn't worth the risk."

"Next time, let me know, and I'll call the doctor." Mr. Davies said.

I scowled and cracked a few more eggs into a bowl. We needed some tea cakes. Penelope railed through them these days. At the rate she was going, I'd need to call the seamstress to let out some of her gowns.

"You don't think he's helping her?" Harriet asked.

I shook my head. "She likes him well enough, and he takes good care of her. I just don't like the way he just loads her up full of drugs before a party and makes her look like a damn fool. That makes things even worse the next time."

"I don't know that anyone likes their doctor," Mr. Davies said. "Mine told me I needed to eat less bacon and sausage! Can you imagine?"

No, I couldn't. The look on my face must have been indication enough because the butler blew out his puffed cheeks. As though I, the kitchen maid, could confirm his diet was proper.

"I just don't like doctors in general."

Penelope was always excited when her doctor arrived, but despondent and inconsolable once the drugs wore off. I wasn't an expert on psyche like the doctor. The drugs might have helped her spirit or whatever, but they didn't look like they helped mentally or physically.

\#

That evening, Mr. and Mrs. Jones took their dinner in the bedroom. Mr. Davies usually held this honor, but when we began compiling the trays, I noticed he tried to pour tea for two. "No tea for her," I reminded.

The butler took the teacup and dumped the contents into the sink. Harriet made boiled fish with potatoes. This was something they served all the time. "Have you ever seen her eat the fish?" I asked.

"I've never seen her eat much of anything, to be honest," he replied.

That was concerning. I frowned at the fish, and it stared back at me. "Perhaps we should debone it first. Or at the very least, behead it."

Mr. Davies glared at me with great annoyance. His moustache twitched on the right side. "Why don't you serve dinner?"

That was exactly what I wanted, but I wasn't in a position to ask for it. "Are you sure?" I asked.

"A lady's maid serving dinner. Might as well," Mr. Davies said. "If it were a proper meal in the dining room, I'd sooner die."

My smile was one of triumph as I deboned the fish and added a few things I knew Penelope would eat. Some sliced apples with a shiny red peel imported from warmer lands, and some bread with preserves and butter. It didn't go with the fish, but at least she'd eat it.

I went up the stairs, positioning the tray on my hip, and knocked.

"Come in," Mr. Jones called.

They were sitting opposite one another on the loveseats. Penelope was facing the door, and her eyes widened at my entrance. Mr. Jones turned with one arm resting across the arm of the chair. "Oh, Mr. Davies is busy?"

"I'm afraid so," I said, setting the tray down between them. Penelope eyed the fish before reaching for the bread and preserves. As I suspected, she wanted nothing to do with the fish.

"I'm glad you're here," Mr. Jones said. "I wanted to thank you for taking the position for my wife. She's come an extraordinary way since you became her maid."

"Thank you, sir, but Mrs. Jones did all the work herself."

"She's being modest," Penelope said, her eyes locked on me, and my face felt like I was standing too close to the stove. "I don't know what I'd do without her."

Mr. Jones paid no mind to how bright my face must have been. He plated some fish before taking a few bites. "Penelope has been talking to me about remodeling the manor."

"Mr. Davies is thrilled with her ideas," I said. Penelope tensed for a moment before smiling.

"A lot has changed since the house was last remodeled," she said.

His eyes remained on her while I stood at a distance, allowing them their space to eat. Mr. Davies acted as a shadow until his services were required, and I would do the same.

"That is true," Mr. Jones said. "But this house was made up by my grandmother. There have been a few additions, like the water closets and the hot water, but it has otherwise gone unchanged. It's nostalgic for me. Reminds me of being a boy, running up and down these halls with my wooden train and kites."

"We don't have to remodel every room," Penelope said. "And I wouldn't want to change the hallways or the woodwork, just freshen it up a bit. After the remodel, we could host a party of our own," Penelope offered.

At this, Mr. Jones's eyes lit. "You'd host a party...here?"

The doubt in his tone was enough to rattle what little confidence Penelope had. She played with her hands in the lap of her seafoam green dress. "Well," she said. "I wouldn't have to leave the house that way. If I felt ill, I could just go upstairs."

This was a sort of compromise. Penelope was offering to have parties at the house to keep Mr. Jones from dragging her out into society. She would have more control of her surroundings this way. It was clever avoidance of a larger problem, but it could also help prepare her for social events outside the manor.

Mr. Jones took a sip of his tea before leaning back into the seat. He said nothing, and I felt as though I were hanging on his word just as much as Penelope must have been. "I rather like it," he said. "It's about time our friends come to our house, isn't it?"

"Your friends," Penelope corrected.

He tilted his head. "Come now," Mr. Jones said, his voice raised in a masculine way that suggested it was not up for further debate. "They just need to get to know you."

Penelope—still bawling her hands together—relented. It must have been a source of quarrel between them. His friends may not like her, but here in this manor, we liked her. She would be around people she knew. I would be here to take care of her.

"We can invite the good doctor to join us as well," Mr. Jones said. "You'd like that, wouldn't you, love?"

She gave a pursed smile and nodded. "English society would benefit from his knowledge."

"Well, that settles it," he said, setting his cup down. "You have my blessing to remake the house however you see fit."

Relief was painted on Penelope's face when she smiled. "What did I do to deserve you?" she asked. She said it for his benefit, but she glanced my way as she said it.

Mr. Jones chuckled before taking a bite of pudding. "Well," he said, eyeing me for a moment. "We won't discuss that in front of the maid."

My heart dropped straight through my chest. Of course they were intimate. They were a married couple and likely trying for an heir. I couldn't fault her for doing her job, but the way he said it... His playful tone warped into a mocking one in my mind.

Another person was suddenly in the room. He was seated in a neglected chair beside the loveseat Mr. Jones sat on. His greying hair and the sagging skin I had seen so many times upon entering my humble flat. Wrapped in that knitted blanket Mary had knitted. My father stared at me with white eyes, void of pupils or iris.

"You love her, don't you?" he asked.

A strangled gasp came from my chest. Penelope and Mr. Jones went on, conversing about plans for the manor. They flirted and laughed as old friends would, but it could do nothing to distract me from my father. I dared not speak. It was all I could do to stand there and pretend I was invisible. This was not real. I was imagining things. It couldn't be him.

"There's no shame in it," my father rasped. "Your mother and I suspected as much. You were always different from the other little girls in the village."

"Mr. Davies brought me a stack of magazines the other day," Penelope said. "He ordered some from New York, too, but they won't be arriving until a few more weeks."

My corset squeezed my ribs, forcing a series of small inhales that merged into one large breath. Sweat rolled down the back of my neck. I clenched my eyes shut and silently pleaded for my father to go away.

He was sitting there, in his chair, plain as day, but no one else could see him.

"They find you quite exotic," Mr. Jones said. "Being a New York woman. Feel free to indulge them, my love. They will be talking of this remodel for years to come."

"You really think so?" Penelope asked.

"This would be the height of excitement in this area," Mr. Jones chided. "They haven't seen anything this big since my mother installed indoor plumbing."

"It's all rather posh," my father said. "She isn't like you. She can't survive outside her world, and you can never live in hers."

I gave a discrete nod in hopes my father would return to wherever he came from. I always had an active imagination, but this was so vivid, so real. I didn't believe in ghosts or spirits. It was just hogwash people made up to explain things they couldn't deal with. I thought I had dealt with my father's death, yet his image gripped my mind with a force he never used in life. It was so unnatural that I couldn't help considering the hogwash.

I cursed myself then, wishing I had done more for him in the funeral rites. Spirit or guilt manifested, had I taken greater care of him at the funeral, I might not be seeing him in the corner of every room. Perhaps we missed a mirror or some other talisman that had trapped his spirit and bound it to me. We only had two mirrors—the small, round one in the living room that was covered, and my mother's vanity in my bedroom.

Oh no! I never covered the vanity mirror. Mary never went into my room—too fearful of my wrath. Did his spirit somehow get stuck in my mother's vanity mirror? Is that why he haunted me? The grandness of the bedroom fell away one wall at a time, exposing my old room. I took account of every detail, but there was no indication of my father that remained when I sold the vanity to Mr. Granger.

Perhaps it was me who carried his spirit unintentionally. A sort of delayed grief that seeped into my mind. He was always with me in spirit, at least, the person he was before he got sick, but why was his sickly version the one that haunted me? I couldn't make him well. I had done everything he asked for, rather than what Mary asked for. What did I miss?

"Ms. Mayweather?" The voice of Mr. Jones pulled me back into the blue bedroom once more.

"Hm?" I asked.

The seat where my father had sat was vacated. It was just the three of us now.

"I say," his voice lined with annoyance. "We're done, I think."

I gave a curtsy and retrieved the tray. "Is there anything else you require?" I asked.

"Are you all right?" Penelope asked.

"Ma'am?"

"You're shaking like a leaf," she said.

"I'm just tired, ma'am," I said. "Thank you for inquiring."

"I'll see you tomorrow, then?" she asked. Her eyes were full of alarm. I regretted letting her worry.

I gave her a smile. "Late morning, as usual, ma'am."

Mr. Jones yawned and said, "I will go to bed early."

"So early?" Penelope asked. "It's still light out."

Mr. Jones got up and kissed her on the forehead. "I know, but I'm so fatigued I can barely keep my eyes open."

"All right then," she said. "I'll read up on radiators."

That night, before I went to bed, I examined my savings. The third jar had been topped off. I would need a fourth. It had been four months since I started working at the manor, and I had saved up nearly seven pounds. I had never had that much money in my life, but was it enough? I had no experience in life outside the village, but I had no illusions that life in the city would have its drawbacks as well.

Life was comfortable here for the most part. I examined myself in the full-length mirror. Mr. Davies was right. I had grown into my uniform. Not in the physical sense, but mentally. The uniform had been eased in the arms and shoulders, allowing me better mobility. I grew accustomed to the stiff fabrics. My skin was a healthy olive shade, and my hair was growing in thicker than ever. So what if I died a little when Mr. Jones and Penelope were together? It was better than actually dying of the illnesses that often raged through the city.

If I saved my money for a long time, I could just open my own bakery. Maybe not in a big city, but in a village where no one knew me. Like the one our bakers had. The family lived upstairs, and the shop was downstairs. It would be a home I owned and a life of my own.

My father's ghost or whatever it was had the right of it. As much as I wanted to be with Penelope, it could never be. The better she got, the more Mr. Jones's interest grew. They were husband and wife, and I was a maid. It didn't matter how much she liked me or I her. There were no women couples in the village, just as there were no men couples. Such things didn't happen. If the villagers got wind of such a couple, what would they say? What would they do?

It would be better if I left once I was secure in knowing that Mr. Jones no longer considered institutionalizing his wife. Not just for my own good, but for hers as well. That noose called upper society was drawn tightly against Penelope's neck. If she tried to escape them, she'd strangle herself. It would be the end of me knowing that I had been the cause.

I went to sleep that night thinking of the future, but it was Penelope I dreamt of. Her silken hair pressed to my face, and the smoke of her cigarette coiling around me. Her rosewater that clung to my uniform.

It wasn't my father who threatened to linger in my doorway. There was no doubt in my mind that it would be Penelope who would haunt my dreams for the rest of my life.

Chapter Eleven

"Oh, come on," Penelope said. "What's the worst that can happen?"

I scowled at the bicycle. Just how was it that Penelope was afraid of her own butler and fish heads, but a bicycle was not a problem? It was my turn to be anxious, it seemed. "I could break a leg."

When Mr. Jones learned of Penelope's interest in riding, he, of course, had to order her a bicycle. It was a tall thing, more for her height than it was for mine. She straddled it and demonstrated how it worked, but her legs were so much longer. There was no way I could do it.

"It's easy," she said. "I used to ride one around the park all the time. It's about speed and balance."

She rode around the yard with all the grace of a swan landing on a still pond before making lazy circles around me. Graceful as a swan, she wanted me to be a swan too. I didn't have the heart to tell her I was more of a gopher than anything.

Even if we did live in a world where two women could be together openly, we'd no doubt be a total laugh. Like when the young parish married a widow twice his age. That was years ago, and the village was still having a go at them. Beautiful people were meant to be with beautiful people, and people like me were meant to be alone.

I could picture it in my mind. Tall, svelte Penelope with her golden hair and wide smile, walking arm in arm with me—a thick, masculine woman. Even with a hat on, I only came to her shoulders. The truth was that I didn't measure up in so many ways, and it was only a matter of time before she saw it too.

Penelope came to a skidding stop. "Now you try," she said, dismounting.

She held the handles as I clambered onto the machine. I wobbled before finding my feet on the pedals. This bloody thing was going to get me killed, I just knew it.

"You got it," she said. "Now, just push hard on the petals. Don't think about it too much."

I shifted my weight to one pedal. Every fiber of my being told me this would end in disaster, but Penelope wouldn't ride by herself. The doctor had prescribed exercise as a part of Penelope's wellness. I found it written in a note beside some vitamins stashed away in a drawer while looking for her winter bloomers.

"Are you supposed to be taking these?" I asked her, holding the bottle.

Her face scrunched with disgust. "It tastes so awful."

Stupid posh girl. These vitamins probably cost several months' rent, and she stashed them away in a drawer. "You don't know what people would do for this bottle." The harshness in my voice gnawed on the heiress. She pressed her lips together and winced.

"You must hate that about me."

I was too rough with her. My shoulders slumped. "No, I can't blame you for not knowing things, I just wish you would take better care of yourself is all."

She hesitated for a moment before marching toward me, her lips a hair's breadth away from mine. Tobacco and coffee lingered. Her breath was hot and shallow. For a moment, I thought she was going to kiss me. Her eyes went to the bottle. Delicate fingers grazed across my rough, calloused ones as she took the bottle.

"I'll take it from now on," she said. "There is a set of bicycles somewhere on the grounds. I'll ride if you come with me."

So, there I was. Propped precariously on one foot, ready to risk life and limb on a contraption that would sooner murder me. A bicycle wasn't that hard to master. If the likes of Robert could do it, there was no reason I couldn't. Just because I was too poor to have one growing up didn't mean I couldn't learn, right?

I clung to the handlebars and gave my lady a nod before pushing off. She ran alongside me, pushing and guiding the bicycle until I gained enough momentum to ride off. It was exhilarating, but nerve-racking. The slightest turn of the handlebars sent the bicycle wobbling, forcing me to pedal faster to keep balance.

A shrill cheer sounded from the other end of the driveway. I turned to see Penelope, a distant figure, jumping up and down. My chest swelled with pride. I was riding a bicycle. The world was a blur as my figure sliced through the air. For the first time in my life, I was light and graceful.

I was also fast.

Perhaps too fast. As I laughed at my own cleverness, something occurred to me. I did not quite know how to turn, and I had no idea how to stop.

My laughter turned into a scream as I rode off the driveway and into the lawn. Unable to release my grip on the handlebars, all I could do was brace for impact.

Fortunately, the grass slowed the wheels, and when the machine tilted to one side, I had the good sense to lean with it. I almost landed on my foot, but the bicycle kept going, and my foot slid on the morning damp. I fell on my side with my face smooshed into a mound of dirt left by a mole.

"Are you okay?" Penelope was panting so hard I thought she'd turn blue.

I just laughed, still stimulated by the ride itself. Oh, it hurt. My whole side was surely bruised, but the corset of all things protected me from the worst of it.

"Dinah!"

"I'm fine," I said at last. Rolling over to face her, poor Penelope was on the verge of tears. She brushed my hair from my forehead.

"I'm so sorry," she said. "I forgot to tell you how to stop."

"Falling was the best part."

Penelope was looming over me. Her face was reddened from cold and tears, but the overcast sky above her promised rain. She directed her attention to the fuss toward the manor. Sitting up on my elbows, Mr. Davies and Harriet came into view. They were by the servant's door, waving and shouting at us.

"I think that means it's time to come in," Penelope said.

She pulled me up, leaving the bicycle where it lay. "Leave it," she said. "Leave it for the groundskeepers."

I did as she said, swept away by her commanding tone and the arm in mine. She pulled me inside through the front door to a waiting butler. "Goodness!" he staggard, before covering his mouth as he chuckled. "What happened?"

"She rode a bike for the first time," Penelope declared.

"It looked as though the bicycle was the one who took her for the ride," Harriet said.

"You want to try?" I asked dryly.

Harriet went back to the kitchen. No doubt there was some beef to overcook.

Mr. Davies dropped the subject. "Should we proceed with teatime as usual, ma'am?"

"That will be good," Penelope said, unpinning her hat. "What are those little cookies that look like seashells?"

"Madeleines?" I asked.

"I'd love some of those if we have any."

There was a moment of panic in my mind. I hadn't made any Madeleines. Penelope had kept me far busier than before, and baking was something I only got around to when Mr. Jones demanded her attention.

Mr. Davies caught my distress and said, "I'll have Harriet make some."

"Thank you!" Penelope said.

"Let's get you changed, Mrs. Jones," I said. "I might need to wash up a little myself."

"Can you start the boiler, Mr. Davies?" Penelope asked.

"Of course," he said with a bow.

Not only did she ride a bike, but she also asked for things from Mr. Davies now.

Her confidence with the old butler was growing. The smile on Penelope's face remained as we passed the parlor on our way to the stairway. The door was uncharacteristically open, revealing Mr. Jones, fast asleep in his chair.

"Freddie, dear?" Penelope called, but Mr. Jones did not rouse.

"Did he not sleep well last night?"

Folding her arms in front of her chest, Penelope frowned at her husband. She was worried about him, but I didn't see what all the bother was about. "Perhaps he's still growing," I chided.

"Freddie?" she paused in the doorway.

His feet, shoeless and sockless, were heavily swollen. It wasn't uncommon to get swollen feet after a day's hard work, but it was mid-morning, and the man had spent the morning in his chair. "Penelope, his feet..."

"Go fetch Mr. Davies," she said. "He needs to soak his feet again."

Before I could turn, Mr. Davies was walking briskly toward us. "The builders will be here soon!" he said with a happy clap of his hands. "I was just going to alert the lord."

"He's asleep," I said. "But his feet are swollen something fierce!"

The butler peeked into the room and sighed. "Yes, it happens quite often. I'll take care of it."

There was a slight tremble along her bottom lip. What was it that upset Penelope? "It's just a little swelling, my lady," I soothed.

"It's not that," she said. "I...can't meet with the builders."

She was the one who instigated a remodel, but looking at her now, one would think it was thrust upon her. It worried me. She had been making such strides, yet in this moment, I half-expected her to flee to her bedroom.

"I don't know how any of that stuff works," she said. "Maybe you and Mr. Davies should see to the men, and I'll stick to the more feminine designs."

"Me?" I scoffed. "I don't know which way is up."

"If the lady does not wish to be in the presence of the men, I will see to it." Mr. Davies said with an air of defense. He was protecting her. As a father of a daughter, he must have felt compelled to protect her from menfolk. It filled my heart to see such a bond forming between Mr. Davies and Penelope.

Her face was awash with relief. "Thank you, Mr. Davies."

The butler bowed and retreated to the kitchen. "At your every command, my lady."

In the safety of her bedroom, Penelope undressed and lit two cigarettes. In nothing but her undergarments, we smoked and talked about the remodeling. In her bedroom, she was still just as excited about the renovation; it was only downstairs where it unnerved her.

"You're a mess," she teased.

I saw myself in her vanity mirror and snorted a laugh. I still had dirt on my face from when I fell. "I'll get cleaned up," I said. "Your hot water should be ready soon."

In my room, I poured some water from the pitcher into the basin and washed with a rag. I changed into the spare uniform that hung on a nail beside the window. The laundresses didn't come for another several days, so I wouldn't be able to do anymore bicycle riding for the week. What a shame that was. I was never so grateful for a dirty uniform in my life.

Freshened up, I made my way across the manor and back to Penelope when her laughter found me first. It echoed in the entryway and through the hallway. The source was within the parlor. At first, I thought my mind was playing tricks on me, but Mr. Davies emerged from the room, closing the door behind them.

"Mrs. Jones's teatime cookies should be ready by now," he said.

"She's in there?"

"Mr. Jones woke when I put his feet in the bath, and he called for her." His eyes shifted from the door and back to me. "Our lady is full of surprises lately."

A heavy feeling came over me then, like a wet woolen blanket draped over my shoulders. She was in there, laughing and enjoying herself with Mr. Jones as it should be, but...

Mr. Davies approached. "There is no doubt in my mind that you are responsible for the changes in Mrs. Jones, but tread carefully. Your corruption cannot infect our lady."

It took everything to stay my temper. I felt like I had steam erupting from my ears! When had I ever gotten so mad at anyone like I did with Mr. Davies? Not when Mary suggested I get a job, not when Mary told me I needed to lose a few pounds, not when the village boys threw rocks at me. But why? He said nothing wrong, yet it felt wrong. The butler was my strongest ally but my greatest source of frustration.

"You think me corrupt?" I asked. My jaw ached with tension. "What have I ever done to anyone in this village other than be different? I don't hurt no one. I don't expect or demand or send people away like your lot does."

Something broke in Mr. Davies then, and I was glad for it. His straight posture was crippled, and he wiped at his mouth and disturbed his waxed moustache. Men could spend their whole lives making choices without giving a second thought to how it would impact the women around them, and it was nice to take at least one down a peg or two, even if I wasn't entirely certain as to why.

"I owe you an apology," Mr. Davies said. "I should know better than to listen to village gossip."

"It's fine," I said, ignoring the churning in my gut. It wasn't fine, but there was nothing to be done about it. "I should see to Mrs. Jones. She probably wants to go back to her room—"

Before I could finish, Mr. Jones and Penelope left the parlor. He had his hand on the small of her back, and she was practically glowing at him. As if the sun rose and set by his smile alone. I swallowed my urge to interrupt them.

"I told him his services were not needed this week," Mr. Jones said.

"What did he say?" Penelope asked as they rounded the banisters that resembled chess pieces.

"He was rather unhappy," he said. "Not so bold as to accuse me of lying, but he was adamant about not enabling you. I told him all about your projects and excursions, but he remained unconvinced. I know he's been in your family for years, but..." The door of their bedroom clicked closed, and the remainder of the conversation was held behind closed doors.

Mr. Jones was turning the doctor away.

I should have been thrilled, but the sinking in my gut suggested otherwise. I didn't want her to go up there with him. It was her job as his wife, and I was a horrid creature for prioritizing my wants before her safety in this moment. Wracked with guilt, I turned around and left without another word.

After spending half the night crying into my pillow, I lay on my back and stared at the ceiling. Mr. Davies probably served them supper. I didn't mind. I couldn't face her in that room while it still smelled like their lovemaking. She always used rosewater after an encounter with him. I swore I could smell it all over the room.

If only I could turn my heart off and switch it back on when it pleased me. Turn it off when Penelope went to bed with him, turn it back on when he was gone, and it was just her and I.

Tried as I might, I couldn't convince myself that her being with him was a good thing. That this was how it was supposed to be. Did she feel as strongly about me as I felt about her? What if this was all in my mind and in mine alone? Dread filled me then. I would need to ask her. Part of me didn't want to, the other part couldn't live without knowing.

The next morning, tray in hand, I knocked loudly on the door. There was a feminine groan, and I entered. She was still in bed, in that damned pink nightgown. I fought with the door clumsily before closing it.

"Why so early?" she just asked. "Fredrick just left for breakfast himself; the bed is still warm."

I slammed the tray down so hard, Penelope jumped in her bed. She said nothing for a moment. It was too dark to see my expression, but my anger was palpable. It seethed from my skin and flared through my nostrils. I had enough money that I could leave today if I wanted.

"You're angry with me," she said evenly.

"If you're awake, you should just go down and eat with Mr. Jones."

"We always eat together," she said.

I sighed to release the building frustration in my lungs. "You don't need to do anything for my benefit."

"It's not for your benefit," she said. "I enjoy our time together."

Penelope got out of bed and turned up the lantern oil. The orange light of the room cast an unseemly grey tone throughout the usually tranquil room. Our eyes met. She studied me then.

"Do you?" I asked. "Or do you just enjoy dragging around a pet that loves you so unconditionally?"

Her face broke into a sullen pout. "I thought I made my feelings for you clear."

"But it's not the same, is it? Not like it is with him."

A slender hand went over her chest. "I am his wife. There are certain things I just can't avoid."

It was too much then. Like the walls were crashing down on me. She was just doing what she must, and so was I. Shame and a resounding foolishness took the place of where all my anger and bluster once sat on my chest. She did love me like I loved her, but we all had our parts to play. Society was not accepting nor kind to unconventional women. I knew that firsthand, Penelope must have known it as well.

"Have you ever…" I struggled to say the words. "Been with a woman like you have with a man?"

The room was silent, but I couldn't stop myself. "Because I've never been drawn to men. Not like the way the village girls swoon over the boys."

"They never told you about boarding school, I take it."

"Mr. Davies said a professor punished you, and the doctor said it was bad for your nerves."

She shook her head. "Just like my family to sweep anything inconvenient under the rug."

And she was willing to tell me? That was a first. I sat down at the edge of the bed, facing the fireplace. "Well?" I spat.

"A few of the girls and I," she started. "We were playing a game of sorts. We dared one another to take off our clothes and, well, explore. Only, one of the girls got scared and left. She told the professor what we had been doing. I was still naked when he yanked me out of bed and made the whole class watch as he beat me with a ruler."

I choked on my own air. The humiliation and cruelty of it. It was worse than anything I had endured within the village. Never had I imagined they treated rich girls just like they did us poor. This was worse. Mr. Davies may have been on to something when he said she feared men.

"I had no idea." I wiped my wet face with my sleeve.

"My parents were called, and they found me covered in blood, huddled in the corner of my room. The professor…" She paused, and a shudder went through her chest. "He was found dead outside the door. Some sort of brain bleed."

"That's when the doctor knew," she said with a sad smile. "He knew what I was capable of. If he hadn't intervened, if he hadn't begun the drug regimen...who else would I hurt?"

Oh no. It was a disturbing tale indeed, but whatever happened to the professor was not her fault. "Wait one moment. You don't think you killed him, did you?"

"You weren't there," she said. "You didn't feel what I did in that moment. The surge of power that made his hand so weak, he dropped the ruler. The sounds he made. He begged me to stop, and I wouldn't."

She was angry then, her fists in knots so tight, spots of blood were staining the sheets. I didn't know what to make of her story; all I knew was that she suffered something awful, and the doctor had her convinced she was at fault. Regret and shame came over me then. I shouldn't have gotten so angry with her, knowing what was at stake. Forcing her to relive something so traumatic for something so selfish.

My skin prickled with heat, and I muttered, "I'm sorry. Sorry," before dashing out the door.

"Dinah, wait," she called, but I was already out the door.

My footsteps knocked and echoed throughout the house, only heightening my embarrassment. My eyes were red and stung with tears; the last thing I needed was for someone to see me like that. In my bedroom, I sat on my bed and had a good cry. Over what, I wasn't sure.

The professor had it coming, regardless of whether it was Penelope's doing or not. She said she threw the vase without touching it. Was she trying to tell me she was telekinetic? That the doctor kept her on a drug cocktail to keep her from unleashing an unseen fury on the men who wronged her in life?

More importantly, did it bother me that she was living in some delusion that she had special powers?

No. It upset me that her doctor had her convinced of these things and that he used drugs to control her. But even if there was some shred of truth to what she was saying, I couldn't hold it against her for using any means to protect herself. The bastard probably gave himself the brain bleed while he was beating the holy shit out of her.

I sighed and trudged to the washbowl and splashed some winter-chilled water on my face. Checking in the mirror to be sure I wasn't blotchy, I emerged from my bedroom. I needed to apologize to Penelope. Poor thing was probably falling apart in her room. It didn't take much to rattle her confidence from that slender frame of hers.

What sort of future did we have if I couldn't come to terms with the fact that I would have to share Penelope with Mr. Jones? It wasn't ideal, especially not in her delicate state. The last thing she needed was to give that doctor a reason to show up with that medicine bag or his ideas of institutionalizing her.

There was a grim satisfaction in it. Imagining Penelope draped across her bed in her sheer nightgown, her golden curling hair shielding her face as she gently wept. No small amount of guilt followed.

It wasn't that I wanted her to suffer, but to have someone care that much for me made for a nice change. After we made up, I'd take her out for a walk in the garden. It was too cold to use the swing, but afterward, we would go to the greenhouse like we always did. I would make her those cakes she liked with her coffee.

Male voices came from inside the parlor door as I passed. I slowed to overhear the conversation. I didn't know anyone was scheduled to visit today, and I didn't hear anyone come in. It must have been when I was in my room. I slowed to a full stop, just short of pressing my ear against the wood to eavesdrop on the conversation.

"It's just that I don't know if your services are required as frequently these days," Mr. Jones said. "She has flourished over the last several months."

"That's wonderful to hear," a nasally male voice said. "However, I know our girl. She has a harder time of it come Christmas."

The words *our girl* ricochet through my mind and soured in the back of my throat. Did Mr. Jones feel the same? The audacity of it. I was new to the etiquette of the upper-class, but even I knew it was wrong to insert oneself into the lives of the upper-class.

"*My wife,*" Mr. Jones enunciated with slow and deliberate meaning, "will decide if and when she needs your services."

Yes! I silently cheered Mr. Jones on.

"Oh, I don't know if that is wise," the doctor interjected. "You don't tell a man to amputate his own gangrenous arm, do you?"

"Of course not—"

"And when someone is sick with a fever you don't let them take a hot bath."

"Well, no, but—"

"It's not fair to leave her ill-equipped for the month ahead," the doctor said gently. "The last thing we want is for her to relapse. I only propose that we continue with the current treatment. Come spring, we can reevaluate her."

There was nothing for a moment, and the doctor followed up with, "I've discussed this at length with her parents already."

The voices were moving toward the door. I scurried up the stairs before the parlor door could open. I braced the banister and dug my fingernails into the hard wood, wishing it was the doctor's face. Mr. Jones's face was the color of a tomato and appeared utterly defeated. Mr. Davies emerged from some shadowed corner in the house to hand the doctor his coat and to escort him out.

Good riddance.

I knocked on the bedroom door, but there was no answer. Fearing for the worst, I entered the room to find Penelope lying on the loveseat. She was disheveled, and her glassy eyes drifted nowhere specifically. "Penelope?" I whispered.

She let out a groan as her head drooped to one side. I sat beside her and took her hand in mine. It was a good thing I had already cried my eyes out earlier; otherwise, I wouldn't be able to keep it together. Then again, if I hadn't reacted the way I did, maybe I could have stopped this.

"I'm sorry," I whispered. "I wasn't angry with you. I know you did nothing wrong. I was just jealous, I suppose."

She didn't need that doctor. Whatever it was he was doing to her wasn't helping anything. Mr. Jones didn't know a thing about being a woman and didn't have the courage to stand up for his own wife. He was too keen on his parties and business engagements.

The mention of her parents changed his tune. What did they hold over his head? They were married, and the dowry was paid. What more could they do?

"I was fine," Penelope muttered. "I told them so."

I squeezed her hand and swallowed the lump in my throat. I stayed with her for the next hour. She wheezed and panted erratically before falling into a near-death lull that frightened the wits out of me. Did anyone see her like this? Did Mr. Jones know, or did he simply avoid the discomfort of this so-called treatment?

Penelope fell into a deep slumber. I put a blanket over her and went to the kitchen to fetch her some coffee. Harriet wasn't there, but Mr. Davies was sitting at the table with a cup of tea that didn't hold so much as a wisp of steam. I was angry at the doctor, not at Mr. Davies, but I could no more stay my tongue than I could swim in a frozen pond.

"He forced her to take his medicine," I said bitterly.

Mr. Davies stared into the tea. "I know," he said. "Mr. Jones and I held her down while he injected it."

I sucked in a quick breath; hot anger went to my head. They held her down while that monster injected poison into Penelope's veins. There were times when she wanted the medicine, but this time was different. She said no, and they violated her. Why?

"How could you?" I gasped.

"Mr. Jones was just as upset about it as I am," he said. "I told him I would sooner resign than do that again, and I've served this house since I was seventeen."

"You'd better put in those papers then," I said. "I overheard the conversation between them in the parlor. The doctor has some sort of hold on Mr. Jones. The doctor mentioned her parents, and Mr. Jones folded like a used envelope."

Long, slender fingers traced the floral design of the teacup. "Mr. Jones doesn't need the monthly stipend her parents provide. I suppose he just doesn't want the conflict."

I was muttering curses under my breath as I prepared her coffee. Mr. Davies interrupted the vortex of my thoughts with a gentle, "Dinah..."

"What?" I asked, too preoccupied with handling the boiling water without burning myself.

"The thing with upper-class people, like Mr. Jones and Mrs. Jones, they are not like us," he said. "They don't live their lives by morals. If they did, they wouldn't be successful. They often make unscrupulous choices because they are without consequences."

What an odd thing to say. Until this moment, I had never heard Mr. Davies utter an unkind word about Mr. Jones or his parents.

This incident must have shaken him to his core and tested his faith in the household. "Would you have done that to your own daughter?" I asked.

He slammed his hands on the table so hard the teacup shattered, sending bone China chips everywhere. "Dammit, Dinah. Don't bring Agatha into this."

"So," I said with a lifted chin. "She has a name after all."

Mr. Davies's gaze returned to his cup. "Your father never spoke of her?"

"My father never spoke about anyone."

The butler sighed. "He was a good man. You have my word. I will not take part in anything like that again."

The kitchen bell rang a coppery note. It was the parlor bell. Mr. Jones required assistance. Mr. Davies stood and silently left the room to serve his master. I remained in the kitchen alone while the coffee swirled into the bottom bowl of the vacuum press and the bitter smell bore its full fruition.

I tried to recall what little I knew about Mr. Davies's family. His wife was gone, and he had a daughter around my age. That was all I knew. Did it matter? I had a deep suspicion it did, and that my father had alluded to something...but what?

"It's nice to be in your thoughts once more," a gravely, dry voice sounded. It was the voice of my father.

Chapter Twelve

He was sitting in the chair where Mr. Davies once sat. Only, my father was in the beginning stages of decay. His skin had shrunken from his face, and his mouth was wide and gruesome. His hair was longer, as were his fingernails, and his nose had appeared to have shrunk. His skin was a ghastly violet shade that made me I was grateful I couldn't smell my imagination. The remains of the teacup sat almost comically before him as if it were his.

This was not real. I was stressed and angry over what they had done to Penelope. Yet my breath was so hot in the room that my breath created white, puffy clouds. Maybe that was my imagination, too. "It's not normal," I said. "People shouldn't be talking to themselves."

"But you're talking to me, not yourself."

"Same thing, isn't it?"

His head tilted to one side. "You had a question for me?"

Did I? My hands trembled so hard I gripped the wooden countertop to anchor them. I shook my head, hoping he would go away.

"About Agatha," he prompted.

What on Earth was he going on about? We lived in a small village; it wasn't impossible, but no one ever told me. My kneecaps were rattling against the counter, and the world began to spin. This wasn't real.

"God, I'd give anything for a good cuppa," he lamented.

Was I being haunted, or was I just crazy? Perhaps I learned these things as a child and forgot. Maybe I was being haunted by the spirit of my father for forgetting to cover the vanity mirror. Either way, he wasn't leaving until he said his peace or until I admitted mine.

"You love the woman. This Penelope."

Was this my own mind working against me? It wouldn't be the first time, but why must it be so visceral, so cruel? Could he really be a ghost? Saliva pooled in my mouth, and I swallowed a gag. If I covered the mirrors or bought more flowers...

"Focus, girl," my father said. "If you don't listen, you'll lose Penelope forever."

My mind snapped back into the hallucination of my dead father. "What?"

"Weak hearts are less forgiving than stronger ones. It takes less to put a stop to them."

He nodded sagely as if I would understand what that blather was about. "What?"

My father shrugged. "I can't spell it out for you, then it would be useful. I'm not supposed to be useful. I'm a ghost, after all."

"Is that what you are?" Pink drool was stringing from my mouth and puddling on the table. I had bitten my cheek...or maybe I was still biting it. My fingernails threatened to buckle against the wood countertop, but I couldn't stop myself.

"I couldn't say, if I'm honest," he said. "All I know is that I am here, and you needed to be told something important."

An incoherent noise came from my mouth, and my stomach lurched, threatening to spill the contents all over the counter. Hot and sweaty, my legs exhausted from the grip of self-control. My vision darkened, and I leaned against the counter, praying I wouldn't faint.

Voices from the entryway echoed through the kitchen corridor. I looked away for the briefest of moments, and when I turned, my father was gone. It was as if he were never there in the first place. I stared at the spot where he sat and wondered if he was ever there to begin with.

After several minutes, my heart stopped banging around in my chest, and I regained some composure. My legs were weak, but they supported my weight once more.

Harriet trudged in with a sack of potatoes. "Help me with this, would you?"

All my strength had been siphoned from my body, but the potatoes were still light enough. Harriet looked me up and down with worry. "What's the matter with you?"

"Before I came on as the lady's maid," I started, not quite sure where I was going with it, but the words came out nonetheless, as if they weren't my own, "you and Anne were in Penelope's room."

Her veined and blotchy brow furrowed. "What about it?"

"Did you see anything you couldn't explain?"

Harriet hesitated. She did see something. It was written all over her face like arithmetic on a chalkboard. Numbers and formulas she didn't understand and couldn't explain. "It's all right, Harriet," I assured her. Blood still lingering in my mouth. "No matter how crazy it is, just tell me."

"She was in bed," she started. "Scratching at herself when she began to contort. It wasn't natural. We tried to stop her, but when Anne ran her mouth about the missus being dramatic, the vase came flying off its pillar. Only it wasn't aimed at us. It flew at the door and shattered."

It was incredible. Maybe I was seeing the ghost of my father, and maybe Penelope could move things with her mind. Revelations often happened in the kitchen, but never quite like this.

"You did good in telling me," I assured her.

"Is it a ghost, you think? Anne often told stories, but I thought they were just for fun."

"We can never be certain of anything, I suppose."

Who were you throwing the vase at, Penelope?

If all this was real, what would it mean for Penelope if others found out? If she hurt someone, they'd lock her away. The doctor used drugs to manipulate her feelings, but why didn't she use her powers earlier? Maybe she didn't have control of them. It explained why Penelope suffered such intense anxiety.

She wasn't afraid of what was out there. She was afraid of herself.

The voices in the hallway pulled me from the miraculous discovery. Just as well, I hadn't decided what to do with the information anyhow. With my tray as a prop, I made my way down the hall to hear Mr. Jones and Mr. Davies in a conversation.

"It's rather short notice," Mr. Davies said. Not bothering to hide his irritation.

"That is the nature of the job..."

Mr. Davies fluttered around the young master, clearly flustered. "It's not appropriate to demand your time at such an hour."

"It's an emergency," Mr. Jones said. "It's only Manchester. I'll be back in a few days."

Mr. Jones was leaving for Manchester in the middle of the day. He wouldn't get there until the early hours tomorrow. I emerged from the hallway. Mr. Davies and I exchanged a knowing glance. Mr. Jones was making up an excuse to avoid Penelope after what happened earlier, the poshy little coward.

Mr. Davies's face was sullen. "Are we to say to Mrs. Jones when she comes around?"

Mr. Jones's face reddened a deep shade of scarlet guilt. "Ms. Mayweather will care for her," he said. "Won't you?"

It sounded so innocent, but the blow was deft indeed. He must have known, on some instinctive level or more, that Penelope did not love him. She was not expected to love him, though; she was expected to produce children and run his household. Her love wasn't a requirement for their marriage, but all men wanted to be loved.

"Someone must," I said.

His eyes locked on mine. Nostrils flared and ruddy cheeks blazed against tanned skin. I planted my feet and gripped my tray. If he was going to call me out, I'd do the same.

"Right," Mr. Davies said, slicing through the tension in the air. "Here's your coat."

Mr. Jones hastily shook on his coat and gave me one final glare before marching out the door and slamming it before Mr. Davies could see him out. The trotting of horses outside signified Mr. Jones's departure.

"What were you thinking?" Mr. Davies hissed.

The indignation of it all. "He was in the wrong," I said. "He had no right to take it out on me."

"He has every right," Mr. Davies said. "He is the lord of this house, and you are in his employment."

I remembered what the butler had said about upper-class people making wrong choices and getting away with them. To call him out the way I did was a good way to lose my job, but in that moment, I didn't care. He needed to be held accountable, even if his social status and bank account stated otherwise. "Someone had to."

"You best start thinking about Penelope," Mr. Davies smoothed his oiled hair back over his receding hairline. "Make her forget it happened. If she raises too much hell, that doctor of hers might get his way."

"Just what is that, exactly?" I asked.

"He is just looking for an excuse to put her in his new, state-of-the-art institution for women with her condition," he said darkly. "If she gives Mr. Jones too much grief, I fear he may concede."

"No," I whispered. He couldn't do that. She was his wife.

"He claims it's like a spa for hysterical women. Her parents already agreed to pay for it. Mr. Jones is the only reason she remains here."

"But she's getting better." The tears threatened to fall down my face. I couldn't bear it anymore. I rushed past him. "Sorry, Penelope needs me."

Mr. Davies turned and said, "It's Mrs. Jones, and you'd do well to remember that."

My father's ghost said that it takes less to put a stop to a weak heart. He must have meant Penelope. She wasn't strong enough to be institutionalized. I saw the papers. They were cruel, barbaric places that promised conversion and guaranteed torture. Electric shock, steams followed by ice baths, padded cells, and stimulation at a doctor's hand. She wouldn't survive it.

The doctor would force her to endure all sorts of experiments to see what made her psyche act up. It was so frustrating, not being able to reveal what I knew to be true. Penelope had abilities this doctor wanted to possess. Was his *spa* full of women with abilities similar to hers?

Mr. Davies was right. I needed to get Penelope to forgive and forget, to play nice with Mr. Jones. Just the other night, he bedded her, but the next day, he held her down for an injection she didn't want. He was no doubt cowed by the doctor. How quickly his affections changed from yesterday to today.

Was there another way to ensure her safety? Only one harrowing idea came to mind. If she got pregnant, there would be no way Mr. Jones would commit her. His heir would be growing inside Penelope. The prospect made me sick to my stomach. Turning her into a brood-mare didn't guarantee her safety; if anything, it endangered her mental stability even more.

Nonetheless, he couldn't take her from me if she was pregnant. She wouldn't be expected to do much with the child—they would hire a nanny. She had a sponge in the bathroom with ties on it that she bought from a catalogue. I could loosen the ties to the sponge or even toss it out altogether. With no form of contraception, there would be no choice but to go without.

No, I couldn't do that.

It was hard enough hiding her doctor's institution from her. I couldn't lie to her about something so important. Not only that, but taking away what few choices she had in this miserable life was wrong. If I could get her to come to that conclusion on her own, it would be better. With a heavy sigh, I knocked on the bedroom door and pushed it open.

She was awake. Sitting up, mostly, but with the help of the back of the sofa.

"How are you feeling?" I asked.

She gave me a playful smirk. Her hair was down and flowing freely around her as she lounged on the loveseat. "Not bad, honestly."

I set the tray down and gave her the coffee. She took tiny sips while relishing the all-consuming scent of roasted coffee. "I understand the doctor was rather insistent."

"I admit I was agitated," she said. "I think our little row had an effect on me. The doctor knew this instinctively. It took two men to hold me down; you would have been proud."

If a heart could disintegrate into grains of sand and slip through gaped fingers, mine did in that moment. She had convinced herself that what happened to her this morning was for her own good. Did she hold the slightest grudge against the men who behaved so atrociously? If it were me, I'd want revenge. I would curse them to a shallow grave and might even put them there myself.

"I am proud," I said, taking her hand.

I couldn't tell her exactly what was on my mind. Swaying her toward feelings she deserved to feel would only be a detriment to her future as the lady of this house. Instead, I had to lie to her.

"I know you're much more confident these days, but your treatments will help you recover faster. I overheard Mr. Jones talking to your doctor. He doesn't think you need as many visits. The doctor is going to reevaluate you come spring."

"Reevaluate me?"

I wouldn't ask her to alter her thoughts or emotions like the men in our lives did. Instead, I would give her a way out. If she could prove to Mr. Jones by spring that she didn't need these treatments, it would loosen the doctor's hold on her. Everyone would be much happier, except maybe that doctor.

"Yes," I went on. "Come spring, you may be seeing that doctor less if you want."

Her eyes searched the tabletop as if it would have an answer. "I don't know," she said.

It was baffling to me that she was uncertain. What did she not know? I searched her darting eyes for answers, but all I found were deep blue wells of internal conflict. I wanted to take her by the shoulders, to shake her, to kiss her. None of that would do any good. "Whatever you decide to do, you have our support."

She smiled weakly. "We?"

"Mr. Davies and I," I said. "He was quite upset with the ordeal and threatened to put in his resignation should the doctor ask him to do such a thing again."

"Oh, Dinah. You weren't there. I was clawing and screaming at them like some wild beast. I was wrong to behave that way. Mr. Davies only restrained me to prevent me from hurting myself. I'm afraid I frightened Freddie. He's never seen me like that."

She was guilty and ashamed. If anything, it was the men who should be ashamed. "What started it?"

Penelope wrung her hands with all the friction she could muster after being doped up. Her eyes went wide, and she shook her head. "I'm not certain myself. I was tense from our fight, but if I'm honest, I was also quite relieved. We said some important things."

The resonance of our declarations remained even if the anger and jealousy did not. "Yes, we did," I whispered.

"Then the doctor came in and examined me. I didn't want him to. His touch made my skin crawl, and I just wanted him gone. Acting like a wild animal did the opposite of making him leave," she chuckled.

"If he was the reason you acted in such a way, why would you want to continue seeing him for treatment?" I asked.

Penelope shrugged. "Is it wrong to admit that I like the drugs? Not before I go out in public, but I like how they make me feel. All my cares and worries are gone with the prick of a needle."

I didn't know how to feel about that or what to do with the information. "It's not wrong to want relief," I said. "But why didn't you use your powers?"

"Don't tell me you believe me!"

I gave her a knowing look. "As if you're capable of lying."

Penelope tilted her head. Her grin was half crooked. I blamed the drugs. "It happens when it happens. I felt something building, but once the drugs kicked in, it was gone." She made a fluttering motion with her hand, like it was flying away.

Just as well. If Mr. Jones got clobbered by a flying vase, he might have given in to the doctor's request. He might have cared for Penelope. He might have thought he was working in her best interest. But when a man decides the best course of action for a woman, he ceases to understand them.

"I'll just go tidy up the bathroom," I said, gently patting her hand.

To my shock, the washroom was empty of all personal effects. The toiletries, hand towels, even the paintings on the walls. "There is something wrong with this bathroom."

Penelope laughed. "We are finally having that plumber in for a remodel today."

I blanched. She didn't know Mr. Jones had fled the house, leaving her to deal with the technical aspects of the remodel. "Oh, um, about that..."

She turned, resting her arm on the back of the loveseat, and regarded me curiously.

Before I could stumble over the words, there was a knock on the door. I gave her a forced smile before opening the bedroom door to answer. It was Mr. Davies. He didn't so much as glance in the room, perfectly content with never setting eyes on Penelope again.

"The plumber is here," he said.

"I should leave the bedroom and let the menfolk see to it then," Penelope said behind me.

The butler's brows raised, and I cringed. "I was trying to tell her."

"Tell me what?" Penelope asked.

"There was an emergency in Manchester, ma'am," Mr. Davies said.

I turned to see Penelope frantically pacing the room, raking her fingers through her hair with a clawed movement. At any moment, she could start scratching at her face. I had to do something to stop her.

"It's no problem, my lady," I said. I moved to her and took her hands in mine. "I'm here, and Mr. Davies is here."

She gave a shaky nod.

"If I may, ma'am," Mr. Davies said. "You are far more qualified to lead this project. Mr. Jones has never had an interest in such things."

"Yes, well, see him in," she said.

Mr. Davies brought in a short, portly old man with frost-white hair and a gentle smile. He quite reminded me of Santa Claus. Penelope—who had recovered some at the sight of him—stood nearly a foot taller.

"Mr. Wilson, ma'am," Mr. Davies introduced.

"Hello," she said in a low tone. "I'm sorry Mr. Jones isn't here to speak with."

"That's no trouble, ma'am," he said with a high, voice thick with a Scottish accent. "I understand you have some pictures."

"Oh, yes," she said before frantically searching her vanity for the correct magazine among the stacks.

"May I just pop in for some measurements?"

"Please," she said.

Mr. Davies and the plumber measured and took notes while Penelope sought her example bathrooms. I helped her look, flipping through various magazines. I opened one and found a sketching on yellowed parchment. It was done in pencil with some penned notes along the edges. It was rather good and unmistakably the work of Penelope.

Before I could give it to her, she was showing the plumber a series of pictures, attempting to piece together a vision for the bathroom. The plumber regarded the images and nodded thoughtfully. "I don't know if we can make that fit…"

"If the sink were to be moved, it should work," she said.

The man seemed very kind, but he lacked the imagination and vision Penelope had. Mr. Davies nodded appraisingly at the sink. "With a newer, more streamlined style, we should be able to fit a clawfoot tub in here."

Penelope beamed at Mr. Davies. Not an ounce of hostility or resentment despite the morning's events. She forgave him completely, from what I could tell. I don't know that she was angry at him in the first place. The only person she was upset with was herself, and it made my stomach sour.

She had done this sketch and had no intention of showing it to anyone. Pinching the edge of the paper, I marched into the bathroom and extended it to the plumber, who was scratching his head as he eyeballed the distance between the tub and the sink. Penelope's eyes went wide, and she moved to yank the sketch out of my hands, but Mr. Davies was quicker.

"Now this is a bathroom," he exclaimed.

The plumber leaned over, and Mr. Davies lowered the paper so he could have a look. "Oh," he said slowly. "Well, that would work quite nicely, I should think."

Penelope slumped against the sink. Too exhausted to be angry with me. The plumber took out his string, made a measurement, and checked her sketch with a nod of disbelief. He followed it up with a measurement of the cabinet, the current toilet, and marveled at the sketch. "Do you mind if I keep this?" the plumber asked. "It would be perfect to jot down my measurements."

"Yes," she said, nodding.

"It's really well done," the plumber said. "If I had someone doing these for me, it would make my job much easier."

"It's quite remarkable," Mr. Davies said. "She managed to get the proportions despite all the built-ins."

The plumber chuckled. "She's a better designer than most in those books."

I couldn't help but grin. They were not attempting to flatter her. It was the truth. The bulky cabinets and built-ins around the tub and shower took up so much of the room that no one could see its potential.

Well, no one but Penelope.

"The process will be quite extensive," the plumber warned. "I'll need to move a lot around. Might be best to take up staying in another room for at least a month."

"We've already got a room ready," Mr. Davies assured Penelope.

When the men finally took their leave, she fell onto the sofa in a wordless heap and chain-smoked for the better part of an hour.

Not a single word was spoken, but I did change out her ashtray and brought her a glass of wine. It was late in the evening when Penelope dozed off on the sofa. I pulled her up and helped her undress. Too exhausted to change into her nightgown, she slid into bed in her underclothes.

In the kitchen, Harriet was tidying up with Mr. Davies. I overheard him discussing the plans for the renovation. "You should have seen it," the butler gushed. "It was so technical and articulated. It's as if she studied design. I was rather proud of her. Mr. Jones up and left the responsibility to her, and Mrs. Jones came in like a professional."

"How about that," Harriet said absently.

The maid wasn't listening. Her mind must have been on the earlier conversation about the vase. I didn't blame her. Penelope's abilities seemed to occupy every vacancy in my mind as well. It was just so hard to fathom. But people believed in all sorts of nonsense. Why not believe in Penelope?

It didn't help that Anne retired and went to live with her children in Kent. Harriet had been rather lonely, and her workload had increased. I didn't know if they intended to hire another maid or not. I hoped they would for her sake. Even Mr. Davies and Harriet's boundless energy wasn't enough to keep up, and the Joneses were talking about receiving guests once the remodel was complete.

"Dinah," Mr. Davies called as I came in to set the tray beside the sink. "The fabrics from New York should be arriving tomorrow. A man from Manchester will be here next week with wallpaper samples."

"When did Mr. Jones say he was going to return?" I asked.

"He didn't."

Harriet dedicated herself to the dishes while singing that sad Celtic song again. Something must have happened. Her eyes were glazed and staring out the window into the snowy garden.

"How's Anne doing?" I asked.

Harriet gave me a sour frown. "How am I supposed to know?"

"Sorry. I just thought you had heard from her."

She gave a teacup a most aggressive scrub. "Am I the authority on former help, or is it because I'm old?"

"You're singing that song," I said. "You always sing it when you're sad."

The stillness in her expression was a portrait of grief. I placed a hand on her arm, and she didn't shrug it off. "I didn't get word from her," Harriet said. "It was her daughter who sent me a letter."

I bowed my head. "I'm so sorry."

"Well, that's just how life goes," she said, shrugging me off her arm. "It's shite, and then you die."

Knowing Harriet, she wouldn't say anything that veered toward the sentimental. It was best to change the subject. There was only one other subject she and I had discussed that wasn't about Anne. "Have you ever seen a ghost?" I asked.

"Funny you mention it," she said. "Anne once said she did."

"You mentioned that earlier. What did she say?"

"Yeah, she told me about how her gran used to slide the kettle to one side after boiling water for tea. When she passed, Anne said that the kettle kept going to the same spot, though she never moved it over."

An unsettling chill ran through my body. "How long did it do that?"

"It never stopped."

Chapter Thirteen

With the renovations well underway, the Joneses were in the next biggest bedroom in the manor. It was settled in the opposite wing above the dining room. It was an even older style than the former bedroom; it had green walls and red velvet curtains with a dizzyingly busy carpet. While the couple did not agree on all things, they both hated the room with equal measure.

"He's getting antsy," Penelope said with a flick of her cigarette. Ashes flittered into the crystal ashtray. "With all the workers coming in and out, staying at home these last few weeks has given him cabin fever."

She hadn't attended a social event in several months despite the fact that he had engagements almost weekly. The renovations had provided an excuse to get out of them. Someone had to see to the workers, and from all the eavesdropping I had been doing, I gathered that Penelope was quite good at it.

When the fabrics came, Penelope stroked each one lovingly before hanging the swatches all around her bedroom. After a few days of "judging the light of the room," Penelope began to do the same throughout the rest of the house. She took notes in a little leather-bound journal.

Mr. Davies was beside himself with the disorganization at first. Various fabrics lying atop everything without order left him believing someone was having a go at him. "Is this a joke?" he asked, staring at the dining room one afternoon.

"It's how Penelope decides which fabrics she likes," I said.

His moustache twitched, but he held his tongue.

After the dining room, Penelope sashayed into the parlor with her armful of fabrics and began draping them all about the room. Mr. Jones remained immune to her actions. He rubbed at his arm as if in discomfort while he worked on a crossword puzzle.

"Freddie," Penelope said. "Which of these do you like better?"

She had been vying for his approval throughout the entire process, but Mr. Jones shrugged at most things. I didn't understand why Penelope needed his endorsement so much, but it was important to her. It was his house, after all. He had clung to his nostalgia for so long only to forget about it altogether. Perhaps he trusted that his wife would maintain some of the tradition, but I found the sudden disinterest perplexing.

"They don't compare to your current dresses," he said, setting his newspaper down.

"These are not for dresses," she said with a laugh. "These are fabric samples for curtains and upholstery."

"Oh," his face went flush with embarrassment. "That explains why you're laying them about?"

"The lighting of the room determines which fabric goes where," she responded.

Mr. Jones gave a glance around the room appraisingly. "I rather like the gold shiny stuff."

"Me too," she commented. "It's overwhelming in our bedroom. I thought I'd leave our bedroom blue but update it."

Mr. Jones gave a grunt of approval. "I rather like all of these. Except that one," he said, pointing the pen he was using on his newspaper. "That one looks like tiny little eyes staring at me."

I couldn't help my snicker. Mr. Jones heard me and grinned.

"Dinah said the same thing," Penelope said with a smirk. "All right. That one is off the table."

"It would make a wonderful tablecloth for when your parents visit," he teased.

"Oh, don't say that. I was having such a wonderful time."

It was the first time I had heard them speak of her parents. He spoke of them to the doctor, but never to her. It was only a matter of time before they would visit, given how involved they were in her treatment. It was funny, they never sent so much as a letter, but they sent that doctor. They had so much invested in this marriage and her "cure," but they never tried to mend what was broken.

"We need to get the Christmas decorations up as well," Mr. Jones grumbled. "Mr. Davies usually does everything. I'm surprised it's not done by now."

"I think the renovation has kept us all rather busy," Penelope said, falling into the tall-back leather chair. "Dinah, be a dear and fetch me some coffee."

"Yes, ma'am," I said with a curtsy and left. Penelope didn't really want a coffee; she wanted to talk to Mr. Jones without me.

Coming to terms with their marriage had been easier as of late. Ever since she told me that she felt the same as I did, and that her marriage was just a fact of life, it didn't bother me as much. She was his wife, and I was her closest companion. I was satisfied with that to some extent. We still hadn't done more than hold hands, but that was out of precaution. Her position here was precarious at best, and I wasn't willing to jeopardize her safety for lust.

The story was different at night. While she slept in the room above me, I tossed and turned, unable to block her from my lonely mind. Helping her dress was never an erotic thing. It was rough business lacing a corset, and hoop skirts and garters were never any fun for anyone.

It was the little smile she made when she knew I was watching her. The shifts in the fabric of her nightgown when she moved about in the evenings and late mornings. The scent of coffee and powder, the whirls of cigarette smoke and her amber-toned laughter. The wide cut of her nightgown often slipped farther than it ought to, and when she caught me staring, she never flinched. Sometimes she'd stare back at me, as if daring me to climb on top of her and...

I let out a groan of frustration and rolled over.

That week, Mr. Davies hired some boys from town to bring in a Christmas tree and decorate it. He stood inside the entryway, guiding the boys as they dragged in the tree corpse and set it upright in its pedestal. "Watch the chandelier!" he warned.

I went and stood by Harriet in the hallway and watched the spectacle unfold.

"Mr. Davies always goes a little mad around the holidays," Harriet said.

The butler was frantically flittering his hands in the air as if he could will the tree to not fall over, crushing the side-table that had been in the family for six generations. I buttoned my smile thin smile. Madness was a fever that had been spreading throughout the manor.

"I think that's normal," I said.

"Oh," Harriet said as if madness reminded her of what she was about to say. "I hired a traveling Medium. She's going to do a reading to see if she can't talk to Anne or help me with a family matter. You want to join?"

If someone told me that I'd be buying into such nonsense a few months ago, I would have laughed them off. But given the current situations, Penelope's abilities and my father's lingering ghost, why not throw a Medium into the chaos? If telekinetics existed, why couldn't Mediums be real?

"Yeah, I'll go halves with you."

"All right, she said she'd be here tomorrow night."

Our conversation came to an abrupt end when the boys attempted to turn the ladder around in the entryway and nearly clobbered us.

The frenzy of the renovation was like bees swarming the hive, and Penelope was the queen bee. Mr. Davies directed the men as much as possible and only involved her when they had questions only she could answer. In the evenings, she fretted over every aspect of the house down to the most minuscule detail.

Sketches covered her vanity, where most women had jewelry or cosmetics. Some of the papers had coffee stains in rings around the edges. Unsatisfied, Penelope would bawl up an offensive diagram and throw it into the fire.

"Penelope, you've done this sketch already," I said one afternoon after hours of watching her work.

Her fingers were stained black with ink and charcoal, whatever she happened to grab first. "I know, but I need to redraw to account for the plumbing."

"How do you even know which way plumbing lays?" I asked.

"I did some digging. Well, I had Mr. Davies do some digging, and we discovered that each of the bathrooms was plumbed differently," she said, pointing at the washroom behind her with the stick of charcoal.

"Now, I have to redraw each individual bathroom before the workers come tomorrow, and there are five of them."

She sighed and tilted her sketch at arm's length. "Not to mention we need to decommission the water closets and figure out what to do with those spaces. I might leave one, just for the sake of antiquity."

I thought of the servant's water closet downstairs and its strong smell. "I don't know if anyone needs to remember those," I said.

"Oh, where's your sense of tradition!"

"In the outhouse," I retorted, and she laughed. I loved making her laugh, and it was so easy lately. I wanted to keep it that way.

There was a commotion downstairs. Shouts and panic filled the entryway, and we both went silent at the same time to eavesdrop. "It sounds like Mr. Davies got the Christmas tree," she said.

Like children, we burst out of the room and leaned over the stair railing to watch. A massive green log tied with rope bindings was being wedged through the doors. Mr. Davies was orchestrating its birth, barking orders to turn left or right, guiding the workers. The hallway had a stack of crates full of candles and red velvet bows, tinsel, and holly.

Mr. Jones was observing as well. He was standing outside the parlor door, arms folded and wry amusement on his face. Penelope went down the stairs, and I shadowed behind. She was going to speak with Freddie. Pine and resin reached us at the stairs and became overwhelming when we stood in the entryway.

Mr. Jones pulled her in close. "Mr. Davies goes bonkers every Christmas."

"My mother is the same way."

Memories of Christmas were sweet and nostalgic for me as well. Ours were always smaller, but the smells of nutmeg and fruitcakes filled our flat, and Father would always have a nip of Brandy. That was the only time he drank. His cheeks would flush red, and he'd tell the silliest stories as the booze went to his head.

"Oh," he said. "I confirmed for a party tomorrow night."

Penelope said nothing, but she shifted. I braced myself for the argument.

"Is the doctor coming?" she asked.

Mr. Jones frowned. "I meant to ask Mr. Davies to send word; I suppose it slipped my mind."

I suppressed a grin. It seemed that Mr. Jones had no intention of calling on the doctor, not after what happened last time. The doctor's grip on the Joneses was being pried away one finger at a time. It was only a matter of time before he would be forced to relent.

"Mr. Davies," Mr. Jones said casually, "did I tell you to send for the doctor?"

The butler turned. His face blanched like linens in lye water. "No sir. Was I meant to?"

Mr. Jones shrugged once again, shoving his hands into his pockets. "Well, I suppose it can't be helped. You'll be all right, won't you, my dear?"

Penelope frowned as if debating how to feel about it. "Maybe it's time to see if I can do it without his help."

The prospect was worrisome but could prove to be rewarding. If she could attend a party without drugs, it would be one less reason to call the doctor. One more finger pried away. With Penelope out for the evening, I was free to join Harriet and her medium.

Mr. Davies had stilled his hands as he gazed up at the ginormous tree as if it were the blessed Virgin herself. "Stop right there," he said. "It's perfect."

Perfect indeed.

Chapter Fourteen

Penelope was still in bed when I came into the bedroom. Fully expecting her dread and melancholy, I brought Madeleines with her coffee instead of the usual poached egg and slice of toast. Harriet's neighbor was selling last year's apricot preserves, so a glob of orange jelly sat in the center of the cookies.

"Morning," I said, setting the tray down before pulling open the curtains. She winced at the daylight that blasted her in the face.

"No..." she moaned before rolling over to stuff her face into the pillows.

I moved to her wardrobe and had a look at her gowns. "Any thoughts on what you plan to wear tonight?"

"A death shroud."

I rolled my eyes and selected a royal blue gown with pale pink flowers trimmed with white lace. "It's not formal, and you'll be home before midnight."

Penelope sat up and lit a cigarette. "I hardly slept a wink last night. I must look ghastly."

I sat beside her on the bed and took a drag off her smoke. "You are inescapably beautiful," I said. "You keep me up at night all the time."

"That explains the bags under your eyes," she teased. "Try some of my face cream."

"You know I don't fuss with those things."

"You're probably better off for it," she said with the cigarette waving like a wand from her mouth as she spoke.

I took her hand—that was currently clutched on the blanket—and held it tight. "You can do this."

"What if I faint?" she said.

"Then you will faint. That's what fainting couches are for." She wouldn't be the first woman to faint. It was perfectly acceptable due to the tightness of corsets. It was even viewed as romantic. Men loved a swooning, unstable, tragically beautiful woman who needed their unconditional love and support. Penelope fit the bill unlike any other.

She frowned. "I'm going to make a complete fool of myself."

"Good," I said. "Be a fool, and have fun doing it. At least you'll do it unhindered by that medicine."

"So, you're saying I should be a fainting fool at my husband's party?"

"What's the worst that can happen?" I asked.

She thought about it for a minute. "Well, I suppose he might stop expecting me to attend."

"Is that bad?"

She smiled, and I knew that I had won the argument. We took extra time that day on our walk. The frigid cold pinkened my cheeks and the tip of my nose. While Penelope's breath exhaled billows of clouds, her face was impervious to the cold. Only the slightest tinge of rose touched the edge of her pointy nose and sculpted cheekbones.

"You're not cold?" I asked.

"No, these winters are much tamer than the weather we get in New York."

That made sense. The snow muted the sounds of everything but the gentle crunching underfoot. We walked by the swing covered in ice, wishing it weren't. Spring could not come soon enough. Then again, with springtime came the return of the dreaded bicycle.

"Too bad the ground is too frozen for bicycle riding," Penelope teased.

"Are you reading my mind?"

She gave a sly grin. "It doesn't take a medium to know your thoughts; you were staring at the spot where you fell."

Was I really that transparent? "You must think me the most boring person."

"Interesting people are never really as interesting as they'd like you to think," she said. "I'd rather spend the rest of my life with you than one minute with any of Freddie's *interesting* friends."

The rest of her life, eh? I could live with that. She always said things like that. Like she knew we were meant to be together somehow. If only I had such confidence.

"Maybe they're not truly interesting," I said while trying to not slip on an icy patch in the driveway. "Mr. Barnett thought himself interesting because he went to India while in the military. He liked wearing a *dhoti* for Easter and Christmas service and made sure to make a spectacle of it by retelling the same story of how he got it. It wasn't very interesting, but he thought it was."

"Sounds like most of Freddie's friends, only they think of themselves as philanthropists."

I cringed. Nothing was worse than a wealthy person thinking they were the savior of the common folk. "Oh, whatever would we do without the rich telling us how to exist!"

We laughed, but I quickly realized that she was also rich. "Not you, of course."

"No," she said. "I can't help anyone. It's all I can do to get out of bed on most days."

As we rounded the stables, a flash of orange dodged through the trees. "Look at that!" I said, pointing.

Penelope squinted. "Is that a fox?"

A pointed white and orange face with black, beady eyes poked out from the snow. It was beautiful and wild all at once. Disgruntled neighs came from the stable. The horses could smell the fox and didn't like it. "I suppose we should scare it off before the horses get too upset."

"We should," Penelope agreed. "Freddie still fancies himself a hunter. He will shoot it and make me wear the pelt, the poor thing."

I picked up a rock and threw it, sending the creature scampering away before anyone else saw it. "Come along," I said. "It's time to get you dressed."

Penelope stared off into the woods where the fox went. "I have half a mind to run off and live with Mr. Fox, but there's ivy in the forest, isn't there?"

"You don't like ivy?" I asked, half-teasing. The smile fell from my face when I realized she was still staring off into the forest. She had this look about her before, whenever she said odd things.

"I told you, it's how I die."

The prospect gave me a terrible notion. What if we ran off together? To someplace where ivy didn't exist. It couldn't harm her if we lived somewhere it couldn't grow...like India! Though ivy could have grown in India for all I knew. The idea had struck me so profoundly.

No more pretending, no more parties, and no more doctor. We could find some busy town and keep Penelope hidden until they had forgotten about her. Would Mr. Jones even look for her? Her parents might, but we could flee the country. She liked Paris. There were lots of bakeries in France.

The ghost of my father didn't think she was strong enough for such changes, but maybe he was wrong. He hadn't paid a visit in a while. Perhaps he decided to stay dead. Either that, or my mother's spirit boxed him by the ear and dragged him back to his eternal sleep.

I shuddered at the thought of his last appearance. It was like I was trapped in my own body as it convulsed out of my control. A bit of my tongue was actually missing. I could feel its absence every time my tongue grazed my teeth. Maybe it would be my mother who answers from the great beyond.

"Come along," I said.

Penelope slowly followed behind me. The cold had finally gotten to her; she was hugging herself, and her lips were quivering. If it wasn't the cold that made her shake, it was the prospect of running away.

She wasn't ready.

Her fleeting desire to run away was met with whalebone stills and a cage that hovered around her middle. Her blue satin dress swayed, and her matching coat was draped over her shoulders. With her curls pinned back neatly behind her bonnet, it was clear that Penelope was every bit a lady of a manor, no matter how desperately she wished she were a fox.

If I wanted to protect her, I would need to find this ivy and tear it out by the roots.

\#

Harriet's home was a three-bedroom flat that was eerily similar to my childhood home. It made sense. They were built at the same time by the same people, but I couldn't help but feel nostalgic when I walked in.

The cozy little fireplace just where I expected it to be. The kitchen was nearly identical, if it weren't for the embroidered dishtowels. Ours were never embroidered. Neither me nor my mum had a head for needlework. Harriet saw me staring and misunderstood the moment.

"My daughter embroidered those," she said proudly.

"They're lovely."

Harriet's husband was one of the farmhands who worked with my father. He was a hirsute man with darker skin. She told me he came from somewhere else; I wanted to say he was Italian or Greek, but I couldn't remember. He greeted me warmly before saying, "I think I'll join John at the pub and leave you ladies to your witchcraft."

"Oh, get off!" Harriet said before pretending to slap him. "She might help us find Alexandra."

I knew Harriet had several children, but most were grown and flew the coop when I was a child. John was the youngest and worked in Chester as a mason's apprentice. "Your daughter has gone missing?" I asked.

"No," Harriet grumbled. "I should have explained, but I had a bit of a falling out with my daughter. What about you? Are you going to try and speak to your parents?"

I nodded, but something about it didn't feel right. There was more to it, but the conversation shifted so quickly, it was clear that Harriet didn't want to say more than she already had. "I was actually going to ask about Mrs. Jones," I said.

"About the thing we discussed?" she treaded.

I straightened out my skirts before sitting on her sofa. "If there's any way to help her more."

"I see." Harriet didn't sound convinced, but further explanation would give me away. We were banded together by our secrets. If I didn't pry into hers, Harriet would leave mine alone in turn.

The knock at the door made both of us jump. Anticipation had a way of eating at the nerves. Penelope often said that waiting caused her more anxiety than the social events or strangers stomping around her house. For once, I understood what she meant.

Harriet welcomed the person in the doorway and escorted a woman who oddly reminded me of Mary into the house. She used a rinse in her hair to make it dark, but a stripe of white went down her center part. The medium most likely left her hair down for a dramatic effect. She wore a heavy black cape and brown scuffed boots.

"Good evening," she said somberly.

"May I take your coat?" Harriet asked.

With ringed fingers, the medium unfastened the latch at her throat and gave the cape over, revealing a faded burgundy dress and several tarnished necklaces. I wasn't sure what to expect, but she resembled something of the cartoons in the newspapers. With the occult being a popular topic these days, it was easy to find a fortune teller. I just hoped Harriet didn't pay too much money.

"My name is Rivers Stoneworth," she said, sitting across from me in a wooden chair.

"My name is Dinah."

She was old. No doubt the cataracts forming in her eyes only added to her overall costume. Rivers said nothing more until Harriet sat beside me on the loveseat.

"Had I known there would be two of you, I would have cautioned you on the amount owed."

If she was psychic, wouldn't she have already known? I didn't want to play into my doubts, but I also didn't want to be taken for a fool either. Penelope couldn't control her powers; maybe this medium couldn't see everything. "I brought coin as well."

One of us was already better at foreseeing the future.

Rivers nodded and closed her eyes. She hummed to herself while slowly rocking back and forth. I looked to Harriet, whose hands were woven together in her lap as she stared at the medium.

"I see a woman," Rivers said between hums. "A woman walks on a dark and busy street unaccompanied."

Harriet leaned in. Enthralled with the vague statement.

"But now a different woman emerges," Rivers said, gripping the armrests. "She is beautiful, but her eyes cannot open. There is something, something grows around her neck..."

I stifled a gasp, not wanting to give anything away. Was she speaking of Penelope and the ivy? Harriet took my hand, as if she knew my thoughts.

"Fire," the medium whispered before slumping in her seat.

"What does that mean?" My voice trembled as I spoke, but I didn't care. I needed to know what she meant.

It was as if the medium couldn't hear me. "She walks in night and in shame. Too proud to ask for help. Too afraid of implicating those she loves."

"Where?" Harriet pleaded. "Where is she?"

The medium's eyes snapped open.

Her once milky white eyes were clear as a cloudless sky. She frowned before saying, "The fates of these two women are tied. If one dies, so will the other."

The medium stood. "I am done for tonight."

I went back to the manor several coins lighter and only more questions to show for it. What sort of fate could bind an upper-class woman like Penelope with Harriet's runaway daughter? That's the thing about ghosts and mediums, I supposed. They were equal in how helpful they were.

Chapter Fifteen

For all the fretting and sleeplessness of the night before, Penelope's laughter sounded her return. I dashed out of my room, but froze in the hallway—not wanting Mr. Jones or Mr. Davies to see me. Penelope was unpinning her bonnet when I came into the entryway. Mr. Jones was grinning from ear to ear.

"I think they were all quite taken with you," he chided.

"Yes," she said. "That banker friend joked about stealing me away so many times I began to worry."

Over my dead body he would.

I didn't want to insert myself into the conversation. They would have to pass me to their room, so avoiding me was impossible. At least, that was what I thought. Instead of going upstairs, Mr. Jones guided Penelope to the parlor. "A little nightcap?"

"God yes," she muttered before turning around. "Mr. Davies, could you bring me my cigarettes?"

She didn't want to see me tonight. It hurt, but it was better this way. Penelope needed to be the wife Mr. Jones desired, and lord knew I didn't need to be witness to it. I crept back into the shadows. There was no way I could go to sleep, not with the thoughts spinning in my head, keeping my blood pumping hard in my chest.

I had a lot of baking to catch up on. It was late, but most everyone was awake anyhow. It's hard to sleep in a house constantly changing.

Madeleines were on the agenda. We'd eat them tomorrow to celebrate Penelope's victory. Her first outing as Mrs. Jones without the drugs. It was one of Mr. Jones's biggest needs apart from an heir, and she provided it.

I whisked the egg whites with a handheld mixer furiously while debating on whether Mr. Jones really wanted children any time soon. It was expected of them, but that did not mean he wanted them so soon.

"Goodness, Dinah," Mr. Davies said over my shoulder. "What did those eggs ever do to you?"

I didn't hear him come in. I was so startled I jumped back, eggbeater still in hand. Fortunately, it was a fully formed meringue by this point. It stuck to the whisks and pointed a cloudy peak at the butler.

"En Garde," Mr. Davies said with a smirk. He too was in high spirits over Penelope's triumph. I thought it strange and endearing that the butler's mood hung on the lady of the manor. He cared for her far more than he let on. Perhaps he wasn't so bad after all.

"Sorry," I said. "I didn't hear you come in."

"Madeleines?" he asked, regarding the bowl of meringue.

I folded in the dry ingredients. "She loves them."

"The social gathering was a success," he said as I mixed. "I'm quite proud of her. You should be, too."

Was he trying to console me? "Of course I'm proud of her. She keeps going at this rate, she won't need me or that doctor anymore."

"It's better to be wanted than needed in any relationship," he said gently. "Trust me on that."

Would she still want me after she got better? Her life would be filled with parties and friends. Sure, she cared for me, and Mr. Davies had explained to me how posh people worked, but she didn't grow up as posh as Mr. Jones did.

If you knew the truth about me, you wouldn't want me.

Penelope had secrets. Her wants and needs were seedlings that were forced to grow in a bed of fear and guilt. No one knew her like I did, and what I knew was that she would never let someone suffer if she could help it. Penelope wouldn't cling too tight to me in case I wanted to leave, but she wouldn't hang on just because I wanted her.

"Either way, I am glad for the wage increase," I said, forcing a smile.

Mr. Davies said nothing further, and I poured the batter into the tins and into the oven for cooking.

The next morning, the party was all Penelope could talk about. The cigarette smoke clung to the tiny bedroom in a way it didn't before, and a nauseating stink clung to the curtains. There was not enough room on the coffee table due to her sketches, but the end table beside the loveseat was enough to set the tray on if I balanced it properly.

"You should have saw it," she said, lighting another cigarette. "They hung on my every word. They wanted to know all about New York. I admit I was a bit out of my element...I haven't seen New York for almost a year."

I was brimming with insecurity and guilt. Penelope had every right to be proud of herself. She deserved to enjoy a night out without being drugged into submission, but I couldn't bring myself to be happy about it. "Um hm."

"What is the matter with you?" Penelope's voice was several octaves higher than usual.

I sat down on the edge of the bed. "I'm sorry," I said. "It's not you. I just had a long night."

Her head tilted as though she were looking right through me with those big eyes of hers. Something in me caved. "I'm just afraid you won't need me after long."

"Need you?" she said with a haughty laugh.

That was the last thing I needed to hear. My love was disposable. Mr. Davies told me it was better to be wanted rather than needed, but when need was all I had, how could I not crave it? The heaviness in my heart soured my disposition.

Penelope did a double-take and said, "Oh, Dinah, I didn't mean it like that."

My head was swimming with self-pity. I couldn't remain in this tacky room any longer. I stood up and said, "If there is nothing else you need."

"Dinah!" Penelope cried, standing up. I moved for the door, but her long legs carried her there faster than I could manage. She stopped me with a forced embrace. Long, thin arms wrapped around my waist as she pulled me against her frame. "It's not need," she whispered. "It's more than that."

"You've changed my whole outlook on life," Penelope whispered into my ear. "I can never be the same now that I know you. No one has ever been there for me the way you have. I've never trusted someone so fully in my life."

Oh, God. That couldn't be true. Surely, that was an exaggeration meant to placate my raging, baseless insecurities. "Not even your parents?"

"Especially not my parents," she said. Penelope pulled back suddenly. "I was saving this for Christmas, but I think it's needed now."

My eyes darted across her face, searching for whatever it was she alluded to. Her lips parted and met mine. A lightning bolt coursed through my body. There was heat and passion, everything I questioned and feared dissolved in one kiss.

Cool air rested on my lips, and I opened my eyes to find Penelope fully flushed and smiling with tears in the corners of her eyes. "Just...try not to look so bewildered for the rest of the day."

Did I look bewildered? I certainly felt like a newborn doe in the woods, stumbling amid the uneven ground. All eyes and shaky legs. Our relationship had crossed the threshold from companions to something more.

My first kiss. For the first time in my life, I could see what all the fuss was about.

The wind outside sent leaves swirling and bare branches whipping through the air. The manor occasionally gasped as a gust here or there found its way inside and was forced back out again via one of the many chimneys.

One loud groan in particular caught us in the hallway on our way to the greenhouse. It was so pervasive that it felt as though the manor were a beast, and we were a bit of meat caught in its throat. Penelope paused and raised a weary brow. "I don't think I've ever heard a house make that kind of noise before."

"What? You mean your penthouse didn't sway a little?" I teased.

She gave a dismissive laugh and kept walking. Her laughter echoed down the corridor, and the house groaned once more.

"I think it's hungry," I said.

"It's not the only one." Her low tone and sharp American accent loomed with threat. My heart skipped a few paces. It took me a minute to register that what she had said did not mean she wished to devour me, but rather, that she was simply hungry.

I sped up to catch up to her. "I made some madeleines last night."

We ate the cookies with coffee and jam. Despite my best attempt, Penelope refused to try the clotted cream based on the name alone.

"It sounds disgusting," she said, dunking her cookie into the ramakin of apricot jam.

"Well, I can assure you it's not."

The greenhouse was nestled into a corner of the manor. Shielded by the wing and the main body, it escaped much of the wind and bluster. The humidity reminded me that spring was just around the corner. We could walk the garden, Penelope and I, in the full bloom of an English spring. It was something I wanted very much.

"Any update on the plumbing situation?"

Penelope rolled her eyes while chewing. "No," she said. "They are scheduled to get a new boiler in, but that was days ago. My curtains are on hold due to the holidays. The wallpaper should be here any day, though."

"Well, that's good."

"It is," she explained. "The curtains are for the new wallpaper. If Freddie sees the curtains with the old wallpaper, he may not trust me with any more decisions."

The mention of Mr. Jones brought up another question, one that I had been putting off. My hands went to my lap while I picked at my cuticles. I had every right to know what they were planning. I may have been a third wheel on the bicycle, but it was important.

"What's wrong?" she asked.

I shook my head, and her eyes narrowed. "No, something is wrong. You're making that face."

It was useless hiding anything from her. I ripped a bit of cuticle from my thumb. There was a stinging pain as new flesh was exposed to the air. It would be best to get on with it. "Are you and Mr. Jones considering children?"

Her eyes fell to her empty plate. "The doctor is against it," she said quietly. "He's afraid the hormones will put me in a permanent episode. There was a pregnancy early on, but the doctor saw to it. Now we take precautions."

I didn't know what to make of it. I was furious that the choice was taken from her. If she and Mr. Jones wanted a baby, they should be able to have one. Just how far did this doctor's meddling go? And yet, what if the doctor was right? I had heard of women going mad after having children. Then again, every woman I knew had children, so who was to say that was the common factor?

"I'm sorry," I said.

"Don't be," she said. "I'd be a lousy mother anyway."

I didn't believe that for a moment. "I'm sure you'd made a better one than me."

"You'd make for a proper spinster," Penelope teased.

"That would be fine with me, honestly."

After tea, we went up to the bedroom to observe how the bathroom renovation was going. From what I could tell, it wasn't exactly going anywhere. The room had been totally gutted. Exposed pipes and a hole for the toilet were all that remained. Even the wall had been stripped bare of its decorative mint-green and floral paper.

"Well," I said, leaving the response open-ended.

Penelope smoked a cigarette with gritted teeth. "I would have thought we'd at least have the boiler in by now. I'd settle for a new toilet. Are they in high demand around Christmas?"

It was a rhetorical question, of course. I wouldn't have the faintest idea. I had never even seen a toilet like the ones in her magazine. Her agitation was mounting the longer we stayed in the room. Her nails seemingly grew overnight and were now drawing white lines along her forearm.

"It will be much easier applying the new wallpaper this way," I offered.

Why did it upset her so? The bedroom they stayed in now wasn't stylish and inconvenient, as the washroom was at the end of the hall, but the stress this was causing her was undue. "It's just a bathroom," I said, stroking her arm. She put her hand down and away from her arm.

"I held up my end of the bargain and then some," she said. "I dealt with the plumber when I shouldn't have, I picked out every detail, attended his social thing, and now, I have to host a New Year's party for all his friends in a half-made home."

Her words took moments to sink in. It was impossible. Words sputtered on my tongue. "Mr. Jones didn't—"

"Oh, but he did."

Of all the selfish, idiotic things he could have done. Did he want her to fail? "I thought you were to host the party."

"I was," she replied. "He had too much to drink and announced it the other night at the party. We're committed to it now."

Well, that was all there was to it, then. Maybe the bathroom wouldn't be ready by New Year's, but there had to be something they could do. "Does Mr. Davies know?"

Thin, bloody lines were drawn down her arm. No, this wasn't the time to lose all the progress she had made. No one could see her arm. They would call the doctor, and he would have the validation of being right. Tempering the fury I held for Mr. Jones, I grabbed her hand and pulled her out of the bathroom.

We retreated to the temporary bedroom where I dressed her scratches and got her a dress of a thicker material than the linen crepe sleeved dress she had been wearing. "Don't roll the sleeves up on this," I ordered.

"What does it matter?" she asked, sitting at her vanity stool. "He should know the distress he is causing me."

"He should," I said. "But you need to use your words."

Penelope bowed her head. Defending herself, especially to men, was difficult for her. I had seen her with multiple men at this point, and I was only beginning to understand the fear she held for them. That damned professor who humiliated and inflicted so much pain was the start of it, but I couldn't help but wonder if there were more secrets in Penelope's closet.

"I would tell him off," I said, sitting beside her on the tiny stool. "But I can't."

She rested her head on my shoulder for a moment. "I think I just need to lay down."

I helped her to bed, tucking her in as if she were a small child before shutting the door as quietly as I could manage. I walked as quietly as I could manage, but I couldn't take it anymore. I lifted my skirt and ran the rest of the way to the kitchen.

Harriet was maintaining the oven when I burst in. She straightened, wide-eyed with alarm. "Dinah—"

"Davies," I huffed. "Where is he?"

Marching across the driveway, the butler's slim frame was a black stick in an otherwise picturesque scene. The expensive, well-bred horses were lined in their stalls, and a wooden fence separated the Jones property from the wooded road and the forest on the other side. Evergreens wore snowy coats, as did the rooftop of the stable and shed, but the landscape was otherwise clean and tidy.

"Mr. Davies," I called, bounding toward him.

I wasn't close enough to see his face, but he had the good sense to understand something was wrong. For me to leave Penelope and come running out here for him in the frigid cold without a coat, it must have been important.

"What is it?" he asked once we were within range of one another.

"Did Mr. Jones tell you about the party?"

He frowned. "No, we're not in any condition to have any callers."

I told him about what transpired at the party Mr. and Mrs. Jones attended. He listened, and his frown did not diminish. "You say he refuses to back down?"

"I don't think Pen—Mrs. Jones is incapable of confronting him."

"No," Mr. Davies agreed. His words were lined with sympathy. "It's not something ladies are taught in civilized nations."

Oh, I'd give him civilized!

The state of the home could not be denied. The Christmas tree had only just gone up recently and had yet to be fully decorated. Half the furniture had been relocated to an unused room to be re-upholstered. There were no curtains, and most of the paintings had been tucked away in preparation for new wallpaper. The bathroom in the main bedroom was the least of our worries.

"Well, what are we going to do?" I asked. "She's falling to pieces over this, and I don't want Mr. Jones to get wind of it."

The butler's eyes met mine. He knew full well why I didn't want Mr. Jones involved. "I'll ride out to the post office, send out some telegrams. If Mr. Jones insists on having a party by New Year's, we will simply need to hire more people and expedite the process. Dinah," he said, clasping his hands on my shoulders. "You did well to tell me. I'll take it from here."

I watched Mr. Davies step into the coach through the window. Christmas was in two weeks and New Year's in three. I paced the entryway for several minutes before returning to Penelope. She was still in bed. I sat beside her prone body and stroked her back. I couldn't reassure her because I had little idea what Mr. Davies was planning. He was calling for more workers, I supposed, but that wouldn't be enough to placate Penelope.

"Laying about won't solve anything," I whispered.

She refused to answer. Her face was stuffed into the pillow, and she was totally ignoring me.

I slipped an arm underneath her and rolled her over. Her body was rigid and frozen in the same position as when she was lying face down. Her eyes were closed and her mouth open, arms stiff and unrelenting. It was as if she had died and rigor mortis had set in.

"Penelope," I gasped. Her back was frozen into an arch. "What is the meaning of this?"

Why was she doing this? Angry and resentful of her immaturity, I grabbed her shoulders and shook her unyielding body. Tears fell down my cheeks when my furious onslaught did nothing. Her bandages were removed, and fresh scratches crossed over the old ones. I had underestimated just how much she was suffering. Something was terribly wrong.

"Just stay here," I said to the unmoving body. "I'll get help."

Bursting out the front door, I ran to the stables. Edward, one of the village boys, was brushing a horse. He was a waif-thin man with pale skin and dark hair. "I need to get to the village," I said.

"You what?" he asked.

"Now!"

I didn't know how to ride a horse. I had to ride on the back, clinging to Edward. Thankfully, he did not ask questions. The brown and white horse galloped down the road, paying no heed to the mud or the cold. My thighs burned as I struggled to maintain my balance, but we were at the village in half the time it would have taken me at full sprint.

I found Mr. Davies at the post office. He was sending telegrams furiously. The butler stood when I walked in. "Call for the doctor," I said.

There were no questions asked; he simply nodded and lowered his head, resuming his series of messages.

Penelope was far sicker than I could have ever imagined. I had demonized the doctor all this time, but she really did need him after all. The fantasies I had of running away with her were shattered. What happened if she had one of these episodes without him? There would be no way to afford a doctor as often as she needed one.

A blast of cold air hit my heated face as I emerged from the stuffy post office. Had I been crying the entire time? I couldn't recall.

"Miss," the coachman called from his seat. "Edward has some errands to run. He'll take Mr. Davies back when he's ready. Would you like a little ride along with me?"

I sniffed back the tears and nodded before clambering on. Unable to shake the image of Penelope's stiff body from my mind.

"You look like you've had a day," the coachman said. He was a small man with white bits of hair sticking out from under his top hat. "I always find a good ride helps me. Why don't you try?"

"Me?"

"Why not?" he asked, putting the reins in my hand.

"Now, pull the lines back, straight back when you want them to stop. To make them go, you flick the whip in the air. They follow commands instead of riding."

I nodded and took the whip. I flicked it a few times before a loud crack sounded and the carriage bolted forward. With some guidance, I took the lines and steered the horses out of town and back to the manor. It was rather fun, and the coachman was right—it did clear my head a little, but the dark cloud of Penelope's mental stability hung low over my head. I needed to get back to her.

The coach made it through the gate at long last, and I nearly jumped off before we came to a full stop. "Thank you," I clipped, rushing back to the manor.

"You're rather good," the coachman called. "Ride with me anytime!"

"Thank you!" My voice carried through the front yard before dashing back to Penelope.

Inside, I found Penelope just as I had left her. I tried pushing her stomach down—her back must have hurt immensely—but she would not budge. Penelope would not bend, and I could not risk her breaking. I sat there beside her. I don't know how long. It was dark when a knock sounded at the door.

"Come in," I called.

It was Mr. Davies with a man stepping on his heels. The doctor emerged with a large leather bag with a brass clip. "Good evening," he said, his American accent harsh and foreign. It wasn't like Penelope's accent at all; this had a different drawl that I couldn't put my finger on. Not that I was an expert at American accents.

"How long has she been like this?" he asked. His leather-gloved hands moved a stethoscope on different parts of Penelope's body.

"Since early afternoon," I said. "Mr. Jones sprung some news on her, and I'm afraid it took its toll."

The doctor examined the scratches on her arms. "I see," he said.

Opening his bag, the doctor produced a single bottle, a syringe, and a rubber tourniquet. "And where is the young man now?"

"He went to Manchester this morning," Mr. Davies said.

The doctor made a grunt of disapproval as he filled the syringe with the contents of the bottle. "This is one of those symptoms of her condition that Penelope cannot control," the doctor explained. "It can come about even when she's feeling well. We don't know if this is brought on by stress or not, but it appears she is experiencing some."

He took out a little notepad with the name 'Penelope' on it and jotted down some notes as Penelope's body eased into the bed. I gasped in relief. She relaxed and appeared now as if she were sleeping. I took out a handkerchief and blew my nose as quietly as I could manage. The doctor moved his stethoscope around Penelope's neck and chest before he applied ointment to her scratches and rebandaged them.

"These should not see the light of day; otherwise, they will scar," the doctor said. "We can't have that."

How could I have been so blind?

Penelope's doctor was not some evil fiend who wanted to steal Penelope away in the night. She really was sick. My love for her couldn't cure her; consistent expertise could. Still...was an institution really the best choice? If it was, I couldn't stand in the way, no matter how badly I wanted Penelope to remain with me.

"I'm going to leave an oral tonic behind," the doctor said, pulling a bottle out of his leather bag. "It's not uncommon that these episodes come in a series. If she does have another, two tablespoons should be sufficient." He stroked her forehead lovingly. His thumb lingered on the bridge of her nose for a moment as if something just occurred to him. The action sent a chill along my spine, but I shoved the warning away—too ashamed of how I tried to ignore and downplay Penelope's illness.

The doctor said nothing more. He was guided out the door by Mr. Davies. I waited a few moments, but I snuck to the door to try and eavesdrop. The doctor waited until they were at the stairway landing before speaking. "Mr. Jones claimed she was going out without the medication?"

"She did," Mr. Davies said. "She had a lovely time."

The doctor frowned. "And the marriage has been going well?"

"They get along quite well," the butler said. "They spend more time together now than ever."

"The maid," he said. "She's attentive?"

"Absolutely."

I pressed my cheek against the frame and closed my eyes to listen better.

"It's always the damn holidays," The doctor griped.

"If I may explain, sir." The butler told the doctor about the agreement between Mr. and Mrs. Jones. How she would be allowed to renovate the home so long as she be more present in social engagements. How Penelope kept up her end, and how Mr. Jones had done nothing apart from financing the undertaking. Mr. Davies didn't say it in that way. He held nothing but deference for the Jones family, but there was an air of defense in his voice.

"Mr. Jones made an announcement that we would host a party on New Year's, but as you can see," Mr. Davies gestured to the ransacked house. "We are not ready for such an event."

The doctor turned around to regard the house. "That would make any woman go catatonic," he chuckled. "That boy could stand to gain an education regarding the fairer sex. I have to notify the parents."

"Sir—" Mr. Davies began to plead.

"It's in the contract," the doctor said firmly. "If her health deteriorates, I am bound by my oath as her doctor. The marriage will be annulled, and the stipends will end. I realize it puts Mr. Jones in an embarrassing predicament, but our girl comes first."

That was why Mr. Jones feared the doctor. He didn't approve of their marriage. No doubt he reported back to her parents every time Mr. Jones so much as sneezed. The marriage was conditional on

Penelope's health, and if she was not well, her parents would not keep her here, no matter how large the scandal. Mr. Jones loved his social events and the prestigious lifestyle. If rumor spread that he was unable to care for his wife, those parties would dry out faster than a coal miner without a pub.

"Yes, sir," the butler relented with a bow. "I will make this information known to him."

I stepped away from the doorway and returned to Penelope. She opened her eyes halfway and let out a small moan. "What happened?"

"It's all right," I said. "Just rest. Everything will be okay."

She tried to sit up. "But the renovations—"

It didn't take much to push her back down on the bed.

That night, I slept beside her. I remained on top of the covers with a thick blanket. It wasn't a romantic gesture in any way, not like how I imagined our first night together. Still, to be close to her, the intimacy of laying in the dark together... It was the only future I wanted. Come what may, I would do whatever it took to stay by her side.

CHAPTER SIXTEEN

The front door was open when I came downstairs. Why would Mr. Davies leave the front door open? I stepped out to find he was ushering workhorse after workhorse. Each had two or three men on the back of carts, along with unknown materials under a tan cover. The butler turned to regard me standing there.

"He won't be pleased with the bill," Mr. Davies said. "But I suspect he will see things my way."

They were men from the village. Workers of various trades, mostly farmers, but they all had sturdy backs and good intentions, which was more than I could say for the single plumber I hadn't seen since the initial consultation. "What will they be doing?"

"These men have enough experience in their own lives to work on our furniture and to move things about. Polish, buff, sew, and most importantly, deliver items from Manchester with utmost haste," Mr. Davies explained. "The fabrics will be coming today, finished or not. The local ladies will finish them. We will have this place done in less than a week."

"What about the bathroom?" It was supposed to be the crowning achievement.

"I took the liberty of hiring several plumbers from Chester," he said. "Not only will the master bedroom be outfitted, but all the bathrooms will be done at the same time."

The cost must have been enormous. This was a wealthy manor, but were they truly that wealthy? My face blanched at the unknown pounds racking up in my mind. It wasn't my money, what did I care? Still, the butler had taken on an executive decision without consulting the lord of the manor. What if Mr. Jones grew angry with the mounting expenses? I was concerned for the butler. He was reaching well beyond his station, and it was solely for Penelope's sake.

"Mr. Jones will be okay with this?"

Mr. Davies gave a reassuring nod. "See to the lady. We will need her consultation."

I also learned that Mr. Jones didn't just leave for the day. He would be gone for several. The butler's plan to employ the whole village in expediting the renovations was likely emboldened by that information. Penelope was up when I returned with a tray of snacks.

"What's all that banging around down there?" she asked.

"They are working on some of the furniture."

"About time," she said before falling into the loveseat. "What am I going to do, Dinah?"

"What are *we* going to do, you mean?"

Penelope looked up at me as I handed her a cup of coffee. "What do you mean by that?"

Did she really think we would stand by and do nothing? Maybe that was how things were done in New York, but not in England. It wasn't just her pride on the line, but ours as well. Debuting a social event in a half-made house would not stand under Mr. Davies's watch. The man cared about his reputation as a butler too much to allow such things.

"You're not alone," I said, trying my best to contain my smile. Dread shifted to concern, then curiosity. As if she were a child on Christmas day, a light returned to her eyes that I hadn't seen in days. Penelope, still in her nightgown, rushed out the bedroom door. I chased after her with her robe.

"Please!" I pleaded with a chuckle. "At least get dressed."

"Right," she said with a fierce determination in her eyes.

Downstairs was sheer pandemonium. There were some fifty people that I recognized and about twenty that I didn't. Makeshift workbenches were strewn wherever there was room. A brigade of seamstresses had invaded the dining room, and Mr. Davies was orchestrating a clawfoot tub up the stairs. "That's it, lads," he said. "Nice and easy."

Penelope froze for a moment, and I feared the aftershocks of her condition were taking hold. I was about to take her arm, prepared for the worst, when she scampered into the parlor. Assessing the situation, she said, "No, this wallpaper isn't for the parlor. It belongs in the dining room."

Walter Bradshaw was working on the bedroom loveseat. He exchanged looks with Mr. Emit before saying, "Who are you?"

She faltered for a moment, as if just now realizing she was in a room full of men. I took her arm and said, "This is the lady of the house, Mrs. Jones."

Their mouths gaped for a moment, their eyes went up and down as if thinking, "Of course, who else could she be?"

"Apologies, my lady," Walter said, "We've been up since the wee hours."

Penelope lifted her chin and said, "Dinah, we've got work to do."

My heart was so full I nearly cried in that moment. Gone was the weepy, nervous outsider, replaced by a stout-hearted, iron-willed Lady Jones.

In the kitchen, Harriet was frantic. Her wiry hair was escaping the bun and hat, the water was boiling over, she was muttering, and I could smell something burning. When she saw not only me, but the lady of the house, the maid gasped and fell back against the counter as if Penelope were a ghost.

Penelope ignored Harriet. She was scanning the kitchen. "I don't know where anything is," she said. "How about you and Harriet make the tea, and I serve it?"

"You?" Harriet asked. "Serve tea?"

"I learned a thing or two in charm school," Penelope said. "How hard can it be?"

Harriet raised a brow but kept her comments to herself. "Let's get to it then."

We lined up six trays. Each with four teacups, milk, sugar, and slices of lemon, along with some spoons. I plated up all the cookies and teacakes we had as well as some scones, jam, and clotted cream. Harriet was responsible for making the tea, while I served tea, and Penelope would be serving the food.

Penelope was nervous at first, but after receiving praise and blessings, she began to venture from my side and check in on different rooms, assuring they were doing as she wished. All around me, I heard the villagers praising the lady of the manor.

"What an elegant lady!" The baker's wife said at her sewing station.

"She's not so stuck up as the last one," a farmer's wife commented.

"She's not afraid to roll up her sleeves, that one," another woman said.

The house was being pulled apart and put back together at the same time. Like a great knitting of lace being pulled and weaved before our very eyes. I wondered when it was the house last saw this much commotion.

I made it to the entryway before my plate was bare. Hands occasionally reached out as I wandered until I glanced down and realized I was carrying an empty tray. At this rate, we'd be cleaned out before teatime.

"Harriet," I said as I reentered the kitchen. "I think we're going to need a stew or something of that sort."

"Can you whip up some more of your breads?" she asked, pulling out a huge silver soup pot.

I nodded and got to work. Penelope emerged through the double-doors. "How far did you make it?" she asked.

"Almost to the entryway," I said.

There was a moment of calm then. The lady of the house was assessing, calculating, and measuring. Like a wartime general, she weighed out the plan of attack. "Can you introduce me to the baker, butcher, and the grocer?"

With restocked trays, Penelope and I navigated the tumultuous happenings within the house, where I found the baker's boy. "Where's your pa?" I asked.

"Upstairs in the guest bathroom," he said before taking a scone.

Penelope frowned, and I knew what she was thinking. She did not plan on remodeling that bathroom. She had only the one in mind. "Stop chewing your lip," I said under my breath.

I received a scowl for my efforts, but her bottom lip returned to its natural place. "What are they doing up there?" she asked.

A pang of fear struck me then. It was laughable to be afraid of someone as docile and easily intimidated as Penelope, but in that moment, she was someone else. A true lady of a British manor, and not one to indulge in servant shenanigans. There was hesitation, but it was entwined with arousal. "I couldn't imagine you being any more irresistible than you are now," I whispered under my breath as we stepped onto the second-story landing.

She grinned and gave me a wink. Full of surprises, that one. We caught Mr. Davies as he was guiding a sink into its rightful place.

"What's all this about?" Penelope asked.

"Ah! Mrs. Jones," the butler said while clasping his hands together. "What do you think?"

Penelope was unreadable for a moment as she assessed the hallway bathroom. "It's the same as the master bathroom?" she asked.

"Well," Mr. Davies started. "There was a slight change in the plans. You see, thanks to modern plumbing, we need to be connected to the sewer line, and only these modern toilets and baths will work. If we only put in a modern system for one room..."

"Oh, of course," Penelope sighed. "We'd still have water closets separate from the baths and washrooms."

"Precisely," Mr. Davies said with a wave of his hands, gesturing to the half-assembled room. "I figured why not buy in bulk and save us all the fuss later. We have builders here now; they can convert the rooms into modern baths, and we won't have to bother with all this again later."

"Efficient," she said. "But how long do you think all of this will take?"

"The plumbing will take the longest, I'm afraid. We will have the men digging the sewage lines once the furniture is done and the wallpaper is up."

I turned to assess the chaos below and noted that the wallpaper was already being applied to some walls. New wainscotting was being trimmed and measured right behind the wallpapering. "At this rate, we'll be done before Mr. Jones comes home," I said.

"That was my hope, actually," Mr. Davies said. "I'd like for all of this to be done before Christmas at the latest."

"Freddie's going to kill us," Penelope groaned, lighting up a cigarette.

"No, Ma'am," Mr. Davies said. "He brought this predicament on us all, and to make matters worse, I received a telegram that your parents are coming for Christmas."

Penelope blanched. She sucked down her cigarette. The fire burned through the paper with an orange hot glow. "What was he thinking!"

"From the sounds of the telegram, he didn't have much of a choice," Mr. Davies said.

She lit up another cigarette. "No one ever has a choice when dealing with my parents."

I was grateful for the bottle of medicine the doctor left. She was going to need it. Bloody hell, I might need it too before all this was said and done. I had overheard the conversation Mr. Davies had with the doctor. It made sense that her parents were worried. The utter disdain Penelope had for her parents clung around her in an ashen cloud of smoke. Her brow furrowed as she regarded the wallpaper that was being spread up the wall.

"I was worried that paper would be too busy for this room, but it's rather gorgeous, don't you think?" she asked.

"It's my favorite thus far," Mr. Davies said. "If I may be so bold."

She soaked in the praise with a proud lift of her chin. "How are the curtains coming along?"

"They are nearly ready," Mr. Davies informed.

The front door blew open as the baker's boy and the grocer returned. Ladies emerged from the dining room in a row of bustling skirts to retrieve wicker baskets like the one the baker's boy used to deliver morning bread before I put an end to it. "It seems the women are done," I said.

"Good," Mr. Davies said. "I'll have them see to the men."

Penelope could use a break. Her lean frame was tall and straight, but just yesterday she was catatonic. I feared she would exhaust herself right back into that half-life. "How about some coffee in the greenhouse?" I asked.

She gave me a coy smile, which undoubtedly meant yes.

The rough voices of men and hammers were blocked by panes of green glass. We were walled in with the blissful silence, and Penelope exhaled as she collapsed on the chair like a marionette cut from its strings. "It is insanity in there," she said.

"The whole village turned up."

"I'm in their debt."

I stood facing the courtyard and watched a new layer of snow blanket what little greenery there was left. We didn't talk about what happened yesterday and what it meant for us. She was overwhelmed with the renovation and the news of her parents. It was selfish to try and bring it up, but I couldn't help it. "You frightened me half to death yesterday," I said.

"I'm sorry," she said. "I should have warned you. It hasn't happened in such a long time, I thought I had grown out of it."

"What does it feel like?" I asked.

"It's the oddest thing. My jaw starts to lock, and I go mute, but I don't necessarily care that I can't speak. I don't feel like I'm asleep, but a great deal of time passes when I'm in that state, and it only feels like a few minutes. I was fourteen when it first happened."

"The doctor thinks it's brought on by stress," I said. "Is that what you think?"

Penelope went quiet then. I turned to find her staring at her plate in a sort of vacant rage. There was something she wasn't telling me. What was it?

"I can't explain it," she said. "But I need you to promise me something."

"Anything." I held fast to her hand, desperate for her to feel my intent through the limited touch we were permitted.

She faced me then. So close our eyelashes nearly touched. "Don't pick the berries on the ivy."

Again with the ivy. I hadn't the faintest idea what she meant by that. I half suspected she didn't either. "You said you see things in that state," I said. "Is that what you saw?"

"I know it doesn't make sense, but if there comes a time when it does, at least you'll be safe."

"Okay." I nodded. Touched that she had the same fight in her to protect me as I did her.

"I need to rest."

We went upstairs, where I helped her change into her nightgown. Free of the confines of the corset and bustle, she eased into her bed, but not before eyeing the bottle on the vanity. "I want some of that," Penelope said, gesturing to the amber bottle with a prescription across the front.

I pursed my lips as I stared down the bottle. Who was I to deny her the medicine? Clasping the thick glass in my hand, I resisted the urge to throw it out the window. Instead, I took the tin tablespoon left beside it and filled it. Penelope poured the syrup down her throat without question and extended the spoon for the other half of the dose. She knew exactly how much was prescribed, but after the second tablespoon, she extended her arm again as if she expected more.

"It says two tablespoons," I said, pulling the bottle back.

Penelope rolled her eyes, her head swaying on her delicate neck. "You're no fun."

I shrugged off the sting of her words. I didn't want to be a mother to her; I wanted to pin her on the bed and make her forget all about Mr. Jones. "What if you need more later or take too much—"

She nodded at the bottle and said, "Take some."

I swallowed hard. Here she was, tempting me in every way she shouldn't. Declining would only confirm her assessment of me being a goody. Penelope would never understand the predicament she put me in at that moment. It simply was not a situation she could ever relate to. If Mr. Davies were to walk in on us, drunk on her prescription, I'd be on the doorstep faster than an empty milk bottle.

It made me envious. Nothing touched Penelope while she walked on the edge of a knife. She was a few steps away from being institutionalized. Even if she knew, I didn't think Penelope would change; I don't think she would even know where to begin. Did I want her to change? I considered it for a moment. Her rebelliousness was what drew me in. From the moment I first laid eyes on her in that sheer, improper nightgown, smoking a cigarette. Penelope was a revolution for what a woman could be, and everyone around her fought to control her. I didn't want to control her. I wanted her to be an inspiration for a new generation of women.

I uncorked the bottle and took two tablespoons of the stuff myself. It was sugary with a bitter aftertaste. As if the sweetness could somehow hide the true nature of what would soon be coursing throughout my body. A heavy feeling in the pit of my stomach was being piped the way one would fill a cake. It wasn't unpleasant, but it made me jittery thinking about what came next.

Penelope sat before me; one leg crossed over the other. She patted the bed, indicating that I should join her. I did, but then I said, "We should be careful. If Mr. Davies—"

"We're not doing anything he can prove," she assured before cupping my face with a manicured hand and kissing me.

That familiar heady feeling, followed by weightlessness, had me spinning. Maybe it was Penelope's medicine, I wasn't certain, but she had pushed me into her feather-stuffed mattress, and I let out a small whimper as the world shifted into a perspective I had often fantasized about. Penelope was directly over me, the folds of her nightgown toppled over the black maid uniform.

She raked her hands over my corset and chest, and I felt her thighs straddling my hips. She thrusted against me, and despite being fully clothed, it was enough to have me gasping with pleasure. The pressure mounted between us, one needing throb after another as Penelope crashed into me like the unrelenting tide.

Arching her back, Penelope cried out as she shivered with climax. As if responding to her clarion call, spasms of pleasure exploded from my mound. I let out a strangled cry, and she applied more pressure than before. Her rueful smile suggested that she enjoyed my climax as much as she enjoyed her own. Moments went by, stiller than midnight, before she rolled off me, and we lay side by side in the quiet dark.

By this point, the medicine had taken hold of my body. It was a smile-inducing relaxation I had never experienced in my life. I had climaxed before, but always by myself. Never had I experienced it with someone else. My head lulled to the side, and I stared at her profile. A cigarette appeared in her mouth, and the grin remained.

I didn't know what to say.

Perhaps it was best to say nothing. I just watched her. The way the light illuminated the curvatures of her face, how big and doll-like her eyes were, even as the lids threatened to close. Her cigarette wasn't being smoked so much as it was burning away. A stack of ash created a tower where her tobacco once was as her eyes drifted closed. With a clumsy hand, I plucked the filter from her lips and squashed it into the ashtray beside her on the bed.

The drugs had taken hold of both of us. My head was swimming. My fingertips were so numb that it made me giggle. For Penelope, the intoxication slowed her speech and exaggerated her accent.

"If you saw what I can do, you'd be afraid, just like them."

Fairly confident I had seen most aspects of her personality over the last few months, I strongly disagreed. "I don't think there's anything that could make me love you less," I replied.

A single tear fell down Penelope's temple and onto her hair.

"What is it?" I asked, rolling onto my side to wipe her tears away. "Is this about the professor? Does it haunt you so?"

"It's my true nature that haunts me. My selfishness. I brought you here because I needed you, and I'll do whatever it takes to keep you."

It was the drugs that made her talk that way. Though she did ask me if I received her messages when we first met, but if I did, I didn't know it. "You know the feeling is mutual."

She was fast asleep. I shook her a little, but her body was limp. She still did not fully trust me, even after we were together. Not that I expected intimate relations to change our disposition, but I was naïve enough to assume that there would be fewer secrets between us by now.

The moon had risen, and the pale light now focused on her chest. The slight swell of her breasts and the dark circles of her nipples could be seen underneath her nightgown. Her face lingered in the shadow of the moonlight, and she reminded me of an angel, sculpted in marble.

The darkness took hold of her features, making her appear like an evil caricature of the woman I loved.

What was she hiding from me, and would it really change how I felt for her?

CHAPTER SEVENTEEN

C hristmas had arrived like a train into a busy station. While everything inside the manor had been finished, the plumbing that connected to the sewer had not. A cold snap followed by a heavy snow froze the ground, making it impossible to dig the networks required. Water closets would need to be used until the bathrooms were connected to indoor plumbing.

Despite the delay, Penelope and Mr. Davies were thrilled with the results. Fresh wainscotting skirted walls with an emerald-green wallpaper with yellow buttercup flowers. The chandelier in the entryway was cleaned and polished, giving it a new life. Maintaining Mr. Jones's nostalgic needs was at the forefront of their minds, and I dare say they succeeded. Everything looked the same, just better.

"Look at the way it shines," Mr. Davies admired.

Once the tarnish and wax stains were rubbed off, the light it emitted was five times brighter. It appeared lighter somehow, as if some terrible curse had been lifted from the house. Penelope broke the spell of English stagnation. The crystals swayed, providing fragments of light to dance along the walls. I nodded in appreciation.

We had most of the house put together before Mr. Jones came home. Penelope was insistent that the parlor be a priority since it was the place he loved most. "You should have seen the look on his face," Mr. Davies said with a chuckle. "He was like a child marveling at his first circus."

"Is he in the parlor now?" I asked.

When the clopping of horse hooves sounded from outside, Penelope went into a mad dash from the bedroom down the newly polished stairs with a new forest green runner and into the parlor. "Get some tea and cakes!" she shouted before shutting the door.

I didn't know if she was frightened or excited. Probably a little of both. Please don't be angry, Mr. Jones, I silently prayed. Please be happy and proud of the results and let it go at that. I went and set up teatime as Penelope had asked, and Mr. Davies came striding in to give me the news.

"Do you think he's angry about the cost?" I asked.

Mr. Davies's moustache twitched on his drawn face. "With her family arriving at any minute? No, I think he will be grateful. With the burden he placed on everyone in this house and village. The price is only fair."

The price Penelope paid was higher than any number of pounds distributed by the Jones accounts. The bottle the doctor left behind was half-empty. I had taken to hiding it now that the renovation was mostly over. She never asked for it, but her eyes searched tabletops, vanities, and other places the bottle once sat. It thumped heavily in my apron pocket as I carried the tray to the parlor.

The renewed upholstery and curtains dramatically lifted the room. It went from being a stuffy old man's dwelling into a sophisticated social room with soft leather furniture and golden sheets contrasting the green and yellow striped wallpaper. Penelope had continued similar color schemes all around the house, but this room had more golden hues to complement the leather furniture.

"I can't get over it," Mr. Jones said, grinning from ear to ear. "It's my home, but better. It reminds me of when I was a boy, and everything was so new."

"You have no idea how happy that makes me," Penelope crooned. "I'm so sorry again about—"

He waved her off with a large hand. "If anyone owes an apology, it's me. I..." Mr. Jones hesitated. "Sometimes the drink and the attention get the better of me. Then your parents had to pile on."

Penelope let out a groan. I handed her a cup of coffee before moving to Mr. Jones, who scooped a heaping spoonful of sugar into his tea before adding a substantial amount of milk. He then put half the butter I brought onto a single scone and ate it in three bites.

"Would it be terrible if we gave them the wrong address?" Penelope asked.

Mr. Jones grinned. "Send them to the Connor house instead?"

The laughter of their inside joke went from small giggles to outright laughter. A pang of envy struck me then. After our encounter, seeing them laugh at some inside joke rattled me harder than I wanted to admit. It wasn't just so much their intimacy—that I begrudgingly came to terms with—it was the mention of people I didn't know and never would.

Their inside joke was one of a social nature. Something that Penelope and I could never share. We would never be able to attend parties together. Not just because of our indecent relationship, but because of my social status. Come what may, Penelope would always walk in different circles than I. It's not that I wanted to join those fancy parties; it was that I couldn't be with her in the ways Mr. Jones could. I gave a stiff curtsy before leaving the room unnoticed. He was back, and I was to be an outsider once more.

In the entryway, I came face-to-face with an enormous ladder with a thin man at the top. "Mr. Davies?" I called.

"Hand me those bows, would you?" he said.

I did as he asked. In a wooden crate, there were dozens of red velvet bows. I extended to the tips of my toes, and the butler still had to climb down several steps to reach it. "And here I thought the decorations were done and over with," I said.

"My work is never done," he grumped. "Decorating the tree the day before Christmas is not what I would have chosen, but here we are."

It was the biggest Christmas tree I had ever seen in my life. It wouldn't have fit in my father's little flat. We couldn't afford velvets and candlelight, so we tied hair ribbons and bits of yarn on ours. The scent of fir and sap filled the flat within the hour it was dragged into the house by my father. His worn leather gloves had dabs of sap stuck to them.

"What do you think, my dear?" he'd ask every year.

"It looks like a tree," I'd say.

He had been sick for months before last Christmas, but my father still managed to chop down a tree and drag it all the way home in the freezing cold. The moment his boots knocked against the door, I was out of my room and on him. "What were you thinking?" I seethed. "Going out in the freezing cold with a cough like yours?"

He took off his hat and smiled. "What do you think, my dear?"

I folded my arms and glared at him. Damn the stupid tree, it wasn't worth it. "You're a fool," I said before stomping back into my room. "That's what I think."

That was our last Christmas together. Had I known it was going to turn out the way it did, I would have said something different. I would have marched out into the snow and chopped a tree down and hauled it back home on a sleigh if it meant that much to him. Maybe he would have had a few more days if I had.

"Are you all right, Dinah?" Mr. Davies's voice cut through the memory.

I blinked back the tears. "Yeah, sorry."

He regarded me for a moment before resuming his decorating. "The first Christmas without my wife was difficult. The first without anyone was even harder. After that, I started to stay here during the holidays. It made things easier."

Without anyone. Did he mean Agatha, the mysterious daughter he never spoke of? Where had she gone? Perhaps she ran off and got married, never to be seen again. Mr. Davies struck the heart of my fears. Penelope and I would never share a Christmas surrounded by friends and family. I would always be a secret. A low-class, perverted secret. I nodded, wiping the side of my face.

"Are you getting anything for Mrs. Jones?" he asked.

"I had thought about taking the carriage driver up on his offer to teach me more."

Mr. Davies caught my meaning. "I believe he makes several trips a week to Chester."

Giving one's employer a personal gift wasn't something most maids did. I rather expected him to lecture me on how inappropriate the gesture would be, yet the butler didn't. Was this an acceptance of our friendship? The butler was aware of how close Penelope and I were. I doubted even he had the full gist of things. Still, Mr. Davies said less and less about our friendship these days. It was as if he had secretly chosen a side after the doctor forced her treatment.

"She said that I wouldn't feel the same about her if I knew her true nature."

"I think that's true about everyone," Mr. Davies said. "Our choices define us, and sometimes we make the wrong ones even for the right reasons."

Mr. Davies wasn't talking about Penelope. His eyes were still on the Christmas tree.

It was easy for me to judge the choices of others because I so seldom had decisions to make. I wasn't faced with losing my job or restraining a hysterical woman from self-harm. Nor was I faced with losing my wife and a steady source of income. She was right to fear my judgment because I was so quick to it. If I wanted her to trust me with all her secrets, I would need to show her that I could make plenty of bad decisions on my own.

\#

That evening, while I made a Christmas bread bigger than Harriet's tits, there was a commotion bursting from the entryway. A sort of clamor with stretched, high-pitched greetings full of falseness. I had to get a peek at Penelope's parents. I gave Harriet a smirk. "Hang on," I said, knocking the flour off my hands.

"Report back!" Harriet said.

They were older than I expected. Mr. Hathaway was hunched with old age and relied heavily on a cane. "Penelope, you look well," he said. His voice was gruff, and his accent had a more rural twang. It reminded me of an Irish drawl after a fashion.

Penelope approached the aging couple with an uncharacteristic coolness. "Mother, father," she said.

The mother was every bit the lady I expected, though she too was old and maybe older than the father. Penelope never told me they had her so late in life. They must have been in their forties when she was born. The mother was dressed splendidly in a rich silver silk embroidered with reds and blacks. Her hat had an assortment of black and red feathers. "Are we to just stand in the entryway?" the mother asked.

Mr. Davies stepped up and said, "Right this way, Lady Hathaway."

Penelope and Mr. Jones trailed behind the elderly couple, exchanging a mutual level of disdain before her eyes flittered to me with an apologetic expression. Her eyes pleaded for me to rescue her, but this was out of my reach.

"The renovations are coming along?" Mr. Hathaway said as they entered the parlor.

"All thanks to Penelope and Mr. Davies," Mr. Jones said. At least he gave credit where it was due.

"The doctor said it took a great toll on our daughter," the mother said as the door was closed behind them.

On the counter lay a great big turkey. Its bones had all been removed, and it was now a flat pile of flesh. Around it were several bowls filled with spices, pickled walnuts, pistachios, suet, carrots, celery, minced pork, and apple chunks. "You going to have a go at that?" I asked Harriet.

"Mr. Davies usually does it," Harriet said. "He has some specific recipe he likes to use."

That was fine by me. I had never cooked a turkey. Hearing it was out of Harriet's rough hands was all I needed. "I need all the time I can get for this bread," I said.

"It's quite a spectacle," she said. "I've never seen anything like it."

It was traditional to have fruit and nuts in a celebration bread. It was plaited into three great circles that interlocked. "Of course you have," I said. "They're called the Borromean rings. It represents the Father, the Son, and the Holy Ghost."

Harriet tilted her head. "Well, it's fancy whatever it is. Fancy enough for Penelope's parents."

The bread needed to proof, so I left the kitchen to find Penelope and see if she needed anything. Only, I was met by Mr. Davies standing outside the parlor door. He saw me and shook his head gently. I was not permitted to enter. Planting my feet, I refused to relent until Mr. Davies made an annoyed gasp and marched toward me. "Mr. and Mrs. Hathaway are not accustomed to staff waiting on their hand and foot."

It was true. Penelope told me her father—a self-made man—never liked the idea of maids and did not employ more than he had to. That wasn't Mr. Davies's concern, however. He didn't want her parents to see me, or rather, he didn't want them to see how my eyes followed Penelope's every move. Mrs. Jones was intended to appear every bit of the adoring wife, and I was to be relegated to the kitchens until they departed.

"On Christmas day, you'll be in the kitchens, and the next day, you'll be riding out to the village to hand out tithes for Boxing Day," Mr. Davies informed.

So that's how it was, then. I pressed my lips together and scowled before whirling back around and into the kitchens. Mr. Davies was tucking me away like some nasty secret he didn't want her parents to see. A tiny part of me was reminded that it was for her safety, but I resented the treatment all the same. I wasn't a bag of dirty laundry. I was a person, and I was a person that Penelope loved. So what if I was just a maid? Then again, the idea of being in the room with those two would no doubt provoke my mouth to run when it shouldn't.

That night when I slept, I dreamt that I was in the garden with Penelope. It was springtime, and the seasonal hedges had not yet developed their purple black berries, but the roses were budding and blooming. Penelope was on the swing, flying high into the clouds and smiling at me from above.

"Come fly with me, Dinah!" she called.

I shook my head. "I can't."

In the gardens, her elderly parents were there, complaining about the flowers. "All this pollen," the woman griped. "It's making my eyes water."

"Penelope," her father railed. "Get down from there!"

I stood on the grassy lawn, lush from rain, and watched her with a knot in my stomach. She wasn't listening to them, but I couldn't ignore their complaints. Their fussing continued in my mind even when they were no longer in the garden. I looked back at the house to find that ivy had burst from the greenhouse and was threatening to strangle the manor.

"English Ivy can be such a nuisance." It was my father who said it. He was standing beside me, looking as alive as he did before the cough took its hold on him. He pointed to where the ivy had broken a window and was now making its way inside. "Impossible to be rid of once it takes root. A single leaf can regrow if left alive, and the whole thing starts all over again."

"What are you doing here?" I asked.

"Where else would I go?" he asked, observing Penelope. She was so high in the sky I could have sworn she was flying.

Fly away, Penelope. No one can touch you up there.

"You can't haunt me forever," I told him. He was grey now, as if remaining here beside me had drained all the life away from his veins.

Penelope was gone now, and I was inside the manor. The lights were out and the hallways dark with shadows. The fires were long dead. The only sign of life was Harriet's Celtic song. Her voice carried down the hallways and into the entryway. It took on an eerie wailing full of grief.

I was ready to wake up. I wanted no part of this dream any longer. I pinched myself, but there was no pain. I tried slapping myself across the face. There was nothing.

"It's no use," my father said. His long fingernails scratched his chin, and lines of blackened blood developed. "See?"

If he did not feel pain, it was because he was dead. I wasn't dead, was I? My father opened the parlor door, revealing a freshly remodeled room; only the ivy had broken through the windows and wrapped around all the refurbished furniture. There was a newspaper and a cup of tea resting on the table beside Mr. Jones's favorite chair, and a green mass of ivy wrapped around something across the sofa where Penelope often sat.

My breath was strangled as it occurred to me that the mass of vines encased a person. A few long, delicate fingers poked between two green ropes. No!

I rushed to the sofa and ripped away the vines. My father looked on as though the love of my life was not being slowly killed. "Help me!" I shouted at him.

Shredded greenery fell to the carpet as I worked to free Penelope. I worked at the neck and face until I exposed her skin, blue from the lack of air. Please, let her go, please.

Something slithered across my calf and around my ankle. I paid no mind to it and continued to yank away vine after vine, freeing Penelope around the chest. She wasn't breathing. I kissed her, and my tears smeared across her cold face.

"Death comes to this house," my father said. "Can you smell it?"

No. I was drowning in the sweet, green smell of the ivy torn underneath my nails. Penelope wouldn't wake, and I sobbed over her unmoving body. Was this why my father haunted me? To warn me that Penelope was going to die?

My legs were held fast to the ground. I tried to wriggle free, but it was too late. The ivy had taken root in the carpet beneath me. It dug into the flesh of my legs and fastened tight to my thighs and hips.

"Help me!" I cried again. My father sat in Mr. Jones's chair and did not move.

"This is a nice chair," he said. "No wonder he spends most of his time here. I imagine his father did the same."

I ripped at the ivy that gripped me, but when the vines fell to the carpet, they regrew faster than before. I was being smothered. Vines squeezed my chest and pulled at my arms. I couldn't breathe. I opened my mouth to scream, but ivy tendrils took the opportunity to climb into my mouth and up into my nostrils.

My last fleeting glimpses were of Penelope before I was forced to the floor. My head cracked, but I opened my eyes, and it was morning.

CHAPTER EIGHTEEN

Harriet said nothing when I came in and began making bread for the next day. She didn't question why I was there with her and not with Penelope. I usually left parlor duties to Mr. Davies as it were, but my exile to the kitchen made me hyper-aware of a station I didn't mind several months before.

"Happy Christmas," I greeted.

"Happy Christmas," Harriet repeated.

"You going to spend Christmas with the little ones?" I asked her as I worked the dough.

The kitchen maid nodded as she cleaned up after me. "Going to visit my son and his children."

"You only have the one?"

"I had seven children," she said, wiping the excess flour off the counter. "Only two survived. My son and a daughter who lives in London."

Her voice tightened at the mention of her daughter. Amid the smell of raw flour and the broth boiling on the stovetop, I asked what I ought not to. "What does she do?" I asked.

Harriet swallowed hard, her fat lips puckered, and she turned away and rushed to the sink. My heart plummeted to my feet. The maid had lost so much in her life. She lost Anne just this year. Yet, here she was, steadfast as always. It was likely her daughter was a beggar and a prostitute. A young woman without a husband or means had few outcomes.

"She was always a stubborn girl," Harriet said, washing a teacup. "Could never get her to listen. She couldn't wait to get away from me."

My eyes fell to the lump of dough before me. I wasn't great with other people's problems; I could scarcely face my own. I unlocked a world of pain for Harriet on Christmas Eve, all because I felt jilted by my married lover. "I'm so sorry," I said.

"When Scarlett fever took the last of the little ones, she was never the same. None of us were. We fought like cats and dogs. My son married the first girl he could and moved out. My daughter couldn't stand being alone with her parents."

"What was her name?" I asked. I wasn't certain it mattered, but if I was going to hear her sad story, I could at least know her name.

"Alexandra," Harriet said, still washing the same cup. "I thought it sounded fancy."

"It does," I agreed. "Posher than Dinah, anyways."

Harriet let out a sound of agreement and finally moved on to another teacup.

"What about your grandchildren?"

"Oh, they are a fun bunch," she said. Harriet regaled me with stories of their mischief, and I laughed at their childish pranks. I knew the children; I had seen them running around the village, the pack of wild beasts they were. More than anything, I just wanted to move Harriet into a better mood.

My celebration bread took hours to bake, but the smell alone was worth it. It was Christmas Day, but I was not cheerful. Not after the dream from the previous night. Mr. Davies came in and hummed as he prepared the turkey. It was quite the lengthy process, but his face was one of serenity as he worked.

He deboned the turkey entirely until it was a husk of meat before laying it flayed side up. The butler placed the nuts, fruit, suet, sausage, and spices all over before sewing the bird back together and tying it off with twine. Then, he wrapped the thing up like a Christmas package in cloth before ceremoniously dropping it into the boiling stock.

"See that this doesn't boil over," Mr. Davies said. "I have to see to the Hathaways."

"How's that going?" Harriet asked. I was so grateful she did. I too was curious but didn't want to appear nosy or too heavily invested.

Mr. Davies pinched the bridge of his nose under his glasses. "Mr. Hathaway goes on and on about how maids and butlers are unnecessary, and Mrs. Hathaway seems to delight in badgering poor Mrs. Jones at every opportunity. I understand now why Mr. and Mrs. Jones did not want them to visit."

I prodded the wrapped turkey in the broth. Penelope never painted her parents in a good light, but I had no idea they were so unbearable. I kept my mouth shut, and Mr. Davies sighed as he dumped the cakes, cookies, and finger sandwiches into the slop bin and left.

"He's been popping off so much these days," Harriet said. "Before Mrs. Jones started coming out of that room, Mr. Davies didn't say a word against anyone."

"What do you know of his daughter?" I asked.

Harriet eyed me with suspicion. "Don't go telling anyone I told you, but his daughter has a lot in common with our Mrs. Jones."

"Is that why he was reading the Nellie Bly book?" I asked, recalling just how weary he appeared that day. Had he put her in one of those institutions like the one they wanted to put Penelope in? There was no way he could have known how bad they were. No one did until that woman faked her way into one. It was in the papers for months when she finally got out. The Bly woman said that most of the women in those places were no crazier than she was, but she had to be a little crazy to try and stay in one.

His words about choices stuck in my mind. He was talking about his daughter, wasn't he?

"You didn't hear it from me," Harriet said with a point of a wooden spoon. "He doesn't talk about her, and neither should you."

I nodded. Agatha had Hysteria, and it was likely the reason the butler grew more vocal about Penelope's welfare. Why he was willing to quit his job after countless years. Institutions were said to be different now. Government put more money into them after discovering how bad they were, but I still shuddered at the thought of Penelope being in one.

The doctor's facility was likely different. I'd never forget the way he made Penelope better during that episode of hers. I didn't doubt he cared for her, but what about the orderlies or the other doctors?

Once Mr. Davies returned to see to his turkey, I took the opportunity to go for a walk by myself.

It wasn't the same without her. The quiet was colder than the winter air. I stood where I had stood in my dream and stared at the empty swing. I hoped Penelope was holding up and that her mother wasn't as awful as Mr. Davies claimed.

The earrings I bought from Chester would have to wait until after Christmas. When Mr. Jones was on one of his many trips. I envisioned her sitting by the fire, her skin aglow with firelight. I'd give her the box, and she'd smile at me and tell me that "I shouldn't have," before gasping as she opened the box. Penelope would put them on straight away, but stash them away before Mr. Jones saw them. Not that he would have noticed a new pair of earrings, she had a jewelry closet full of them.

I gave the house a suspicious glance, searching for any signs of ivy. There was none. It was the dead of winter; of course ivy wouldn't grow. The hedges were without their characteristic violet berries.

What was it that the ivy signified? Penelope was deathly afraid of it, and now I was having dreams about it strangling us all. These were not just any vines Penelope prophesized about. This species grew fruit. I didn't know a blooming thing about horticulture. Maybe Mr. Davies would know. If I just knew what I was looking for, I could fix it, yeah?

That night, I retired to my empty little bedroom for bed. Stripping off my uniform and corset, I hung them up on the nail embedded in an empty whitewashed wall. I was about to climb into my bed when there was a soft knock at the door. Excitement leapt into my chest. It might have been Penelope coming to see me.

I pulled open the door to find her looking down at me. Her golden hair was hanging about her shoulders, and she was wearing a white knitted robe over her pink nightgown. Seeing her like this sent flash-backs of our encounter just a few nights ago. Her body pressed to mine. Her hands raking down my chest. She couldn't possibly be here for that, not with her parents having the run of the house.

She glanced around the hallway before stepping into my room, kissing me in a most ferocious manner. How I needed this today. A reminder that I wasn't just some utility item for her to discard, that what we had was real. Her lips broke free of mine, but her embrace tightened. "Happy Christmas, Dinah. I missed you today," she said in my ear. "I can't wait for them to be gone."

I muttered a "Happy Christmas" under my breath, still dazed by the kiss. I wasn't one for Christmas. My thoughts went to the pair of earrings I had stashed in the vanity drawer. They were pretty at the time, their silver and blue glass shone so brightly in the store window...but they were nothing compared to her.

Suddenly, the idea of Penelope wearing those earrings felt as absurd as serving a burnt biscuit on a golden plate. I couldn't give them to her.

"You can't stay here long," I warned. "You'll get caught."

"I know. I told Fredrick I needed to use the water closet. We're back in our room now, but the bathroom isn't operable yet."

All the water closets were on the first story, so her alibi made sense. Still, we didn't have long. "How is it going with them?"

She clicked her tongue and sighed. "Abnormally well. We gave them the tour of the house. Freddie praised me for spearheading the renovations. Mr. Davies made it sound as though I'm the people's champion. My father loved that."

"Well," I said. "He's not wrong. The whole village is in love with you now."

She broke free and walked into my bedroom, almost as if she were searching for something. "All I did was hand out tea and talk to them," Penelope said. "It's not like I saved their lives or anything."

That was more than anyone in the Jones family did. No one was ungrateful for their employment or economy, but they never interacted with the villagers any more than they had to. "Sometimes it's nice to be seen," I said. "And treated like a fellow human being."

Penelope glided around my room, like a specter on the verge of a haunting. The flicker of the single candle followed her just as we all did. "Tomorrow is Boxing Day," she said. "You're going out to the village?"

"I am."

She frowned at this. "We're not supposed to give the maids and butlers gifts on account of their Christmas bonus, but I wish there was something more I could do for that kitchen maid who helped us make food for everyone."

Mary was usually the recipient of Boxing Day, along with a few other elderly people. She would no doubt scoff if the Jones maids were seen on the doorstep of Harriet's son, but that gave me an idea. "There might be something you can do for Harriet," I said, stepping forward. "Harriet has a daughter somewhere in London. I think she's a prostitute."

Penelope winced. "That must be awful."

"She doesn't know if her daughter is alive or dead. I don't know if you can help, but her name is Alexandria Clarke."

She paced back and forth in my room for a few moments. Her eyes were searching for something, darting back and forth as she deliberated. "It's a longshot. London is a big city and there are a lot of prostitutes. I could hire a few investigators, make some inquiries. I'm certain Mr. Jones will know someone."

"Don't let him know Harriet's daughter is a prostitute," I said. "I don't know how things are in New York, but here that kind of scandal can get you sacked."

Her eyes went wide as if the thought never occurred to her. "I'll have Mr. Davies proceed with discretion then, but I should go."

I showed her to the door. "Goodbye," she whispered.

"Goodbye."

The next morning, I rolled over in my bed and smiled. Our visit was brief, but sweet. It would hold me over for a little while at least. Mr. Davies was storming up and down the hallway calling, "Boxing Day! Boxing Day!"

I rolled my eyes. No one should be that animated so early in the morning. I dressed and emerged from my room straight into a row of maids that spanned half the hallway. It was like payday, only today, we would be the ones paying.

"I realize this is a first time for some of you," Mr. Davies said. "So, I'll reissue the rules. You cannot give the tithes to the families of people working within the house. They must go to the poorest within the village. If in doubt, donate to the family that took in several orphans from Chester and the church. No one will hold it against us for giving more to either."

The coachman offered me the reins of the carriage. I gave him a sly grin and ushered the horses to the village. It took several carriages, but when we arrived at the village, people were waiting on their doorsteps excitedly. Maids in their black and white suits poured out of the carriages and dispersed throughout our village like missionaries, each with a white envelope in their hand.

I too had a white envelope, and while everyone moved inwards and around to the more distant reaches of the village towards the woodcutters and the farmers, I was left no other avenue than the one that led home. Of course they left me to deal with Mary! I should have expected as much; she was my neighbor since I was a small child. It would be only natural to assume there was some affection between us.

The little row of flats was always grim in the winter. With the vegetable garden withered, no foliage bloomed around the old picket fences, providing the flats the cottage whimsy of the spring. The barrage of snow and rain dampened the old wood and puckered shingles. I could smell the wood rotting from the road.

Mary was standing on her doorstep, clasping her hands together with a gentle smile. "Happy Christmas, Dinah."

Sucking in a deep breath, I approached her side of the flat and gave her the envelope. "Happy Christmas."

"Come inside," she said.

I would have rather not, but my fingers ached from the cold. I had become accustomed to a sufficiently warm house, and it had made me more susceptible to the biting cold. If I didn't agree, I'd be sitting outside waiting for everyone else to return in the cold. The carriage was a little bit warmer, but nothing compared to a cozy fire. "Sure," I said.

Her flat was a mirror image of the one I once lived in. She had similar furniture–built by the same village carpenter years ago—and her knits were all over the place, much like they were in the flat next door. I took off my cape and shoes and hung them by the fire.

"Tea?" Mary called from the tiny kitchen that made my heart ache. I practically lived in that kitchen. I used to create makeshift counter spaces out of trays and whatever was flat to set my bakes on. I always had to be mindful of my minuscule workspace. Now I had a kitchen the size of this flat to work in and countertops the size of a mattress.

I shifted beside the fire, unwilling to sit until invited. Mary had been my adversary for so long, but looking at her now, she was just an old woman. She was nosey and annoying, but she bore no ill will, and she provided much companionship to my father while he lived. She had shared much with us and had incidentally led me to Penelope.

"Sit down, dear," she said, motioning to the loveseat my father once sat at on the other side of the flat.

I did as she bid and took the teacup with a mismatched saucer. It was a rough cut of ceramic that grated against my skin. Nothing like the thin and supple bone China of the manor. I never knew better until I was exposed to it, and now, I couldn't stop noticing.

"How is life in the manor?" Mary asked, sitting in a single wooden chair across from me.

The heat from the hot tea burned my frozen fingers, and I pressed all the harder into the teacup. "It's wonderful, really."

"The lady of the manor made quite the impression on the village."

"Yes." I took a sip of my tea to hide any trace of interest in Penelope. The last thing I needed was town gossip. "She's American."

"I know," Mary said with a smirk. "You're her handmaid, and that's all you have to say about her?"

Shit. I trapped myself by trying to appear disinterested. "She's nice," I said. "Eats like a bird, though, and she spends a lot of time reading magazines."

"Magazines?"

I nodded and took another sip of tea. "Home décor magazines. The renovation is nearly finished, but she still reads them."

Mary chewed on that crumb of information for a moment.

"Has anyone moved in next door yet?" I asked.

"Not yet," she said. "But the landlord has been showing it. I think he wants too much for the place."

"He wanted too much when we lived there, too," I mumbled.

There was some chatter outside. I craned my neck to look out the window. I couldn't see anyone, but that didn't stop me from saying, "Oh, I think they're nearly finished."

I stood up, and Mary gave me a hug. I braced for it, reminding myself she couldn't hurt me, and returned the hug before opening the door. A blast of chilly wind blew into my face. I stepped out, closed the door behind me, and regarded the small porch a few feet away where a man stood.

Initially, I assumed it to be the landlord, but it wasn't. My heart stopped, and I gasped. It was my father. Not as the decaying figure that

I last beheld, but a younger version. My legs went to jelly, and I braced myself on the porch post. He was carrying something in the door with both arms and laughing, only there was nothing there. He nudged the door open with his boot before maneuvering his invisible quarry over the threshold.

That was when it hit me. He was carrying his bride. My father's ghost was repeating a memory of when he was a young man, newly married and without a care in the world. His face was smooth and unmarred by harsh weather and wrinkles. His hair was thick and dark like my own. His soul had remained in this world, and it was my fault because I never covered the mirror to my vanity.

My mother was long gone, and a sinkhole fell through my ribcage as I wished it was her ghost that haunted me.

"Dinah, are you ready?" A gruff male voice asked. It was the coachmen. I turned to him and said, "I'll be right there."

One more glance at my porch confirmed my father's ghost was gone. It was. Ghosts never stick around when you need them.

It was an empty porch of half-rotting wood once again. What I had witnessed was not for my benefit. He didn't know me then. It was just a repeated cycle of his last fleeting thoughts before he died.

The chain to whatever anchored my father to this world needed to be severed. It was me, of course, but what did he need before he departed for good? As his daughter, it was the least I could do.

CHAPTER NINETEEN

Returning to the manor and its snowy rooftops, hiding behind the trees and gardens, filled me with more Christmas joy than any gift could. I was going home to her. Even if I couldn't see Penelope, knowing she was there in the house was enough. Her parents would leave soon; I just had to be patient.

Pulling the leads to a stop, the horses whinnied, and I hopped off the carriage before they had fully halted. Something was amiss in the house. I stepped in and squinted as if it could help me hear better. Strained voices could be heard from the parlor.

"They've been at it all morning," Mr. Davies said, materializing from the hallway.

It wasn't appropriate, but I pressed my ear to the parlor door. I eyed Mr. Davies, whose moustache twitched, but he did not argue.

"I can't believe you!" Penelope shouted. "All of you!"

"My dear, it was just a precaution," Mr. Jones said. "We didn't know if you could handle being my wife—"

"It's not just a precaution," Mrs. Hathaway said. "Honestly, you're being a child, Penelope. If your condition worsens, we must consider all options. The doctor has been reporting to us—we know everything."

"Everything?" Mr. Jones countered. "Like how she's managed a whole renovation and attends social engagements without his medicines? How she leads the household and the villagers? She has come a long way since we first got married and...I'm rather proud of her."

There was a silence then. I said a silent thanks to Mr. Jones. He was defending Penelope. He didn't want her to go to any institution. If ever there was a time for him to buck up, it was here and now. Penelope needed to hear him say it.

"Be that as it may, you've been irresponsible as a husband," Mr. Hathaway croaked. "You've forced her to more engagements than we agreed on per the contract. You thrust this, this massive undertaking, on her unwell shoulders. Penelope may be getting better, so you say, but you have not kept up your end of the bargain.

We agreed to pay a stipend on top of her dowry with the understanding that it would go to her medical expenses only to find that you have not been paying the doctor and you've been using the money for this!"

"So I am to be punished for it?" Penelope asked.

"Don't be so dramatic," Mrs. Hathaway said. "The facility is in Europe, you love the Swiss Alps. It's a beautiful establishment, and you'd have your own room."

"It's not what I want!" Penelope said. Something was thrown. It broke and clattered to the ground. Mr. Davies was uttering a prayer beside me. He too was now pressed against the door.

"Not the cherubs..." Mr. Davies groaned. I glared at him. This was not the time to fret over figurines, no matter how costly they were.

The room was silent. Chewing on my nails, I waited for anything. Mr. Davies frowned.

"You see now why she must go?" Mr. Hathaway said with a trembly voice. "We have done everything in our power to give her a normal life, but she's dangerous."

"She is my wife!" Mr. Jones said.

"And we have a contract," Mr. Hathaway argued. "This was a mistake."

"Get out of my house," Penelope roared. Another priceless item ricocheted and shattered, and Mr. Davies whimpered.

We didn't have time to move from the door when it was swung open. We came face to face with the lined face of Mr. Hathaway. "This is exactly why we don't employ maids and butlers," he said.

Mr. Davies pulled me away from the door by my arm. I had half a mind to punch the man, old or not. Those awful people were going to take Penelope away.

"Hear this, Jones," Mr. Hathaway said, ushering his wife out. "Let the doctor collect her, and you'll still receive the stipends. We honor our bargains. If you don't, you'll be hearing from our lawyers."

My knees went weak at the thought. I didn't know what frightened me more, Penelope being sent to an institution or the fact that she now knew about it.

I clamped my hands over my mouth to keep from crying out loud. Mr. Jones emerged, disheveled and red-faced. He was panting hard as though he had been running to and from the village. Sweat dripped around his thick hairline.

"Mr. Davies," he said. "See those people out."

"My pleasure," Mr. Davies turned and followed the couple to their rooms. I rushed past Mr. Jones, not waiting for his orders.

Penelope was staring out the window at the greenhouse. Broken ceramics lay waste where they once sat. They weren't thrown, I realized, they had simply exploded on their designated pedestals as if they had chosen death rather than endure an eternity of stagnation.

Her eyes were watery and full of sadness. I lifted my hand to place it on her shoulder, but hesitated.

"Penelope..."

What could I say? I looked out in the direction of the greenhouse, attempting to understand what she was watching. It was likely nothing, just a distant speck to focus on to keep from crying. Despair was the only way to describe the moment.

Mr. Jones was still panting, but he had recovered some. "I'm sorry, Penelope," he said. "There's nothing more I can do."

Her eyes lit, and she whirled around. "You're going to call a lawyer and fight this."

"I can't," he said. "Their lawyers penned it, and I signed with my lawyer."

Was he just saying this because he wanted the ongoing stipend? The greedy bastard. I wanted so desperately to defend her, but I would only make matters worse. If I were going to act, I couldn't say or do anything suspect in these critical moments.

"You snake!" Penelope flared. "You miserable little snake! You knew all along. You signed this agreement?"

"With the way you're acting, I have half a mind to send you off myself!" he shouted, red-faced and chest puffed.

"I'll show you just how crazy I can get!"

The air electrified as the windows rattled from an unseen wind. Pressure mounted in my ears so fast that I thought my head was going to pop like a cork. Clamping my hands over them, I watched as the room shuddered like there was lightning inside the house. The chandelier rocked from the entryway, sending fractals of light in every direction.

Mr. Davies stood in awe of the situation, but Mr. Jones tripped over his swollen feet on his way out of the room. All the while, Penelope stood in the eye of the storm, unaffected by what was transpiring around her. Not a single strand of her golden hair strayed out of place.

"Penelope..." I cried, my voice muted like I was speaking in a bottle. The pressure was too much. I dropped to my knees, swallowing hard to try and ease the pressure.

She turned, horror-stricken, and fell to her knees beside me. "Oh, Dinah. I'm sorry."

Something popped between my ears. It was so loud in my head I wondered if she could hear it too. I glanced at Mr. Jones, who was up against the wall, gasping. His face was one of realization. The face of a man who waded into the shallow end only for the bottom to give underneath his feet.

There was no denying this was Penelope's doing, but it was so hard to fathom. How could a person be capable of such things? Her hands trembled on my face. She was scared, not scared of what she had done, but rather, she was afraid of how I would react.

I was petrified. There was no denying it, but it was also incredible. I smiled the best I could and said, "Scare him anymore, and there will be a big brown stain on the new wainscotting."

Penelope was still distraught, but that didn't stop the laughter sputtering from her lips.

"I'm going to Manchester for a few days," Mr. Jones said, edging along the wall towards the door. "Mayweather, control her."

As if she suddenly remembered his betrayal, Penelope lunged toward her husband. He may have been done with her, but she certainly wasn't done with him.

I grabbed her arms and pulled her back. "It's not going to help," I said, my face pressed against her shoulder blades. "Believe me, if I thought it would, I'd deck him myself."

Mr. Jones didn't pack a bag. He simply went out the door. Did he have clothes at his office in Manchester? I wasn't certain that's where he went half the time. He came and went so smoothly as if he had another home to attend to. "He didn't pack his bags," I said. "His briefcase is still sitting beside his chair."

"He's not going to Manchester," Penelope said. "He's staying with his mistress."

I was so shocked that I let go of her arms. All this time, Mr. Jones had a mistress. Where did this woman live? Likely in Chester. Penelope stormed upstairs without further explanation. Not that she needed to. I was blind to not have seen it sooner.

But I had bigger worries than Mr. Jones's mistress. The Hathaways had every intention of annulling Penelope's marriage and sending her to an institution. Then there was the inexplicable indoor storm. My mind struggled to process everything that had transpired in those few minutes.

Mr. Hathaway railed at Mr. Davies as they made their way down the stairs, oblivious or unconcerned about the storm. Perhaps they had experienced it enough firsthand that it no longer phased them. Unable to control their daughter, they sought out anyone or anything that could.

How far would they go to keep Penelope tight in their grip?

There was a whack with a cane on something soft, and I knew Mr. Hathaway had hit the butler with his cane. Bloody bastard. I closed myself into the parlor, hoping never to see them again.

When a disheveled Mr. Davies entered the parlor, I was examining the greenhouse. "Are they gone?" I asked.

"Thankfully, yes."

"Did he really hit you with his cane?"

"And not for the first time, sadly."

"What happened earlier..." Mr. Davies started, though we both knew he had no intention of finishing that sentence. He needed a rational explanation. One that would restore order to a mind that could not comprehend the truth.

Penelope wasn't some frail, hysterical woman who needed others to make choices for her. She was an entity more powerful than those around her, and the only way they could think to contain her was by poisoning her or locking her away.

"The boiler was never decommissioned," I said. "It should be removed before it does something like that again."

"Yes," he said. "I think you're right."

What was it she stared at so intently before the storm?

I looked out the same window, hoping to glean any insight into her mind when a sharp groan crept from outside. At first, I thought perhaps Penelope's storm reached the emerald panes of the greenhouse, but something was pushing against the panel.

My stomach lurched as a bit of glass fell, exposing a bit of ivy, coiling around the shards of glass. My dream was a premonition of sorts. If Penelope could throw vases with her mind and cause indoor storms, was it so outlandish that I could see the future that she warned me of?

Perhaps my father wasn't a ghost at all, but rather a way for me to tell myself things I needed to know. Things I couldn't make sense of otherwise.

Jarring me from my thoughts. Mr. Davies cleared his throat. "Dinah..."

Pushing the ivy from my mind, I turned to face him. "Yes?"

"Do you love Mrs. Jones?"

My eyes cast downward, and I nodded. "You were right about me," I said. "I tried my best not to, but she took root in all the empty spaces in my heart. I didn't know how alone I was until I met her."

Mr. Davies frowned. "It's wrong, you know."

"Is it?" I asked. "We've seen so much wrongness today. Is it wrong to care for someone? To protect them? You may call me a perversion or a deviant, sir, but we haven't hurt anyone. Penelope cares more about us than Mr. Jones ever did."

"Us?" he said without blinking.

"You, me, Harriet, and the people in the village. You know that."

I was referring to Boxing Day. When Penelope sent him to the village. He sent the telegrams to London on her behalf to find Harriet's daughter. If they found her, they would bring word to us and let Harriet know her daughter was safe.

"I'm not asking for your acceptance," I said. "Just don't tell Mr. Jones about us. If you want, I'll put in my notice and leave, but don't make things worse for her than they already are."

"You would do that?" he asked, his right hand fidgeting slightly. "You would leave and never come back just so long as I promised not to reveal your dalliance?"

I nodded. "I just want her safe."

There was a long moment before Mr. Davies said, "I will not ask you to put in your notice just yet, Dinah." The butler left the room without another word.

I swallowed back my tears. Relieved that our secret would be safe from Mr. Jones and from the doctor. It was strange to be in the parlor room alone. It was as if I had one foot in my dream and the other in reality.

"Well?" I said out loud. "You can say it. You can say, "I told you so.""

Silence was all that replied. Not even the chill whisp along my collar. I was alone. Utterly alone in this room. There would be no help from a ghost when they came for Penelope. And there would be no easy victory. Someone was going to die at the end of this. Something in me knew it and couldn't make sense of it, so it took the face of my father and forced me to see it.

Someone was going to die soon. I just had to make sure that person wasn't Penelope.

CHAPTER TWENTY

I found Penelope in a pile of lilac broadcloth and ivory lace. She was sobbing uncontrollably. I could have fallen to pieces with her in that moment. The unbridled sorrow and helplessness were unbearable. I snorted out a sob before falling to the floor and pulling her close. "It's never going to happen," I promised. "I'll never let it happen."

Long arms draped around my shoulders, and her cries softened. "I knew they had talked about it, but I didn't think they had put it in my god-damned marriage agreement."

I shook my head. "I just...I can't understand the cruelty of it."

"That's just it," she said. "They don't think it cruel. They think they are saving me from myself. They're probably right."

Not for one moment did I believe that. In the library, the professor...she had only ever acted in self-defense. I pulled her up and guided her to the bed, then lit one of the cigarettes waiting in the filter. She took it from me and sucked down the fumes. "Maybe we can convince Mr. Jones to banish the doctor, agree to see a new one," I said.

She chuckled and stroked my face and hair. "What's done is done, my love."

Penelope wasn't wrong. Mr. Jones was a coward in the ways a man should never be. He could shoot a boar charging at him, and he could make speeches at the drop of a hat, but he ran from difficult conversations. She had every right to be angry with his complicity in all of this. Still, the easiest way to keep her safe was to keep the coward on our side. I couldn't blame her if she never forgave him.

"Make nice with him," I urged. It stuck like bile in my throat, but I was desperate.

Her sour expression said it all.

I sat beside her and took her hand. It was frail and warm like the flush in her cheeks from the confrontation. "You have every right to be angry," I started. "But he is the only thing standing between you and..."

I couldn't say it.

"The loony bin?" she chuckled grimly. "Maybe I belong there."

I shook my head.

Her eyes met mine, then. Her perfect oval blues. "You saw it, didn't you?"

"The Ivy," I said with a nod. "But how do I stop it, Penelope?"

Penelope's tears mingled with my own when she kissed me. "You still don't understand. It grows over everything, strangles everything. The only way is to save yourself before it wraps around you as well."

As if she witnessed my dream, she plucked the intrinsic fear and let the note waver in the air. There was no weeding out the ivy, my father had told me as much. No poison could kill it without salting the earth, taking everything with it.

"There must be another way," I pleaded. "Any other way." Her hands smoothed over my uniform, and I forgot my failures briefly just as a forgotten weight slipped from my pocket.

"You know what I am. What I'm capable of. I didn't mean to get you tied up in this; I just wanted to be near you. Even if it was just for a little while."

She was in a dark place to be sure. Before I met Penelope, I was so bitter and unhappy, so I could relate. But she couldn't remain here. I wouldn't let her.

In a blur of pink, Penelope shot across the bedroom. I sat up, thinking she was having a sort of emergency when the sound of a cork popped. Penelope was chugging directly from the half-full bottle. She had slipped it out of my pocket when I wasn't paying attention!

I was on my feet, rushing toward her. Penelope's long legs glided up the table, and she stood on the loveseat to take another swig. Anger flared within me as I glared at Penelope. Of all the childish hogwash...

"Put that down!" I demanded, staring up at her. "Or it will be me sending you to the looney bin!"

I instantly regretted saying it, but Penelope was unfazed. She was too busy tipping that medicine down her throat with reckless abandon. Was she trying to end it all? She wasn't suicidal, but current events might have driven her to the edge.

Mustering all the strength my stout legs had, I jumped on the loveseat. Reaching my hands up over my head, my hand clasped around the hard glass bottle. Penelope was no longer drinking it, but it remained firmly in her clutches.

In a moment of genius, I used my short stature to my advantage. The back of the loveseat had a wooden railing that scrolled into a square base on the center back of the sofa. Holding the bottle, I planted a foot on the flat spot and pushed myself up with one leg. The bottle was jarred downward as I swung my other leg over the back side of the love seat before jumping down.

I hit the carpet with a thud. My thigh muscles strained with the sudden excursion, but it worked. Penelope didn't see it coming. She stared at me for a moment from up high, half impressed and half annoyed. Full of my success, I retrieved the cork from the corner of the room and plugged the bottle back up. In my hubris, I assumed that I had won the encounter and there would be no more. Penelope had other plans.

She turned to me fully as she lifted her skirts to get back down off the couch. "You give that back!" Penelope demanded with a low, threatening rumble. The air began to crackle, and the hairs on my arms stood on end. She meant business, but so did I.

It was then that I understood my error. She could outrun me, even with a corset laced shut. Without an alternative, I wedged the bottle down the front of my uniform and between my breasts before clambering over the bed and away from Penelope and toward the door.

She dove to the side as if she meant to chase me over the bed before feinting and running around the four-poster, but I was just out of reach. I was out the door, but not before something heavy landed on my back, forcing me to the ground.

It was a slow, clumsy fall. I wasn't injured, but delicate hands were searching for the neckline of my uniform. Penelope rolled me over and straddled me, tugging and yanking at the unyielding fabric. The absurdity of it all made me giggle. She, too, had a smile on her face.

"I'll strip you in the hall if I must!"

That was fine by me. I was about to say so when a man cleared his throat.

If I could have fallen through the marble floor and into oblivion, I would have. We both turned to find Mr. Davies standing at the base of the stairs, his skin awash in various shades. A dark crimson was falling away, revealing a paleness that even the most Celtic blood could not possess.

We exchanged a panicked glance before returning to a butler who was turning the shade of an unripe tomato.

"We—"

Penelope started to interject, "She—"

It was the butler who cut us both off. "Just tell me the vases are intact."

We burst into full-bellied laughter. Penelope slid off me and onto the carpet. My ribs ached. and my lungs could no longer contain air. I was wheezing when the butler stepped over me and into the bedroom to check on his beloved vase.

I turned to Penelope just as reality and the drugs kicked in. Her pupils were large, dark orbs lined in daylight. "Remember what I promised you?"

She gave a nod. "You won't let them put me away."

"We'll run away before that happens."

Uncertainty lined her features. What kind of life would we live together? "What's stopping us now?" Penelope asked.

My heart stopped in that moment. "You would leave all this behind?"

Penelope hesitated, and I closed my eyes. "I don't know..."

Why leave this place when she had everything she could ever need? Penelope knew nothing of real life. Still, I could work while she stayed home. "With the amount of jewelry you have, we could buy ourselves a nice little home—"

"How?" Penelope asked. "You're unmarried and without a father or brother. You can't own property, and I can only own property inherited by a husband or with permission."

She had pored over enough home magazines to learn a thing or two about property rights. "We could rent." Desperation thinned my voice.

"My doctor would never stop searching for me."

How she feared the doctor! My experience with him was limited, but he was nothing if not attentive and knowledgeable. He cared about her well-being, but something about his presence had a grip on Penelope just as it had on Mr. Jones.

Mr. Davies appeared in the doorway. "Nothing is damaged. Thank goodness! What on earth were you two doing?"

"Just horsing around, Mr. Davies," Penelope said with a sudden sharpness. "You're dismissed."

She managed to remain upright, but the moment the butler was out of sight, Penelope fell against the doorframe. Her eyes went all glazy and distant. The air softened, and the little hairs on my neck went smooth. The drugs were taking effect. She would be a docile little housewife for the time being.

The churning in my belly readied me for the unknown threat. I hated that lost look she gave. It always meant she would say something awful. "All this time. You knew. You knew about the agreement."

I stuttered and shook my head in denial. "I...I had no choice."

Her head lolled to one side as she narrowed her eyes. "You could have told me."

She was angry at me for something I couldn't help. "I would have been sacked," I said. "I would have lost you."

"You think lying to me would change that?"

What was she saying? My mind spun, and I reached out for her, but Penelope stepped away. "Not everyone has the privilege of risking everything."

"As if keeping it from me would somehow make me better?" She saw right through me. I had—we all—had thought that by hiding the doctor's plan to institutionalize her, she would get better. But how was I to know the agreement wasn't conditional to her illness but rather her telekinetic abilities?

"I can't turn off the hurt the way you can, and I can't pretend things are okay when they're not."

"Please," I said. "I'm sorry, but you can't give up—" She couldn't move quick enough to dodge my hug, but her posture slacked, and she relented.

"Is that what you thought?" she asked, stroking my back. "That I would fall apart? All this time, you've been trying to keep me from being put away."

My tears were staining her dress. I was wrong. We were all wrong, but it didn't mean I loved her any less. All this time, I had been keeping a secret from her, thinking it was in her best interest when it wasn't my place to decide what was best for her. I said I didn't want to make her choices for her the way everyone else did, but there I was standing with the pack of liars.

"I'm so sorry," I blubbered. "I wanted to be different. I love you, and I just want you to be safe. I can't... If anything happens to you, I don't think I can—"

I couldn't go on without her. She frowned at the notion like it was some disagreeable child that needed a lolly. She grabbed me by the shoulders and pulled me into her chest. Buried in frilly lilac fabric that smelled of lavender, only then was I able to breathe.

Penelope shushed me and said, "Settle down. I don't want you to worry anymore. I'll take care of it. You'll see. I'll take care of everything."

The more people learned about her abilities, the more likely they would agree with the doctor and her parents. Mr. Jones was her only chance, and he ran to the arms of his mistress. She had to convince him that what he saw wasn't real. It was the new plumbing settling in, or a strange storm.

"You'll make nice with him then?"

She smiled down at me. "I'll do whatever I must."

Penelope wasn't angry with me anymore, and the secret was out. There was some relief in that at least. She understood now why it was so imperative to make up with Mr. Jones. All would be as well as it could be, for now at least. She would make up with Mr. Jones and convince him to hire more lawyers.

They could fight the prenuptial contract. Her parents were old; they would tire of it all and relent. They had to.

That night, we sat beside the fire, and I brushed out her hair. "How long have you known about Mr. Jones's mistress?"

She wrapped her arms around her knees and stared into the fire. "She had been there since before we got married. She is some house-keeper of one of the properties he manages. He was always forthright about it, and I didn't care as it lessened my duties as a wife."

That made sense. With a mistress, Penelope did not need to bed Mr. Jones as often. There was a satisfaction in knowing she encouraged the mistress. I wondered just how often they did their marital duties. With the time he spent away, it must not have been often.

"Maybe he could bring her here," I suggested. "He can have his mistress, and you can have yours."

Penelope giggled at that. "It would be fair, wouldn't it? That's not how men work. I am his, she is his, the house is his, my money is also his."

"Does he need the money so badly?" I asked.

"He wouldn't if he didn't spend so much of it on his mistress. I don't know what they do that requires so much of it. How much can a mistress really need if her home is saw to?"

"It doesn't make sense," I said.

I had almost eight pounds in jars in my bedroom saved up since I started working here. I didn't pay rent or meals. None of us did; it was part of our payment. If we were to break something, it would be taken out of our pay, but that hadn't happened to anyone that I knew of. The mistress would have been paid more if she was head housekeeper.

Penelope's hair was brushed and gleaming in the firelight. Her curls were drawn from all the brushing but had begun recoiling once I had stopped brushing. "You have the most beautiful hair," I told her. "It's downright sickening."

Normally, this would make her laugh, but her eyes were dark as they stared into the fire. Her face was lined with shadows, giving her almost a menacing appearance. As though she were a plotting villain in one of those novels men deemed a sinful distraction for women.

As if Penelope could manage anything remotely evil. The idea was laughable. What would she do? Scratch her parents to death? A sure foot on a stairwell would be enough to take them out. The idea made me smile. It was a good thing God didn't punish people for thinking evil thoughts, though I supposed it didn't matter since I was already damned for being a Tom.

Just so long as Penelope wasn't damned with me.

Chapter Twenty-One

When Mr. Jones came home, Penelope played the part of the doting wife. She rushed to his side and clung to his sturdy arm. "I was being ridiculous," Penelope told him as they entered the parlor. "Could you ever forgive me?"

He smiled like a benevolent god, and I wanted to hurl. "How could I not?"

"You only want what is best for me, and I know that."

"It really was just a precaution," he explained. "Your doctor was so against our marriage. It was the only way to get him to give his blessing. If your parents attempt anything, I will fight them tooth and nail. I've already contacted my lawyer."

The parlor door closed behind them, and I stood alone in the dim hallway. A chill tickled up my spine, and the hairs on my neck straightened. My breath was visible. An unbearable sense of dread weighted my feet. I turned just enough to see the ghost of my father. I swallowed the lump in my throat. Why was he still here? "What do you want?" I asked.

My father no longer resembled the man who had died in the fall. It was a rotting frame of a man with long fingernails and stringy hair that lay across his ears. "How do I make you go away?"

"Let me go, my dear," he said before letting out a slow, whistling groan that climbed up the walls and made my vision blur. I snapped my eyes shut and put my hands over my ears as the scream squeezed my heart.

Suddenly, it stopped.

I opened my eyes, and he was gone. I leaned against the wall for a long while. Any desire to do anything had left with the specter of my father. Why was this happening to me? I managed to get to my bedroom and onto my bed, where I remained for the rest of the evening.

Something about hauntings leaves one feeling utterly isolated. There was no one I could go to. No one I could tell about the poltergeist. Not even Penelope. I sat up in my bed and stared at the wooden cross nailed to the wall. It was a remnant of the previous occupant. He said I needed to let him go, but how? If it was all in my head, how could I make myself stop thinking about him?

The plumbing in the bathrooms had been carried out regardless of the weather outside. The ground had thawed enough that the men could dig the trenches from dawn to dusk right up until the eve of the New Year. They were miserable and cold, but we kept the tea hot, and the stew was full of meat.

Penelope watched from the bedroom window while I straightened her bedroom.

"Everything will be ready today," Mr. Davies assured her.

"Will that ghastly line in the lawn remain?" she asked.

"Unfortunately, it will," he said with a bowed head.

Penelope was already on edge in anticipation of the party. Dressed in one of the new gowns from Manchester, she was the vision of a proper Victorian lady. "Have the boys move those bushes over," she said, moving away from the window.

"The Belladonna?" Mr. Davies asked with enthusiasm.

Penelope went to her desk and flipped open the top magazine. "I love the colors," she said. "They will be a nice backdrop for the violets."

Mr. Davies took note of the bushes and gave a nod. "Six should do."

"Will they bloom on time despite planting?"

"I should think so," Mr. Davies said. "Just so long as they are mature."

Penelope gave a nod of consent. "As soon as possible, if you can."

\#

That night, the men had finished their work, and after several hours of Penelope pacing back and forth outside the bathroom, the plumber emerged and said, "Give it a go!"

It was an exciting and funny moment. Mr. Davies, myself, Penelope, and even Mr. Jones all gathered in the bathroom, huddled around the toilet.

"Would you like to do the honors, love?" Mr. Jones asked Penelope.

"The first flush!" she declared.

Long fingers wrapped around the cord hanging from the tank. She pulled lightly, and the water in the bowl was evacuated and refilled within a few minutes. There was a moment of silence in the room. The toilet signified the coming of a new century and a new era for the manor.

The toilets were all the rage the night of the party. Throngs of people were packed into tiny rooms, cheering with each flush of the toilet. I was relegated to the kitchen for the evening, but the plumbing sloshed through the pipes all around us.

Harriet and I would give a knowing smirk each time we heard it. "So easily amused," she chided. "You'd think none of them have ever seen it before."

I wanted to mention how many times she had made trips into the bathroom herself, but I let it go. For us, it was a modern marvel, but it was something many of the guests already had installed within their own homes.

"Posh people," I muttered as I checked on a rack of lamb.

At midnight, the toilets ceased to flush as everyone gathered in the parlor.

When Mr. Davies was busy in the wine cellar, I snuck in armed with champagne flutes. I just wanted to see Penelope in her dress. I hadn't seen her since I helped her get ready.

I spotted her straight away amid the crowd. My breath fell out of my gaping mouth, and I forgot how to inhale again. She was wearing a pale pink gown with pear beading along the low neckline. Her hair was an intricate pinning of wide loops crowned around her head. The candlelight warmed her skin and golden hair. She was an angel amid the black suited men who surrounded her.

I didn't blame them for wanting to be close to her. In my maid uniform, I was invisible. People took drinks off the tray as if I were a piece of furniture. I rather enjoyed it.

There was only one person in the room I wanted to be seen by, and she smiled brilliantly when her eyes met mine. I felt a small pat on my shoulder and found Mr. Davies standing by my side. My face felt hot with embarrassment. How long had he been standing there? "I was just making sure she was okay," I said.

His wry smile was tucked away under his moustache. "Of course."

I had been standing there with an empty tray for several minutes. "I should collect some glasses..."

"She's happy with you," he said without looking at me. "If only my daughter had found someone like you, things might have been different."

The words he used made it sound like his daughter was dead. I didn't recall hearing anything about it. "She passed away?" I asked. "I'm so sorry, I didn't know."

"Few do," he said. "There was no funeral."

Mr. Davies's eyes were filled with a profound sorrow, yet didn't so much as glisten. All that pain was bottled up inside, where it would likely be the death of him. There was only one circumstance in which a person did not receive a funeral, and I understood then why the butler seldom spoke of his troubled daughter.

Heaven was barred to those who took their own lives.

"We don't admit our feelings," I said. "It's something Penelope can't understand."

"Well, no one likes the inconvenience of empathy. Americans have their own ways, I suppose."

Penelope raised her glass, and several crystal flutes reached upward and clinked in a symphony. Mr. Jones was not one among them. I searched the room to find that the lord of the home was not in the room at all. "Where is Mr. Jones?" I asked.

The butler eyed me cautiously as he gauged my expression. "He's giving a lady a tour of the house."

The manor was not a large one. With three stories, including the wine cellar and two wings, there was no reason why a tour would take that long. Was it the famed mistress who stole away all his funds, or another woman who walked the wings?

"The Jones men have always strayed," Mr. Davies said. "It's nothing for Penelope to concern herself with."

I gave the butler a doubtful look. "Until he knocks someone up."

"And those things are discreetly taken care of."

My stomach churned at the thought, and I was reminded by Mr. Davies's earlier assessment of posh people. They don't live by the rules the rest of us do. I had had enough of the upper-class frivolity for one night. "If you have no further use of me—"

"Goodnight, Dinah," the butler said before taking the tray from my clammy hands. "I've got it from here."

That night was a long one. Despite going to bed early, there was no rest. I tossed and turned at every scratch of the woolen blanket and every thin spot in the mattress. On most nights, my thoughts were of Penelope, but that night my mind wandered to Mr. Davies's daughter and my own losses in life.

Since my father's ghost informed me that it was I who kept him shackled to this world, I searched every dark corridor for the answer. I didn't want him here dead any more than I did when he was alive, yet something in me refused to let go. I grabbed the flat pillow and folded it in half before wedging it under my neck, facing the mirror.

When he died, Mary insisted that I cover all the mirrors. In theory, spirits could travel through mirrors and get trapped instead of floating up to heaven. I never covered my vanity mirror. It wasn't like a real haunting, it was just in my head, but maybe if I carried out the funeral ritual, it would be enough to put that part of my mind at ease.

I left the vanity behind; no doubt Mary kept it as a memento of my family. Maybe she sold it. It was the only thing in the house worth anything.

If he was trying to tell me something important, it should have been how to get rid of him. Then again, he had yet to say anything that wasn't cryptic. I groaned and squeezed my eyes shut. No, this had nothing to do with a mirror. Besides, my father hated superstition. He said that I needed to let him go. I never said goodbye, not even at the funeral. Maybe all that was required was to accept that he was dead in my heart, and my mind would follow.

It sounded too easy, but like that grave dirt I clutched in my hand, I struggled to let go.

CHAPTER TWENTY-TWO

I had just finished the breads when Mr. Davies came into the kitchen.

"Mr. Jones has taken ill," he announced. "All that champagne last night gave him a rip-roaring headache."

"He's still in bed?" If he was, I had no intention of going in there. Penelope would go to the greenhouse if she woke to find him beside her.

Try as she might, she hadn't forgiven him—not really. Her eyes narrowed sharp as daggers at the back of his head when she thought no one was looking. But whenever he turned to her to point out something that struck his fancy, an advert about guns or train sets, her face would morph into one of utter devotion. If I didn't know better, I'd say she hated him, but she'd never say it out loud. Even to me.

Mr. Davies' jaw tensed so hard I saw his muscles buckle. "He is in another bedroom."

That was when I noticed it; the butler had set tea for two.

My face went all hot at the realization. Penelope told me she didn't mind his dalliances, but...under the same roof? Bold as brass, that one.

It was as if he had no idea or care as to how it would make anyone else feel. The Jones Manor wasn't that big. Did Penelope know?

"Best not say anything," Mr. Davies said as he lifted the tray.

Penelope needed him to fight for her, but I got the feeling that no matter how loving and devoted she was, Mr. Jones was slipping away regardless. It wasn't right. Her very freedom relied on the moods and whims of that man, and he didn't have the sense enough to care.

Our heads snapped in the direction of the bell mounted on the wall. Someone was at the front door. I wasn't sure who was more eager for a diversion, the butler or myself. "I'll get it."

Pulling the double doors open, who would be standing there but the doctor. I don't know why I was surprised to see his greasy head standing on the porch, but I wasn't expecting him, and I doubted Penelope was either.

"Are you going to let me in?" the doctor asked briskly. "Or must I stand out here in the cold all day?"

His calm doctor demeanor was gone, and a twitchy, bitter little man had taken his place. The doctor wasn't even looking at me as he spoke; his eyes were shifting from the parlor to the upstairs behind me. If I didn't fear being fired, I would have slammed the door in his face, but I bowed my head and opened the door.

Not another word was spoken to me as he brushed past me and strode right up the stairs without invitation. I was frozen with uncertainty. Mr. Davies usually handled this. Was this normal? Something in my gut told me it wasn't.

"The lord and lady are still in bed," I said, omitting the fact that they were in separate beds.

My words went ignored as the doctor with his leather bag went up the stairs. I followed behind him at a safe distance, compelled to witness what happened next. "Sir, she's not awake yet."

I gasped as he walked right into the bedroom without so much as a knock.

Penelope was already awake and sitting up in bed. The commotion must have woken her. "What is the meaning of this?"

Mr. Davies materialized in the doorway as if he sensed something was amiss on his watch. "Doctor Forester, this is highly inappropriate—"

"The Hathaways are concerned about Ms. Penelope's welfare," he started. "They notified me of the occurrences during their visit."

Mr. Davies waded into the room. He was a head taller than the doctor and used every bit of that height to stand over the doctor. Penelope was sitting up in bed, wide-eyed, and her bottom lip was quivering. She looked at me and nodded. Her meaning was plain. Mistress or no, I had to get Mr. Jones.

Not a moment to lose, I rushed down the stairs and across the house to find Mr. Jones meandering down the hallway in his slippers and bathrobe. "Dinah, can you fetch me the newspaper?"

"Mr. Jones," I stammered. "The doctor—"

His blue eyes went harsh then. Mistress or no, it seemed that Mr. Jones had no intention of giving up his wife. "Come along then."

I filled him in on the doctor's intrusive behavior as we hurried up the carpeted stairs. We could overhear Penelope talking to him. "Really, Doctor Forester, my parents are old," she said as evenly as one could manage when their freedom was at stake. "They have a penchant for exaggeration."

"It is true our new plumbing required some settling. I must admit, it frightened me as well." Mr. Davies smoothed.

I glanced at Mr. Jones. He had deflated some as he drew closer to the bedroom. Penelope had struck the fear of God in him that day, and the reminder of it might have been too much for him. "She's your wife," I told him. "He has no right to come into her room, to try and take her away from you."

"Right." He didn't sound as convinced as I would have liked, but he stormed into the room all the same. "What is the meaning of this?"

"How dare you put Penelope in such risk?" The doctor hissed. "It's bad enough that you thrust a massive remodel on her just before Christmas, but to host a party so close after the altercation on Christmas day..." The doctor was gripping the handles of his bag, and his hollow cheeks were enflamed.

"The party was her idea and on her terms," Mr. Jones shouted. "If she didn't feel well, she could retire to her room at any time."

An air of giddiness coursed through me. This was the moment I had been praying for. The doctor had finally overstepped his bounds, and Mr. Jones would finally have enough. With the doctor in ill-favor, the idea of institutionalizing Penelope would diminish without his pressing.

"I've told the Hathaways, and I shall tell you now, she is my wife," Mr. Jones said with a puff of his chest. Both Mr. Jones and Mr. Davies were bearing down on the doctor, forcing him to take a step away from Penelope's bed. I choked back a squeal of delight. Get 'em, boys!

"The Hathaways have sided with me on this," the doctor said. "You cannot understand what's at stake. She is dangerous, and her powers are growing out of control. Tell me you've never seen anything unusual."

The room moved in slow motion then. Mr. Jones bowed his head.

"It's only going to get worse, son. What happens if she gets angry at you, and I'm not here to sedate her? She's already killed once. Did you know that?"

He looked to Penelope for a response. My poor love; she couldn't lie, and no matter how I tried to convince her, she still thought the professor was her fault. "No," I whispered. I tried to rush to her side, but Mr. Davies held me back.

"Is that true?" Mr. Jones asked Penelope.

She tried to speak, but no words would come. Mr. Jones could only look at her in horror. No doubt he feared that his life was at stake.

"You see why her parents are so heavy-handed," the doctor said. "Why I am so involved. Should she kill again, I might not be able to protect her. My facility is far preferable to a prison or a noose."

"I...understand," Mr. Jones relented. The anticipation of the doctor's dismissal slumped with Mr. Jones's shoulders. As his face went pale, my stomach twisted so hard I nearly vomited. He nodded and said, "Very well then."

I must have been shouting. Two arms braced me and dragged me from the bedroom as I kicked and flailed. I could hear Penelope shouting and crying as I was pulled down the stairs. The doctor was going to take her. He was going to lock her up in his institution, and I would never see her again.

The constraints of my corset stifled my breath, and my vision went dark. I must have been upright, because Mr. Davies couldn't possibly carry me. We slammed against wood and walls. I kicked against a banister. The sound of wood splintering and the smell of Mr. Davies's cologne. It took all his strength to pull me away, and his pants turned to gasps as I struggled all the harder.

I had always been strong, much stronger than most, but in that moment, I wasn't strong enough.

Suddenly, I was in my room, and my door clicked closed. Mr. Davies stood between me and the exit. "We can't let them take her," I started. "You know what they do in those places, you read the Nellie Bly story, you know what it's like."

"I know firsthand what they do," he said. "Because they did it to *her*."

The butler was pacing the room, his hair wild and mustache crooked. His pain and loss were lost on me. What would have been a harrowing realization of my cousin's fate was overlapped with Penelope's near future. I stood up and charged him. "We can't let it happen!"

"And what are you going to do about it, exactly?" An abrupt anger hollowed his voice. "You are no one. You have nothing."

That wasn't true. I shook my head with a vision drowning in tears. "I have her!"

He shook his head. "You stupid girl—you never had her. They had this planned from the beginning. Why do you think he was dawdling with other women? His mistress is poised to take Penelope's place, and he will keep the inheritance."

"No!" I fell to my knees and sobbed. How could he be so cruel? "She was getting better."

"This has nothing to do with her nerves," Mr. Davies said. He was staring at himself in the free-standing mirror as if he were sneering at a stranger. "This is about controlling a dangerous woman without a scandal."

Male voices were shouting from outside my room. Mr. Jones was calling for his butler. Mr. Davies gave one last look at himself in the mirror and straightened his vest. "You are dismissed," he said. "I suggest you take your earnings and leave straight away. If I see you in that maid outfit again, I will not provide a reference."

I didn't see him leave. I hoped I'd never see that horrible man again. I trembled all over as I disrobed from the uniform. I stood there with my bare feet like ice blocks on the hard ground as it occurred to me that the only clothes I had were the ones I used for working outdoors.

A pair of trousers and a white linen shirt that once belonged to my father. My square jaw and dark hair. My dark brown eyes lined with a grayish tone. My thick bushy brows. With my hair still pulled back in the cap, I could have easily been mistaken for a man.

Where would I go? Numb and grief-stricken, I took my money and the few trinkets I had and dropped them in a potato sack before slinging it over my shoulder. Harriet caught me in the kitchen. I tried to push past the kitchen maid, but there was no moving around her wide frame.

"Is it true?" Harriet asked. Her eyes were red-rimmed as though she too had been crying over the news.

"You don't see me making coffee, do you?" I muttered as I squeezed past her.

Her eyes were stuck to my back as I pulled open the door. There was nothing left for me here. Numb with the loss of all faith and hope. There was nothing. Everything was lost to me without her. I failed her.

"That's just it, then?" Harriet challenged. "You're just going to up and run?"

What else could I do? Storm into the room and drag Mr. Jones out of her room and away from her family and doctors? Still, Harriet's words stung my irritated eyes. I needed her to quit before she said something that made me change my mind.

"There's no winning for people like us, Harriet. Would have thought you'd have learned that by now."

"She found her," Harriet said, her lip trembling. "I don't know how she did it, but she found Alexandra and brought her home. I know you've had it tougher than most, and that it's easier to shut off those feelings and run, but you can't do it now. She's worth fighting for."

I cried out as my wafer-thin resolve snapped. Penelope had found Alexandra in London. She had Mr. Davies hire multiple detectives to find the woman. Penelope didn't just send word, she brought her home. There was no stopping that woman when she had something in her head. I couldn't shut Penelope out like I did my parents. Well, like I tried to shut them out. I failed at that, too.

"Do you know when they're leaving?" I asked.

"Tonight," Harriet said. "Mr. Davies told me so."

I ruffled at the mention of that traitor. It was still early. I could do something. Without another word, I went to the stable where I found the carriage driver. He was sitting on a rough stool, drinking a cup of tea while he held a conversation with the stable boy.

"Are you driving tonight?" I asked.

He did a double-take before replying. "No, I have nothing on the schedule. Dressed like that, I gather you want to take the carriage out on a drive."

I promised I would get her out before they took her, and that was what I was going to do. I'd need help. I just hoped the village would agree to come to my aid. The impulse to sneak Penelope out in a stolen carriage in broad daylight was a temptation I had to avoid. I would be better off on horseback. I could barely ride, but Penelope had lessons at finishing school. "I just need a ride to town, actually."

"Like that?" the driver asked with his white brows raised.

"It's dirty work I have ahead of me," I said with a grin. "I don't want to mess up my uniform."

The day was just starting for the people in the village. Mary was no doubt still asleep. I banged on her door with a bawled fist until she opened.

"Dinah!" she screeched. "The way you were pounding, I thought you were the landlord."

I walked past her and into the house. "I need your help."

Mary straightened and gave a sullen nod. "Right. I'll put on the kettle."

I told her about Penelope. Not about our relationship, but the doctor and the agreement her parents had with Mr. Jones. She soaked up all the potential gossip just like I needed her to do. "When I found out about it, I was so upset they had to sack me."

Mary was hanging on every word in the same way she clutched her teacup. "Mr. Jones senior must be rolling in his grave. They already got enough money! I can't believe he's exploiting that wonderful woman for a trifle more."

"I couldn't stay there and serve him after knowing what sort of man he was," I said. "I'm going to buy a horse and head north."

Mary cocked her head. "What's north for you?"

I shrugged. "I just need a fresh start."

There were a few moments of silence as she regarded me. "You look just like him, you know."

She meant my father. It was something I already knew. There was a heaviness on my shoulders then. He and I had unfinished business that needed sorting today as well.

Mary stood up and reached for the top of an old coat rack and pulled down a pleated cap with matching vest. "These were your father's."

I took it in my hands and brushed against the wool. He always wore this. His sweat-laden scent was imprinted on the lining, and I resisted the urge to hold it to my face and inhale. These things took me back to Sundays on our way to church. The way he used to look down and smile at me as if I were the brightest star in his sky.

Penelope said that I shut off the hurt, but that wasn't it. I clung to the pain as though it was the only thing I had to remember them by, but that wasn't true. I had memories. Wonderful memories of a mother who passed down her love of baking and the kindest father any girl could ask for. I even had fond memories of Mary, telling me stories at night when my father worked late.

I had more than just pain in my heart. I had their love, and I had Penelope's too.

"I'm going to visit his grave before I go," I told Mary.

I was out the door and running to the church at the end of the street. Mary was calling in the distance. "What was it you needed my help with, dear?"

"Just go about town and do what you do." I grinned back at her dour expression. This wasn't the first time I accused her of being a busybody, but this time I relied on it. Penelope depended on it.

The church was a white-washed building with a single steeple. The picket fence was of the same cut as the fence surrounding my yard. Mary said that after the church was built, they used the scraps on our flats. I had no reason to not believe her; she was a gossip, not a liar.

The church had seen better days. It was tucked into a cove of tall, old trees, and as a result, it developed a shaggy moss on the rooftop. Wild ivy climbed along one side and threatened to break its way into the building itself. No one cared about what the ivy did or where it climbed, just so long as it didn't get in their way.

Besides, if the church siding was broken, we might get some slightly warmer air inside the building. I used to sit in those pews as a child, breathing onto my numb fingers, flexing them back to life. How could one building be so cold?

Mary said it was due to the location of the church. It was shaded by trees and was never touched by daylight. The cobblestones used as a foundation leached the frost from the ground and reserved it especially for Sunday sermons.

My father's grave was around the back. The little wooden marker had his name carved in it, and a similar, yet broken cross sat beside it. I sucked in a heavy breath before kneeling. The damp earth soaked into my pants along the knees and shins, and it itched, but now wasn't the time for trivial matters.

The birds chirped in the afternoon, and the slight breeze gave the impression that I wasn't entirely alone.

"I hated her for leaving me, leaving us," I said. "On the day of her funeral, it was like the light in your eyes went out as well. Might as well have lost both parents years ago, because you were never the same after that."

I refused to cry, but my nails were digging into my palms so hard the smell of iron lingered in the breeze. "I understand now. You were living a half-life. Doing the best you could for my sake. If I let go of Penelope now, I might as well set up a marker next to yours. I love you..." I swallowed the hard lump in my throat. "Both of you."

Awkwardly, I stood on tingling feet and dusted the moss off my knees. No more ghosts. I had to release him instead of trying to cling to him with resentment. It made so much sense now, it was laughable that I didn't figure it out sooner.

The farmer my father used to work for sold me a horse and a saddle. It was a brown mare with white spots, and the saddle was dry and frayed. "Neither are in their prime," the farmer said, patting the mare gently. "But if you're not trying to win any races, she will carry you north."

I hadn't told him I was going north. Mary's gossip had taken root and found even the most remote parts of town. She no doubt went to the post office, grocery, and the baker first. From there, the news of Mr. Jones's deception and mistreatment of his wife reached most of the town by mid-afternoon.

The mare was a calm beast. She trotted leisurely to town along the road she had taken so many times. "You're just happy to be out of the stall, aren't you, girl?" I said, running my fingers through her blonde mane. A pang of fear struck me then as it reminded me of Penelope's golden hair.

I urged the horse to pick up the pace. If I didn't get this right, Penelope would be the one to suffer for it.

CHAPTER TWENTY-THREE

I tied off the horse in the stable. She blended in with the others. The only person who would notice the new addition wasn't here. The stable boy was gone, as was the coachman. The manor grounds were void of the usual maintenance crew, and the flat landscape was developing a shroud of fog that could put London to shame.

There, I waited in the stables until the sun began to set. Anticipation nipped at my fingers and toes in the way no cold would. My saddle bags held all my money and personal effects, including the pair of earrings I bought for Penelope. I couldn't give her the life she was accustomed to, but it was better than spending the rest of her life in an institution. I only hoped she would agree.

With the cover of night, I slipped into the kitchens to find Harriet crying while peeling potatoes. She gasped when she saw me, and I put a finger to my mouth to remind her to be quiet.

"She's been locked in her room," Harriet whispered. "I don't know how you're going to get to her without Mr. Davies seeing."

I didn't know either. "There's a ladder somewhere around here, isn't there?"

The maid nodded. "Around back, behind the shed."

"Good luck, Dinah."

I thanked her. I was going to need it. Navigating the yard with its columns and brick privacy wall, among the hedges and behind the replanted bushes, a small wooden shack without windows slanted all too profoundly to the left. Resting against the side, as if holding the whole building up, was a tall ladder.

My breath made white puffs in the winter air as I tried to pick up the ladder. It was wooden, and wet with rain, and it weighed several stone. I was forced to drag it to the side of the manor to a dimly lit bedroom window. I positioned the steps on the wet grass and hoped it would ground itself on the soaked lawn as I scaled to the window.

The curtains were drawn. I had no way of knowing if Mr. Jones or Mr. Davies was in the room. I pushed open the window, and it let out a squeak in protest. I winced and ducked down for several agonizing moments. The last thing I needed was to get caught. I'd be hauled off to jail for sure, and then Penelope would be lost forever.

I pushed the window open a little bit more. It was silent this time. Reaching my hand in, I shifted the curtain just enough to find Penelope in bed. No one else was in the room. I should have figured as much. Mr. Davies did not enter the room unless Mr. Jones was present, and the coward wouldn't sit in the room with the wife he was about to throw away.

Pushing open the window the rest of the way, I stepped in. Penelope didn't stir. They must have had her sedated, or perhaps she had given up.

I touched her hand, and her eyes opened. "Dinah?" she asked.

Who else would it be? It was only then that I realized I was dressed in a man's clothes. I had my bun tucked into my father's cap, and I was wearing his vest as well. "Let's get out of here," I said.

Penelope gasped and clambered out of bed. She was drugged, al-right. I helped her up and hastily helped her dress. I didn't have time for corsets and stockings, just a plain dress she used for gardening. She was groggy, but upright. I would need to be cautious with her on the ladder.

"You look rather dashing," she said with a weak smile. "Where are we going?"

"Far from here."

"Wait." Penelope groped at her vanity and pulled open the cen-ter drawer. She pulled out ropes of gemstones, rings, earrings, and bracelets before stuffing them into her purse. "This might help."

Her treasure trove would be enough to set us up. It would be difficult to sell without garnering interest, but we'd worry about that later. "Come on."

I went down the ladder first and stayed behind her as much as I could. My arms gripped the rails around her in case she fell. Penelope slipped halfway down, but she recovered as quickly as anyone could in her state. "Take a deep breath," I told her. "Go slow."

We made it down the ladder. I led her through the gardens in the dark with only the moonlight as a guide. Just as we rounded the kitchens, when we were almost free, lanterns sprang to life in the front of the manor. My breath caught as male voices carried across the lawn. "Stay here," I said to Penelope, who was leaning against the manor half-crying.

I peeked around the corner to find two large carriages and several men standing out front. They were the doctor's people, dressed in white and waiting restlessly. We didn't have much time. Once the doc-tor discovered she wasn't in her room, they would search the property.

Returning to Penelope, who was panting and wiping her eyes. I reached up to cup her face. "Hey," I said. "Look at me. We're getting out of here."

Penelope mustered what little grit she had and gave a determined nod. I took her hand and we skirted away from the manor in a round-about fashion. The place where we once rode bicycles together, and the day I knew I was in love with her. The stables were also lit. I would have to go alone.

"Stay here," I told her. "I'll get the horse."

"No," she whispered. "Don't leave me. Let's just run."

"We won't get far on foot," I reasoned. "They'll take me for a stable boy taking a horse out."

She shook her head, but I couldn't delay. I pulled away from her grasp and moved toward the stable. It was a few yards away. If I could just get to it. Get the horse and ride away. She would be okay for a moment. We'd head south—the opposite direction of where Mary thought—and as far from here as the mare could carry us.

All my plans came undone as the front door swung open. The doctor and Mr. Davies emerged.

"She's escaped!" the doctor shouted. "Spread out and find her; she couldn't have gotten far."

I backpedaled into the hedges and out of sight before bolting to the place where I left Penelope. The frenzy on the front lawn could not compare to the chaos in my mind as I crashed through the clearing to find she wasn't there. Had they found her already? Stupid! I should have never left her.

"Penelope?" I called as quietly as I could.

There was no answer.

I clamped a hand over my mouth to keep from wailing. I needed to keep calm. Taking a deep breath, I looped back around the side of the house searching for any sign of her. A man in a white uniform spotted me. I nearly jumped out of my skin when he said, "Sorry, I didn't mean to startle you. Do you need a lantern?"

Why was he offering me a lantern? It took a moment to recall that I was dressed as a man. The orderly confused me with a stable boy who was also tracking down the wayward wife. "No," I said as manly as I could. "I work better in the dark."

"Suit yourself," he shrugged.

"I'll check the back if you take that side," I said, pointing to the part of the yard where I had just searched. The orderly nodded and ran off, and I exhaled.

My muddy boots squished along the wet grass as I made my way into the back yard. There was no way to be silent. If I couldn't get Penelope to the horse, I would need to get her off the property and into the woods before bringing the horse to her. But how could I do that without getting caught? Riding a horse at night in the woods wasn't going to work. No. I had to get her to the main road somehow.

A faint squeak of a wooden board sent me sprinting. I knew where Penelope was. Afraid of getting seen, she must have gone to the place where she knew I would find her.

Penelope was perched on the swing, her head resting against a rope. Checking to make sure no one saw me, I went between the row of columns and said, "Penelope."

She turned and smiled at me, but the color in her face was gone. "I'm sorry," she said as her head bobbed back and forth. "I can't fight it."

I caught her just as she fell backward off the swing. The drugs had taken their toll on her. Desperation crept into my mind, but I refused to cry. I wouldn't give up. Not yet. Scooping her up, she wrapped her arms around me and rested her head on my shoulder. If it were any other circumstance, carrying Penelope the way a groom carries his bride would have been the highlight of my life.

I carried her to the outside of the property. She was so light, but the additional weight made me slow and ungainly in the wet terrain. If I could haul eighty-pound sacks of flour over the summer to pay the rent, I could carry her with ease.

The lanterns continued to move about the yard as orderlies called her name. It was easy enough to avoid them. The stables were in sight, and Penelope became that much lighter. We were almost there!

"Hang on," I whispered. "We're almost out."

We reached the stable when a stringy, male voice came from inside. "You found her!"

I gasped and choked. It was the doctor. His face was even more menacing under the lantern light. "It's good to see that there is some loyalty from the village."

"What?"

"You came to work when the rest of them went home. They claimed we were mistreating the lady and quit—all but you and Mr. Davies."

"Harriet?" I uttered, slowly realizing he did not recognize me. Of course he wouldn't, the arrogant old toad.

"She gave notice. Today will be her last day. Just as well," the doctor said. "Her cooking was terrible. It's a miracle the Joneses kept her on as long as they did. Come along."

I bit my tongue at the remark about Harriet. True, it may have been, but the woman deserved better. I eyed the mare, still saddled and waiting. There was a pitchfork and a shovel nearby. I moved to set Penelope down. If I was going to go to jail, at least I'd get to take that bugger out.

"She's here!" the doctor called loudly.

"The stable boy found her!"

I didn't have time to be furious.

Orderlies swarmed the lawn and were coming for us. In the night, they appeared to be many, but as they came closer, I counted six. Why so many? The doctor was exercising his authority to the highest. He wanted Penelope and expected a fight. Women couldn't gamble, but I knew bad odds when I saw them. I couldn't fight all of them, but it might come down to it. Clutching Penelope close, I followed behind the doctor and toward the house.

My knees threatened to give out as a cold sweat ran down my back. The doctor didn't recognize me, but Mr. Jones and his damned butler certainly would. It was over. Penelope was going to be taken away, and I was handing her over like a prized ham.

I'm so sorry, Penelope. This wasn't how it was supposed to happen.

I bit my lip to keep from crying. A hot, metallic taste coursed over my tongue as I carried the love of my life over the threshold—not to hold her in sickness and in health—but to death do us part.

"Goodness," the doctor fussed. "James, take her off his hands and into the parlor. I need to check her vitals."

In the entryway where we once decorated a Christmas tree, she was taken from me. Refusing to be separated from her, I followed with the group. I'd meet whatever fate had in store for the both of us.

She let out a groan, and the orderly paused. "Doctor," he said. "She's cool to the touch."

"Likely from being outside," the doctor dismissed with a wave of his hand. The orderly hesitated as though he wasn't convinced.

"I'm afraid she was overdosed—"

The doctor whirled around, nostrils flaring as he practically growled at the man twice his size. "Would you rather her wake? I would have thought that after your altercation with Francis, you'd know better than to pity these women."

These women.

Penelope wasn't the only one?

The orderly turned, and the firelight revealed a brutal scar carved down his cheek. A woman named Francis had done that to him. Someone with the same abilities as Penelope.

"She is my responsibility, and if you have any doubts about my authority or expertise, you, sir, may take your leave."

"Sorry, sir."

The doctor wielded fear like a sword. He used people's fears of uncontrollable women to claim absolute control over them. What purpose did he have in store for these poor women?

"Now," the doctor straightened. "Let's get the lad who found her a brandy!"

With one hand, he dominated, and the other, he rewarded. Giving a stable hand a taste of fine brandy like Mr. Jones had was a reward indeed. Right up there with offering grapes. It wasn't even his brandy to give, but Mr. Jones was about to be one stipend poorer if he spoke a word. It would take more than a nip of brandy to calm the rage within me.

Penelope's head rolled back, exposing her neck. From either the banister or the chandelier, a shadow curled around her neck, and she gasped. I didn't believe in omens, but that was as good as any. Penelope's life was in danger.

CHAPTER TWENTY-FOUR

T he doctor led the rotten procession through the parlor door. The room was lit by the roaring fire and nothing more. Wood crackled in the hearth, and a red hue radiated off the gold curtains Penelope had selected so painstakingly for her husband. The doctor marched in like a man who had single-handedly won the war.

"I was right to suspect something," he announced. "She had a ladder outside her window."

"Her maid must have done it before she left," Mr. Jones said. His voice was brittle and brimming with resentment. Not directed at me, but rather the doctor. He wiped his sweating brow with his handkerchief. The lord of the manor wanted this done and over.

"Is she still here?" The doctor asked.

My heart seized in my throat. If he turned around, he'd find me just behind him. I did my best to blend into the background. "No," Mr. Davies assured. "I sent her away this morning. Word is that she took a horse and rode north."

"Good, good," the doctor said, eyeing Penelope on the sofa. "I don't want any more obstacles. That woman was like a bull."

Like a bull? I'd show him obstacles. Once I could get out of this room, I'd go to their carriage and jam up the wheels, maybe even sneak on the back and throw something into the spokes to disable it. I'd need something strong, like some iron. Out on the road, in the dark, the doctor would be forced to send his orderlies for help. I could fight one or two of them before stealing the carriage.

"Your tea, Mr. Jones," the butler said. Mr. Jones took the cup and saucer, avoiding any glance at his wife, whose labored breathing was apparent even to me in the back. At any moment, she might stop, and everything would be over.

"She tried to run, but one of your stable boys found her. It's a good thing I had her so thoroughly sedated."

"Yes, yes, you were right, let's get on with it," Mr. Jones said.

The butler frowned briefly at the mention of a stable boy, but he resumed his stoic demeanor without a word.

At a snap of the doctor's fingers, the orderlies surrounded the loveseat Penelope was draped across. A stethoscope slipped over the doctor's ears while he checked her pulse. There was a brief scowl on his face. He was worried, and my knees threatened to buckle.

I stood there with my back against the wall. At any moment, Mr. Jones or his butler would recognize me, and the gig would be up. I'd be jailed for dressing as a man for certain. I mused at the possibility that the doctor would take me to his fancy institution, too, but I didn't have telekinetic abilities.

"I'll see to the boy," Mr. Davies said.

An oddly sweaty Mr. Jones waved him off without lifting his eyes from the admittance forms. I stepped back, shrinking away from the butler. Fury was in his eyes as he opened the door and said, "Right this way, lad."

I half-expected him to expose me right then and there, but he didn't. I followed him out of the room, where he took me firmly by the elbow like a misbehaving child and led me into my room. "What were you thinking!" he hissed.

"I...I promised I wouldn't let it happen," I said.

"By kidnapping a wealthy man's wife? They would hang you for that!"

"I don't care," my voice quivered. "I couldn't live with myself knowing she was in there. There are more like her. He's going to use them for something awful, I just know it."

Mr. Davies's expression was unreadable in that moment. "I cannot stand against Mr. Jones."

"Why?" I practically shouted. "What he's doing is wrong!"

"You remember our conversation about high-class society?"

I nodded. He said that they didn't live by our rules and that sometimes we must act. I was doing precisely that, but he refused to budge when her life was at stake. "I'm going to get her out," I said.

"Your stubbornness will be your downfall," he warned with a finger pointed at my face. "She couldn't live out there even if you pawned all the jewelry in her handbag."

"At least she'd have a chance," I said. "And she'd be freed of that monster. He's been planning this all along."

"And what if she cannot control her powers? Did you ever think of that?"

It was the first time the butler acknowledged Penelope's abilities. I wondered just what he made of them, but I didn't have time to ask. I didn't care if she could walk in the sun just so long as she was safe, and currently, she wasn't.

"Her powers only surface when she's in danger," I argued. "And anyway, I don't care what she can do. I loved her just as much when I thought she was sick."

The butler straightened his vest and stepped out of the room. Before he left, he said, "I won't stand in your way, but I won't oppose Mr. Jones, and I cannot save you from whatever fall you're about to take."

He didn't understand. I had fallen months ago. There was no turning back for me. No shutting her out. Penelope was a part of me now and always. There was nothing for it. I would need to distract everyone in the parlor. I could get in through the back doors by the greenhouse.

I snuck back out of my room and out of the kitchen. Harriet was crying over a pot of soup too loudly to notice when I went out the door. I ducked around the windows and checked on the parlor. They were where I had last left them. Mr. Jones was sipping tea before breaking into a fit of coughs. The doctor was pacing back and forth in front of Penelope, who was still asleep.

I'd need not only a distraction, but a way to get Penelope out of the room. Even then, how would I get her on the horse? The only option was to steal a carriage outside. It would mean leaving behind all the money left in the mare's saddle, but we'd manage without it. We'd have to.

The stable boys were likely at the pub back in the village. I could bring the carriage to the village and bribe one of them to return it and bring me back the mare. It was a long shot, but it was better than trying to make off with the carriage without any money. If I was going to jail, it better not be for stealing a carriage of all things.

Running back to the shed, I grabbed a wheelbarrow and rolled it back to the window. The faint light from the dining room inspired a most criminal idea. With both hands on the wooden handles, I grinned at the idea. Mr. Davies said he wouldn't get in my way, and there was no staff to look after every room.

Parking the wheelbarrow beside the drawing room window, I ran back around and pushed open the window to the dining room. Inside, several unattended candelabras were lit and dripping all over the wooden table.

A thought occurred to me then. One could not weed ivy out, nor could they poison the flowerbed to be rid of it. The best solution to rid an evasive plant was fire. I reached out a shaky hand, poised to strike. There was no going back from this for sure.

I clenched my eyes shut before knocking the candelabra on the floor. The rug caught fire with an audible "Pfhhh," and I left as the room filled with the nauseating smell of burning carpet. Crawling out the window, I made my way back around to the parlor and waited.

Come on. Come on! I wanted to shout at them before the damage became too extensive, but that wouldn't do me any favors in my current predicament. My whole body was on edge. At any moment, there could be another threat. My breathing was rapid, and my mind surged with hyper-awareness.

After what felt like days, the orderlies began to look at one another. Their noses wrinkled, and there was discourse among them. Mr. Davies said something, and they resumed guarding the door. The butler had served this house for decades. He knew every smell this house could produce, and he would have known if something was amiss. He must have known something was wrong, but he chose to delay alarm.

Mr. Jones's pen was on the paper, but he paused and said something to the others. He was on his feet, and everyone was out the door, all save the doctor, who closed the door behind them. I took the opportunity to sneak through the window.

Of course he had no intention of leaving. If I managed to get through this night unscathed, I would be wanted for theft, arson, posing as a man, trespassing, kidnapping, and assault.

I remained behind the curtain for a moment. Readying myself for what was to come. That was when I heard Penelope murmur. "Shh," the doctor soothed. "I'll give you more medicine. When we go to the facility, you'll be able to try out your powers in earnest."

"No," she moaned.

"Now, now," the doctor said. "I know what's best for you. I always have. You don't have to keep up the charade any longer."

"No!" Penelope was swatting him away, but she was too drugged to really put up a fight.

I grabbed the poker off the rack before picking up the rack itself and throwing it out the window. The doctor stared at me with a wild expression in his eyes. "You're not a boy at all!" he said, extending a finger in accusation. "You're that handmaid!"

"What are you planning?" My voice quivered with rage and adrenaline. All this time, she was trying to tell me. She thought I wouldn't love her anymore if I knew what he was doing with her.

"She can't control her powers until she learns how to properly use them." The doctor said. "There are many powerful people in the world who would pay good money for what they can do."

I gasped at the admittance. The sheer audacity of it all. He was going to train her up and sell her to the highest bidder. He convinced everyone she was sick and needed his help, but in reality, he was going to profit off her.

His eyes narrowed as he sat down in a high-backed chair adjacent to the loveseat. He drank his tea as if he didn't have a care in the world, but I could see the cup tremor ever so slightly. I gripped the poker. "You're going to tell them, you're going to tell all of them."

"No, I won't," he said. "Mr. Jones has already signed the paper-work. She is legally in my custody, and you will go to jail."

"No!" Penelope wailed, forcing herself upright.

"Now if you don't mind," he said, "I have a patient to see to."

Extending my poker forward, he remained seated. "No, you won't," I growled.

My eyes shifted to the paperwork, but the doctor was quicker. He leapt from the seat, the empty teacup smashed on the floor, and we both dove for the papers. We grappled over the stack of paper and rolled on the floor. He was much stronger than I expected, but Penelope was on her feet.

"Find Mr. Jones!" I yelled. "Tell him."

The doctor's fist fully connected with my face. Stuck by blinding pain, my vision was thrown by hot white flashes. His weight had lifted from my body. As I rolled over, he muttered, "Dress like a man, you'll get hit like a man."

He was going after Penelope then. I was struggling to get off the floor, and she had tripped over her lagging feet and fallen to the ground. "Freddie!" she shouted. "...Freddie."

If I didn't stop him, he'd load her up with more drugs, and it would likely be the end of her. He'd tell them all that I attacked him. With Penelope incapacitated, Mr. Jones would never learn the truth. The poker was thrown across the room out of reach, but the doctor was so distracted by keeping Penelope sedated that he abandoned the paperwork.

I grabbed it and made my way to the fire. Along the way, I encoun-tered his leather bag. I grabbed that too and threw it all in the fire.

"No!" he roared. Dropping Penelope on the floor, he ran for the fireplace. I was ready for him this time. Grabbing a wooden chair, I swung it at him, knocking the doctor to the floor. I didn't let up. I was on him and hitting him in the face as hard as I could. My knuckles stung with each hit, fresh scrapes stinging in the open air. The paperwork was burning, and his leather bag warped and blackened in the raging fire. The bag wasn't burning as fast as I would have liked, but Penelope was crawling to the door.

In that flickering moment, the doctor threw me off. My face collided with the ground, and in my sideways vision, I watched him stalk over to Penelope. Grabbing her by her golden hair, he dragged her back to the loveseat.

"It's for the greater good! Think of all the wars that can be prevented with a snap of your fingers. All the death and horror that can be avoided. I know you don't see it now, but one day, you'll fell nations!"

This was something well above my paygrade. The ambitions of men never failed to shock. I was up and charging him again, but the doctor was weirdly spry for an older man. It must have been all those years forcing women into submission.

Penelope was sitting on the love seat, staring at the ground. Now wasn't the time to check out!

The doctor was gaining ground. He was pushing me back toward the fireplace. My body was drained of its previous energy, and fatigue was setting in. My head ached from the injuries. I stepped back, and the doctor stepped forward.

But not before Penelope stood and outstretched her arm. The doctor and I stared as the medicine oozed out of her veins and dripped onto the floor. "You're right," she said. "With a snap of a finger. Move from that spot and I'll snap your neck."

That was my girl! I wanted to cheer and shout as Penelope strode forward, pulling me up into a kiss.

"No," he cried. "Please, I'm your doctor!"

She scowled at him but made no move. "It's not entirely out of my system, but I'm conscious...Do you smell something burning?"

If someone were to tell me a tale of a woman who could pull poison from her veins and smash vases with a glance, I would have laughed. Nowadays, it was just a Tuesday. "I love you," I told her.

"I love you too," she slurred.

"Say it again when you're sober, love."

We emerged from the parlor together. Smoke billowed from the dining room, and Penelope's side eye could not be avoided. "My newly redecorated dining room?"

Of all the times to be fretting over a dining room! "I had to distract them somehow."

The doors were opened, and the chilly night air flowed into the hallway. The fire had been put out, but the men were still in the dining room and greatly distressed. "Let's just run," I told her. "We can leave now; no one will stop us."

Penelope shook her head. "I can't do that. Not just yet."

What did she mean to do? Probably confront Mr. Jones, but to what end? A spine that bent one way was just as likely to bend another, but the doctor's hold had proved strong. In awe of her bravery, I couldn't tell her no.

I nodded as her hand slipped from mine. I followed behind her into the dining room, where we found Mr. Jones on the ground. The orderlies were attempting to revive him. The butler stood in the corner with his head bowed.

"What happened?" I asked as Penelope rushed to Mr. Jones's side.

"We suspect a heart attack."

Penelope fell to her knees, sobbing, the back of her hand pressed to her lips. "Freddie..."

"I'm sorry," he said between gasps of air. "I..."

She shook her head. "It doesn't matter. Just be okay."

The orderly who was checking his pulse regarded Penelope and asked, "Does he have a history of heart issues?"

"No," she replied. "He was always so healthy. Always."

"Was there anything out of the ordinary?" Another orderly asked.

Penelope looked to Mr. Davies. "I wouldn't know," she said. "I was drugged most of the day."

The butler stepped forward, his expression as sullen as the grave. "The only new addition was the tea the doctor brought with him. He insisted that we drink his special blend from Sweden."

What reason would the doctor have to poison Mr. Jones? He already had what he wanted. I shook my aching head, eyes stinging from the smoke. It just didn't make sense. Poor Penelope sobbed quietly, clutching his hand in her own.

Mr. Jones stopped breathing before Scotland Yard could arrive.

He groaned with immense pain until his heart gave out entirely. The orderlies bowed their heads as Penelope said goodbye to her husband. The single constable from the village arrived on the scene. He was an older man with a dark, thick moustache and tan skin. Constable Elling was a good sort. I had known him since I was a child. He introduced himself to everyone in the room he did not know, making a note to remember their names.

He took everyone aside individually and spoke with them before any of us could talk as a group. He took Penelope first. Then Mr. Davies, myself. "Dinah," Mr. Elling called.

Mr. Davies and Penelope both gave me a nod of support. I told the constable the truth, even if I left out some things. I told him about how I suspected the doctor was mistreating Penelope and how he was trying to make off with her. "I couldn't let him do it," I said. "So, I came back to try and rescue her, but when I did, I found the house in chaos."

"Mr. Davies is certain that the fire was an accident. Did you see anything to say otherwise?"

I shook my head and bit my tongue. "No one used the dining room except for Mr. Jones at dinner and at breakfast. He took his meals at the same time every day. I glanced at the clock and nodded. I suspect Mr. Davies lit the candles anticipating the meal, and it was forgotten."

"Do you think the doctor poisoned Mr. Jones?"

I honestly had no idea. I shook my head, unable to link one with the other. "Poison? I thought he had a heart attack."

Mr. Elling shook his head and gave me a sympathetic nod. "You're a good lass, Dinah. Come, it's time to deal with the demon."

There was a relief in knowing he believed me. I had the law on my side. That probably wouldn't have been the case in a big city, but here, a person's reputation mattered.

An irritated groan came from the parlor. I nearly yelped as I clung to the constable. That damn man was awake. What would he tell Mr. Elling? I was one step away from jail, but at least Penelope would be free. Mr. Elling squeezed my arm. "There, there, Dinah. He won't be hurting you again."

It was only then that I felt the wetness dripping from the side of my head. Warm and sticky. My face throbbed, and my lip was fat. What a sight I must have been. No wonder Mr. Elling was glaring at the doctor.

"Let's all convene, shall we?" Mr. Elling asked.

In that moment, I wanted nothing more than to hold Penelope's hand. Such notions would have to wait. For now, I would have to be satisfied with the fact that she was safe, even if we were not out of the woods just yet. The doctor stirred on the floor as Elling used the poker to fish the charred bag out of the fireplace. "Leather is a tough one to burn," he said.

"Oh, thank goodness," the doctor purred. "Arrest that woman at once! She assaulted me."

The leather bag rolled out of the fireplace. The metal handles were too hot to touch, so the constable squatted down with a carving knife and cut the bag open. Various bottles came spilling out, as well as a bottle full of dark violet berries.

"What are you doing?" the doctor demanded. "That's my bag!"

The constable picked up the bottle of berries and twirled them in the light of the dying fire. "I suspected as much."

"What is it?" Penelope gasped.

"Belladonna," Mr. Elling said. "It causes the chest to seize up like a heart attack. It affects the heart as well as the respiratory system. For a healthy man, this wouldn't kill him outright, but if there was an underlying condition, this would do it."

There were gasps, including my own.

"Mr. Elling, I didn't know you took an interest in botany," Mr. Davies said.

The constable shrugged. "Not so much in botany but crime, Davies. You mean to tell me you've never heard of Aqua Tofana? I imagine our doctor here would know what these berries could do."

I hadn't the slightest clue what he was referring to, but evidently the berries were Belladonna, and they were poisonous.

"Those are not mine!" The doctor was up on his feet, glaring up at the constable.

"You think she did it?" he asked, nodding in my direction. "Went off and found some berries she knew would exacerbate an underlying heart condition?"

My mind whirled with the possibilities. Mr. Jones had been murdered, but had the doctor done it? Mr. Jones signed the paperwork; that was all the doctor wanted of him. There was no reason to poison him. Maybe it was a safeguard in case the lord changed his mind.

"I certainly didn't kill anyone," the doctor said. "I didn't brew the tea he drank. Don't you think a butler would notice berries of this size in a tea? What point would they serve?"

All eyes went to Mr. Davies for a brief moment, and even I found myself doubting the evidence. Mr. Davies spoke of how sometimes we must make choices on the lord's behalf, but he couldn't mean murder.

The butler's face remained impassive. "Tea given to me by you," he repeated. "Your special blend from Sweden."

"With chamomile!" The doctor roared. "I didn't know anything about Mr. Jones's health. I didn't treat him."

"No, but you commented on his condition frequently," Penelope accused. "You always asked questions. It made no sense to me then, but now..."

I didn't know what to think. Someone was a murderer, and there was a pinching in my ribs every time the doctor denied the accusation. I believed him. God help me, I hated that man, and it took all my will to keep from throttling him right then and there, but he didn't do it.

"Her!" the doctor pointed at me. I was stunned by the accusation. Of all the crimes I had committed tonight, the irony of going to jail for something I didn't do was too great. It was all I could do to keep from laughing.

"She threw the bag in the fire, did she not?" Mr. Elling asked.

"Well, yes!" the doctor said with indignation.

Constable Elling tilted his head to regard the doctor. "Why would she try to burn her own planted evidence?"

The doctor didn't have an answer. His face turned red, and he began shouting his outrage, spittle landing on Mr. Elling's face. For all his patience, even the constable appeared as though he wanted to slap the belligerent doctor.

"How dare you? I am a man of learned rank and social class you couldn't reach in your highest dreams! I tend to patients all over the world and—"

"What about Alexandra Clarke?" Mr. Elling asked. "She wasn't some rich dame, nor was she suffering from any illness, but you took an interest in her all the same. She had quite the story when she came home last week."

What did Harriet's daughter have to do with all this?

"I was interviewing her."

"She said you beat her and then locked her up in a garden shed, and the only reason she escaped was because some detectives came looking for her."

"I did no such thing."

"She's got the bruises to prove it!"

My mind went back to that night at Harriet's home. The medium said that Penelope's fate was tied to another woman. This was what she meant. The doctor was searching London for more women like Penelope. He thought Alexandra was one when Penelope inadvertently came to her rescue. Now it seemed that Alexandra was coming to hers.

The doctor had been caught. I burst into tears from relief. Mr. Davies wiped a tear from his eye but remained in the backdrop as a good butler should. The men in the room must have interpreted it as sympathy or distress from the night's events.

With your permission," Mr. Davies said. "I'd like to escort the women out of the room."

"I think they've suffered enough," Mr. Elling agreed.

"Can't you see her clothes?" the doctor shouted as the orderlies braced him. "She's dressed as a man!"

"Aye, she is," Mr. Elling said. "While the law may not make exceptions, in this village, Dinah is allowed to wear pants."

CHAPTER TWENTY-FIVE

Spring was in full bloom in the garden. I laid out a wool blanket and waited. It had been several months since that fateful night in January. The newspapers were going on about the trial for months. Penelope was fortunate that she did not have to take part.

The doctor's journals did most of the speaking where his accountants could not. Sums of money from seemingly nowhere and women from all parts of the world were rescued and sent home. Alexandra Clarke testified that the doctor urged her to move apples with her mind, and when she couldn't, he beat her and left her locked in a shed for dead.

He was deemed insane and locked in an institution he helped found. For what person could believe that women had such unseen strength?

The greenhouse that was once our shelter had been tainted by one final act of betrayal from Mr. Jones. Before the trial, we sat in the room as we often did, but I noted the broken pane of glass. "When did ivy get planted?" I asked.

"I don't know," Penelope said, frowning. She turned in her chair and noted the odd grouping of ivy. It was intentionally planted in a cluster by the window. I stood up and investigated the area. Amid the potted plants and the wooden planter boxes was an odd, single box without a plant.

Penelope grabbed a shovel and struck the lock, muttering, "You son of a bitch," under her breath.

The lock dented and caved in on itself, and Penelope lifted the lid with an icy glare. Inside were pounds and pounds stacked neatly in the box. I stood blank in my astonishment. "Mr. Jones?" I asked.

"He wasn't paying his mistress. He was stashing everything away."

"Why?" I asked.

"Some banker friend sold him on some investments. I said it was a stupid idea, and so did my parents. He must have been saving it up to buy in."

He told Penelope he was broke because of his mistress when he was planning on buying stock? "What an odd thing to lie about," I said.

"My parents would tolerate a mistress, but they wouldn't tolerate him buying in on investments that went towards my father's competition in the mining industry."

"I'll never understand posh people."

Penelope smirked at me as if she were hiding the fact that she, too, was a posh. I had made peace with her social standing the night the whole village quit on the Joneses. They didn't do it for me, they did it for her.

Every single one of those bastards stuck their necks on the chopping block for her. They saw what I saw; she was one of us. Even Rodger joined the protest despite what I had done to his bicycle. I may have accidentally misplaced Penelope's bicycle somewhere along the fence line of his house.

Amid the English roses and the lush greenery, Penelope's golden hair shone in the daylight. She was wearing a simple blue dress and held a wicker picnic basket in the crook of her arm. She smiled when our eyes met. "Hello there," she said.

"Hello," I teased.

Penelope plopped down beside me, and we set the picnic on the blanket. We ate and chatted about little things. It was nice to talk about the trivial things, and we avoided serious conversations as much as possible. "I fear I may have set Mr. Davies into a frenzy," Penelope warned.

"Oh," I asked, taking a bite of a cucumber sandwich.

"I've decided to convert the parlor into a library," she said. "Never again will there be a lord of this house, so there's no reason for a parlor."

"A library would be wonderful," I agreed.

Penelope would be the grief-stricken widow who never recovered from her young husband's murder. She was quite the sight at the lord's funeral. Dressed head to toe in black, her long veil swayed in the winter air. No one expected Penelope to marry again, not after the whole ordeal.

"He's been in there with a ruler ever since."

Mr. Davies stayed on even after Mr. Jones passed. He insisted that it was his duty as the butler to see to the lady of the household. While I was not technically employed, I wore my maid's outfit when we took trips to Chester. High society was never Penelope's style, and she did not miss Mr. Jones's friends who stopped calling on the manor after a few months.

"I feel a sense of responsibility for the two of you," the butler admitted. "I am to blame for what happened to Mr. Jones. I knew he had a condition of sorts. Had I been more diligent, seen the signs for what they were... Now, it's my duty to safeguard his widow."

We kept him on. Only a fool would have sacked the best butler known to this county. Harriet stayed on as well, but Penelope hired an actual cook. She said she couldn't stand my prickly expression at every meal. "Really," she said. "It's just food."

That was a generous description of our meals. Even though we had a cook, I still prepared our picnic basket for the day. There was something special in it I was waiting for Penelope to find, if she'd ever look.

"There's something else in there," I said.

"Oh?" Penelope reached in and produced a little black box. She tilted her head and gave me a funny smile.

"I got you a pair of earrings for Christmas, but when I remembered all the beautiful things in your vanity drawer...I couldn't." Her pained expression said it all. She would have cherished those glass earrings. "So," I continued. "I took them back and used all my saved wages to buy you this instead."

She opened the box, and a ruby ring sparkled back at her. Penelope gasped and put it on her finger where her wedding ring once resided. "It's beautiful!"

I had spent a great deal of time deciding on that ring and even borrowed one of hers to make sure I got the size right. Ignoring the flush to my cheeks, I searched the basket for a corkscrew. "Oh," I whined, wagging the bottle. "I'll need to go back inside."

The pressure in the air changed then, and the cork freed itself from the wine. We seldom spoke of it out loud, but with Penelope sober, she was able to tune her abilities so that my ears didn't pop. She never really used them, though. Said she didn't like relying on powers.

The first few days after Mr. Jones's death were the worst.

At first, it was a headache followed by vomiting. We thought she was just grieving, but Penelope shook so hard and sweat dripped from her face like tears. She thought she was dying. "Maybe this is what I deserve," she said.

That was worse than the whole ordeal with the doctor or Mr. Jones dying in front of me. The way she gasped for breath as if she were being strangled. How she cried. Everything hurt all over, and there wasn't a thing I could do for her. Maybe she was sick with Hysteria after all, I didn't know.

Mr. Davies called on a doctor from Chester. A nice old man and his wife came and saw to her. "This isn't Hysteria," Dr. Gosling explained. "This is toxicity leaving the body."

I didn't understand exactly, but the medicine the doctor was giving her made her sick when she went too long without it. Yet somehow, through it all, Penelope held my hand and promised me that it would all be okay.

I supposed she was right. Things did get better. Dr. Gosling and his wife called on us every few weeks just to check on her. They said she was doing better, and I was inclined to agree. Penelope still had nightmares, but so did I. She still scratched at herself sometimes, but she hadn't gone catatonic since the last time.

All of that was a distant fading memory as we sat among the chirping birds and wild hares that twitched their whiskers at us along the green grass. The wildflowers were already up to my knees, and bees were everywhere. This was the English garden I longed for her to see, and she made it. We both did.

Penelope frowned and pulled an envelope out of the basket. "My parents wrote me," she said.

"Took them long enough," I said.

They almost handed her over to a monster and ruined her marriage before it had even begun. After the nightmares, the trial, the toxicity, and even Mr. Jones's funeral, now they wrote.

"Do you think I should read it?" she asked.

A different question came to my mind then. Did she do it? If anyone had just cause, it would be Penelope, but could she really? She appeared as perplexed by the bottle in the doctor's bag as I did.

Her grief was also genuine. She still wore black on most days, and sometimes she would fall into spells where she talked about Freddie and how she missed him. "Not in a romantic way," she'd say. "I just enjoyed his company. He was such fun."

Penelope held the envelope with both hands and stared at it for a long moment before tearing it up. "Maybe one day I will write them, but I don't want them clouding our perfect day."

"The choice is yours," I reminded her.

She regarded me then with a sad little smile. "I have one, thanks to you."

www.ingramcontent.com/pod-product-compliance
Lightning Source LLC
Chambersburg PA
CBHW051103030726
47504CB00006B/1763